Praise for
*Only Mostly Devastated*

"A delight! This heartfelt, queer update on *Grease* features a diverse cast of teen characters and a charmingly earnest protagonist in Ollie. Gonzales handily balances lively banter with somber issues, and the compelling will they/won't they story line warmly illustrates a timeless truth: love is love is love."

—Jenn Bennett, author of *Alex, Approximately*

"There can never be enough queer stories about romance—and when they are told with this much heart, humor, and a swoon-worthy story line, you never want them to end."

—Angelo Surmelis, author of
*The Dangerous Art of Blending In*

"Oh my gosh, *Only Mostly Devastated* is SO GREAT! Funny and sweet and super gay; fans of *Simon vs. the Homo Sapiens Agenda* are going to be all over it. It's totally swoon-worthy!"

—Cale Dietrich,
author of *The Love Interest*

"Outrageously funny and terribly sweet, *Only Mostly Devastated* will tug at your heartstrings until they break, then weave you new ones made of pure gold."

—K. Ancrum, author of *The Wicker King*

"Wry but earnest, sweet but irreverent, heartbreaking but hopeful. With wit and authenticity, *Only Mostly Devastated* tells the story of what happens to a summer romance after summer is over. You'll be rooting for Ollie and his messy, wonderful friends from the first page to the last."

—Hannah Capin, author of
*The Dead Queens Club* and *Foul Is Fair*

"With razor-sharp wit, masterful comedic timing, and heaps of heart, these hilarious, lovable, heartbreakingly real characters make *Only Mostly Devastated* an instant hit and Sophie Gonzales one YA author to watch."

—Julia Lynn Rubin, author of *Burro Hills*

"Summer lovin' gets a Southern twist in this addicting coming-of-age gay romance. Sweet and tart in equal measure. . . . Poignant, piquant, and not to be missed."

—*Kirkus Reviews*

"Sweet and earnest. . . . A worthwhile romance for any collection." —*Booklist*

"The power of this fun *Grease* retelling is that it normalizes the spectrum of sexual orientations. Recommended for all teens." —*School Library Journal*

"Narrator Ollie is deeply sympathetic, but both teens' feelings—love, hate, lust, grief, and, for Will, insecurity about coming out—are convincing. . . . Though Gonzales is Australian, she gets most US details right in this *Grease* reboot, creating an inclusive cast and giving weight to many parts of Ollie's multifaceted life."

—*Publishers Weekly*

"Heartfelt and charming, *Only Mostly Devastated* is a touching and delightful YA contemporary romance. Highly recommend for fans of Nicola Yoon, *Simon vs. the Homo Sapiens Agenda,* and *Sick Kids in Love.*"

—*YA Books Central*

"*Only Mostly Devastated* is the next queer coming-of-age novel."

—*The Nerd Daily*

"If you loved *Love, Simon,* add this one to your reading list."

—*OUTinPerth* (Australia)

## ALSO BY SOPHIE GONZALES

*The Law of Inertia*

*Perfect on Paper*

# ONLY MOSTLY DEVASTATED

## Sophie Gonzales

WEDNESDAY BOOKS
NEW YORK

Published in the United States by Wednesday Books, an imprint of St. Martin's Publishing Group

ONLY MOSTLY DEVASTATED. Copyright © 2020 by Sophie Gonzales. All rights reserved. Printed in the United States of America. For information, address St. Martin's Publishing Group, 120 Broadway, New York, NY 10271.

www.wednesdaybooks.com

Excerpt from *Perfect on Paper* copyright © 2021 by Sophie Gonzales

Designed by Anna Gorovoy

The Library of Congress has cataloged the hardcover edition as follows:

Names: Gonzales, S., 1992– author.
Title: Only mostly devastated / Sophie Gonzales.
Description: First edition. | New York : Wednesday Books, 2020.
Identifiers: LCCN 2019044429 | ISBN 9781250315892 (hardcover) | ISBN 9781250315908 (ebook)
Subjects: CYAC: Gays—Fiction. | Secrets—Fiction. | High schools—Fiction. | Schools—Fiction. | Dating (Social customs)—Fiction. | Cancer—Fiction.
Classification: LCC PZ7.1.G6532 Onl 2020 | DDC [Fic]—dc23
LC record available at https://lccn.loc.gov/2019044429

ISBN 978-1-250-78743-9 (trade paperback)

Our books may be purchased in bulk for promotional, educational, or business use. Please contact your local bookseller or the Macmillan Corporate and Premium Sales Department at 1-800-221-7945, extension 5442, or by email at MacmillanSpecialMarkets@macmillan.com.

First Wednesday Books Trade Paperback Edition: 2021

10 9 8 7 6 5 4 3 2 1

*To everyone who, in their quest to be cared for
by another, forgot to care for themselves.
Your needs matter, too.*

# 1

It was late afternoon, on the very last Wednesday of August, when I realized Disney had been lying to me for quite some time about Happily Ever Afters.

Because, you see, I was four days into mine, and my prince was nowhere to be found.

Gone. Vanished.

"I'll definitely never forget you," he'd said.

"I don't think I've ever been this happy," he'd said.

"Please don't lose contact. I need to see you again one day," he'd said.

So why was I here, sitting at the kitchen counter and banging my head against a metaphorical wall, weighing up the pros and cons of sending *yet another* message to him?

Like, okay. Yes, if I sent another it'd be three in a row. *Yes* that was semi-stalker level. But I could rationalize this. The first message he'd ignored was in response to his own text on Saturday night. He'd said good night, and I'd said good night. End of conversation. He wasn't required to respond. So I could barely even count that.

Then the second message I'd sent didn't exactly *demand* a reply.

**Sunday, 11:59 AM**

> Totally failed at sneaking
> home. Mom killed me.
> #worthit. Please don't judge
> me for using a hashtag. I'm
> too cool to abide by your
> mundane social expectations.

Read Sunday, 2:13 PM

I mean, he could've glanced at that on his drive home and smiled, and not realized he was meant to text back, right? There wasn't strictly a question there, so it was possible. Or maybe he'd seen it, gotten halfway through a reply, and been distracted by something.

Like a house fire. Or an alien abduction.

For four days.

Really, if you thought about it, I had to message him again. In a cool, casual, not desperate kinda way obviously. But with a question this time. So if he saw it and didn't reply, then I'd know *for sure* he was ignoring me.

Okay. I could do this. This wasn't a big deal. It was just a guy texting another guy. A guy who knew all my biggest secrets, had spent the better part of seven weeks making out with me, and had *Seen. Me. Naked*™.

A guy who'd convinced me he really, really liked me.

A guy who'd *better* have been abducted by goddamn aliens.

So maybe a little bit of clinginess from me was justified. As long as it didn't *come across* as clingy, of course.

Simple. Okay. Go.

Hey Will! So I

Nope. Backspace. Too planned looking.

Dude, you'd never guess what I

What I *what*? There was no way to complete that sentence.

So, I'm assuming you've probably been abducted by aliens, but on the off chance you haven't been

"Ollie. Do you have a second?"

I jumped so hard I almost pressed Send. And let's be honest, if I'd done that, I might as well have thrown myself in the lake. I tried not to seem too flustered as Mom sat on the wooden stool next to me. For good measure, I backspaced the message-in-progress. Just in case. "Uh, sure. What's up?"

Uh-oh. She had that *look* on her face.

My first thought was that it'd happened. Aunt Linda had passed away. I held my breath. As in literally. Like if I was caught breathing it'd make it true, and our family would fall right off its precarious perch on the edge of a cliff called cancer.

That was the reason we'd come to North Carolina in the first place, after all, when Aunt Linda's health took a turn for the worse and she'd needed some time away, to chill out and see family and actually enjoy herself for once. Obviously, my family wanted to see her, so we met her here at the lake, the farthest she could safely go for a holiday. It was the biggest trip I'd taken from California in years, so I'd been more than up for it. I'd been appointed the unofficial, unpaid, uncomplaining—but only because they're so damn cute—nanny to her kids, and we'd rented side-by-side lake houses. Things had been good. Great, even. Best summer of my life I'd have said.

But now it was almost over, and it couldn't be ending like this. It *couldn't* be.

"Well, sweetie . . ." Mom started.

*Dead. Dead. Dead.*

"Aunt Linda is—"

*Dead.*

"—well, you know, she's not doing great. You've been such a help over the summer, but before that Uncle Roy was run thin trying to care for the kids and Linda, and they can't afford child care with the hospital bills. Not to mention all the extra things they could use a hand with at the moment. She's my sister. I want to make sure I'm here for her."

Wait. So Aunt Linda *hadn't* passed away? The relief hit me so hard I almost missed Mom's next words, too dizzy with happiness to focus.

"Your father and I have decided to put the house up for rent for a while. Maybe for a year or so. We have a place we can stay in Collinswood. Only a few streets away from Roy and Linda, actually. We'll go back to San Jose next week to grab our stuff and say good-bye to everyone for now. You'll be back here in time to start the school year."

Wait, what? What, what, and what, exactly?

"Stay . . . here? Move here, you mean? To North Carolina?"

But we were supposed to be going home next week. How could we *come back*?

Mom shrugged. Her blue, deep-set eyes had heavy bags underneath them, and her lightweight black cardigan was inside out. The tag, poking meekly out of the side seam, rustled as she dropped her arms by her sides. "Ollie, we don't have a choice."

"But . . . do you . . . could I stay at home, and you guys can stay here?" Hey, the more I thought about it, the more sense it made. Just because I had fun playing babysitter for the summer didn't mean I wanted to drop everything and make it a permanent role. "Yeah, actually, that could work. I can take care of the house, and I can drive myself around. I can pay the bills myself. I'll pick up a few extra shifts at the store. I can come up later, if it looks like you'll be here for a while, but . . . I mean, Mom, the band. And the guys. I can't . . ."

Mom rested her elbows on the counter and buried her forehead in her palms. "Ollie. Please. Don't make this any more difficult."

I slumped back, staring at my phone. What was I supposed to say here? It's not that I was a brat or anything, but this was a lot to take in. My mind raced as it tried to process the enormity of it all. Senior year without any of my friends? At a totally unfamiliar school, with teachers who didn't know me, right when grades actually started to matter? I'd have to quit my job, and my band, and I'd miss homecoming . . .

Then I peeked back at Mom, and I only had to take one look at the expression on her face to realize this was non-negotiable. Reluctantly, I shoved all the reasons why this would ruin everything to the back of my mind. I'd come to terms with it all later. In my room. After finding an appropriately melancholy playlist on Spotify.

*But—but—but,* a part of me piped up. *It's not all melancholy. Now you live in the same state as Will. Seeing him again might actually be plausible now.*

My stomach flipped at the thought. You had silver linings,

and you had platinum linings. This lining was firmly of the platinum variety. "Okay. Well, it's . . . sudden. But okay. We'll make it work."

Mom brightened, and pulled me into a hug. "That was easier than I expected."

My voice came out muffled against her chest. "I reserve the right to complain constantly moving forward. I'd sound like a monster if I said no and you know it. Not that I had a choice, did I?"

As Mom let me go, she gave a brief laugh. "No, God no, but I appreciate the cooperation all the same."

"At least you're honest." I forced a smile, and Mom hopped off the stool to start lunch preparations.

"We *will* make it work, I promise," she said as she clattered around in the crisper to retrieve some tomatoes and lettuce. "Sometimes we have to make sacrifices for the people we love, right? It might not be ideal, but we may as well do it with a grin."

I nodded absentmindedly and went back to my phone. At least the first problem was solved. This totally counted as a good enough reason to send multiple text messages.

Now he'd have to reply, right?

# 2

Wednesday, 6:05 PM

Hey. So. Funny story. I'm
moving to NC for a while.
I'm going to be living in
Collinswood. Any chance
that's near you?

Unread

I was joking about the aliens thing, but it was starting to
seem like the only plausible explanation. Who doesn't touch
their phone for twelve days? *No one*, that's who. Seriously.
Since I sent that text, I'd:

- Packed.
- Left the lake house.
- Flown home.
- Packed up my *entire house*.

- Said good-bye to all my friends.
- Consumed three milkshakes of pure misery. One with Ryan, one with Hayley, and one more with Ryan because he had a late-night craving after already officially saying good-bye to me.
- Flown to freaking Collinswood, A.K.A. Podunk Nowhere.
- Unpacked my *entire* house.
- Cried in secret twice.
- Cried a little bit in front of my parents once.
- Made a blood vow with myself to stop freaking crying.
- Taken a tour of Podunk Nowhere and cried on the inside a bit when I realized all my shopping was going to have to be online from here on out.
- Watched *Frozen* three times. Twice, with my cousins in the room. Once, on my own because it was already in the DVD player and I couldn't be bothered to change it.

And in all that time, not one message from Will? Screw that. I was officially over it.

Not so over it that I didn't want to vent, though. And tonight was my chance. After several failed attempts, Ryan, Hayley, and I had finally found a time we were all free to Skype. I'd intended to take the call in my room, but Mom decided at the last minute that she needed me in the kitchen to peel the cucumbers for the salad. So I multitasked, with the laptop on the dining room table and a cutting board beside it.

Mom and Dad were cooking a special dinner to celebrate the grand opening of our new kitchen. Trouble was, our special meals were usually takeout, since we never had people over for dinner and therefore had no one to impress but ourselves. And pad thai from the restaurant down the street had historically impressed all three of us without fail in San Jose.

By the time Dad cracked (no pun intended) and pulled up a Gordon Ramsay tutorial on YouTube to copy from, tensions were running high. To make things worse, joining us in the kitchen were my very bored and crabby cousins, Crista and Dylan.

Basically, the house was chaos, and adding a Skype call into it all didn't help.

"It's a *little loud* on your end," Ryan said, making a face into the camera. On the bed beside him, Hayley burst into giggles.

"Right, sorry. Just try to ignore it," I said. I had to speak on an angle in order to peel the cucumbers.

Ryan said something in response, but he was drowned out by Crista's whining.

"Aunt Catherine? Aunt Catherine? Aunt Catherine?" She followed Mom around the kitchen, holding onto her bowl of apple slices and cheddar cheese, while Mom pretended she couldn't hear.

"Sorry, what?" I asked the screen.

Ryan and Hayley gave me matching amused looks. "I said, have you unpacked yet?" Ryan yelled.

I opened my mouth to reply, but ended up with an apple slice shoved unceremoniously in my face. "Don't like the *skin*," Dylan said in a firm voice, waving the apple around.

"It's a little late for that, buddy," I said. "Just eat around it."

"The *skin*."

"I'm busy right now, I'm peeling something else. It'd get

cucumber juice all over your apple. Go get Aunt Catherine to help you."

"Aunt Catherine" gave me a warning look, and I ducked behind my laptop.

Hayley's face had taken over the screen, so close I could almost count her pale blond eyelashes. "So, we wanted to tell you in person, but we've been asked to play at Nathaniel's!"

My mouth dropped open. "Wait, *really*?" Nathaniel's was the dream when it came to underage gigs. Sure, it wasn't *exactly* our audience, but the people who went there tended to be pretty open-minded when it came to music. If anything, we'd be likely to end up with a bunch of new fans who'd never heard of us.

Well, not "we," I guessed. They. They would end up with new fans.

"Ollie, Ollie, Dylan wants you to cut the skin off his apple," Crista said, appearing at my side out of thin air.

"I heard him. I'm just trying to talk to my friends right now."

"Your hands are free, aren't they?" Mom asked from across the kitchen. "Can't you grab a fresh knife?"

"Be right back," I said to Ryan and Hayley, but Hayley held up a hand.

"No, look, we can barely hear you. Go hold the fort. We have to practice, anyway. We'll tell you more when we can talk properly."

But I hadn't even had a chance to tell them about Will. Or Collinswood. Or how Aunt Linda was. "Oh. Oh, okay. Sure. We'll Skype soon, then, I guess?"

"Yeah, when we're all free. Soon."

I wrapped up the call, then dutifully removed the offending apple peel, to Dylan's delight.

Over by the stove, Mom hovered behind Dad, helpfully critiquing his cooking choices. "There's some more room in the skillet," she pointed out, leaning against the counter. "Why don't you put it all in? It'll speed things up."

"Gordon says if I put too much meat in the pan it'll cook unevenly."

"Well, God forbid you disobey Gordon."

"Woe betide the fool that tries, Catherine."

Outside, a car engine rumbled up the driveway. Crista and Dylan perked up as one, and, abandoning their snacks, sprinted to the front door, with me following after them. *"Mama's here, Mama's here, Mama's here."*

Aunt Linda had barely walked through the door when she was barreled over by two pint-sized missiles. "Ooff! Oh my gosh, I was only gone for a few hours." She laughed, pulling them in for a hug.

Tonight, she looked weaker than usual. She'd lost her thick black hair a while ago, and while I was used to seeing her bald, tonight she still wore the paisley scarf she wrapped around her head when she went out. Weirdly, the scarf reminded me how much things had changed more than the hair loss did. Maybe it was because Linda had been so anti-headwear for longer than I'd been alive. I couldn't even picture her in a sun hat, or beanie, or anything.

"They're attention-starved," I said. "We've been neglecting them."

"I know, that's why I leave them here. It makes me look better by comparison, and they're *so much more grateful to have me*," she said, poking the kids playfully in their stomachs as she spoke. They shrieked with laughter.

"How was it?" Mom asked as we entered the kitchen.

"Oh, you know. It's a hospital. Glad it exists, but always

gladder to be leaving it." Aunt Linda lifted her handbag and nodded toward the living room. "Just let me put my things down, I'll be two seconds."

"I hope you're hungry," Mom said to her retreating back.

Aunt Linda's voice was bright and cheerful as she replied. "To be honest, Cathy, I don't remember what hunger feels like."

Mom rolled her eyes, then caught sight of me slumping back down at the dining room table. "How's the salad coming along?"

"Oh, fine." I reached for the peeler again.

"Sorry we interrupted your call."

I nodded, not trusting myself to reply without getting all emotional again. I'd just really wanted to talk to Ryan and Hayley. So much had been uprooted. I just wanted something that felt normal.

Mom pushed down on my hand to get me to let go of the peeler. "Ollie, you need to relax. You'll have plenty of opportunities to talk with your friends. Everything will be fine. I want you to practice some mindfulness."

"No, Mom—"

"*Yes*, Ollie. With me." Experience told me I'd best play along. Fighting would take longer than giving in at this point. "Now, I want you to picture all the things you're grateful for. This lovely big house that costs an eighth of the rent of the one in San Jose. How's that for a start? Big houses, and clean air, and having your parents around to cook you a nutritious meal . . . are you experiencing the gratitude?"

"Oh, totally."

"Oliver, I don't want any of your sarcasm. Picture your

fingertips. How do they feel? How does the wood feel underneath them? Ollie?"

"Mom, honestly I feel a little claustrophobic right now."

She took her hands off my shoulders with a sheepish grimace. "Sorry. But work with me here, Ollie. You need to be relaaaaxed, and caaaallmm."

See, Mom has some ideas about the world. She's not super religious. Just more, I guess . . . spiritual? Basically, she believes in a Great, Ethereal Being out there in the universe that gives us whatever we want as long as we pretend that we're totally happy and satisfied and positive. If we're angry about something, though, it gives us more of it. A Great, Ethereal, petty-as-fuck Being, casually chilling out in the universe.

Which could've abducted Will, now that I thought about it.

Not that I cared about Will anymore, right?

Well, if I kept saying that, maybe the Great, Ethereal Being would make it so.

It took me so long to assemble a decent first-impression outfit for my introduction to Collinswood High that I practically sprinted downstairs, intending to dive straight into the car. My plans were thwarted, though, when I found both my parents in the kitchen, determined to put together breakfast for me. And, to my dismay, they wouldn't take "no time" for an answer.

They'd decided on scrambled eggs. Which sounds simple, and fast. And it probably is, when you don't go through three failed batches. By the time they managed to produce an edible meal between them, the floor was littered with meal detritus in the form of eggshells, burnt toast, salt, pepper, and errant smudges of butter. It was apocalypse by breakfast.

I inhaled the eggs as quickly as I could, dripping butter down the front of my jacket in the process. *Fantastic.* I debated changing, and ended up abandoning it altogether. I sprinted to the car, nearly tripping over my own feet.

First day, the very first day, and I was going to be *so* late.

I made my way to school with all the speed of a ninety-year-old on their way to bingo night. Not my fault, I might add. I just happened to hit every single red light. Straight flush. How lucky can a guy get?

Luckier than even that, it would seem. I was apparently the very last person to get to school, because every single parking space was occupied. Swearing, I turned down the blaring music and crawled around the Collinswood High parking lot.

No spots.

Still no spots.

And yet, somehow, still no empty spaces even after five full minutes of scanning. This was simply joyous.

Finally, I found a place, right at the edge of the lot. It was under one of those trees that drop sappy, sticky blossoms over everything in the vicinity. Silver lining: shade. Not-so-silver lining: I'd be spending the weekend with a hose and rag in my driveway in exchange for the privilege of parking here. Did I accept the trade-off? Well, put it this way: I was late enough by then I'd have parked on top of a portal to hell if it meant I could stop circling this damn lot.

I ripped my keys out from the ignition and launched myself out of the car. Except I vastly overestimated my skills of dexterity. In other words, I may have failed to properly unhook my left arm from the seat belt before leaping out the door. Which *may* have resulted in me being yanked backward with enough of a jolt to throw me into the car's side, and then to my knees like a human pinball. God almighty, this morning was some sort of sick joke.

In the brief seconds I spent slumped on the concrete, one arm dangling above my head in a seat belt sling, I had an epiphany. Everything happened for a reason, and somehow, something out there had been looking out for me after all. *That's* why I was running so late. So, when I made a spectacular idiot out of myself, I'd have precisely zero witnesses.

While I was in the process of practicing mindful gratitude and disentangling myself from the seat belt I realized I was, unfortunately, mistaken. The Great, Ethereal Being of the universe hated me after all. Because a girl stood two spots over, clutching her books and staring at me.

She was pretty, in a polished, "it's the first day of school and I want to impress" way, dressed in a blazer, skinny jeans, and high-heeled boots. Her dark brown skin was totally pimple-and blemish-free, her lips wore a swipe of clear lip gloss, and her curls sat fluffy and voluminous on her shoulders.

Well, this was mortifying.

"I," I called out to her, "am fine. Just to clarify."

The girl shifted her rather large pile of books to lock her own car. "That's a relief," she said. "I was concerned for a minute."

"No need." I straightened and grabbed my backpack off of the passenger seat. Semi-smooth recovery.

"That's okay then." The girl shot me a quick smile, then turned her attention back to her car. I figured the conversation was over, and started the awkward journey past her.

As I got closer, though, I realized why she was staring at her car. Her clicker thingy wasn't working.

Obviously, I couldn't afford to be any later on my first day. But it so happened I was quite the expert in the operation of clicker thingies. So I couldn't very well justify walking past without helping, right? Not least of all because it might further anger the Great, Ethereal Being of the universe.

"Can I give it a shot?" I asked as I reached the girl.

She hesitated. Which was fair, given what she'd seen of my competence levels so far. I straightened and tried to twist my face into an "I've totally got this" expression. It must have worked, because she shrugged and passed me her keys. "Go for the gold."

Stepping around to the front of the car, I brandished the clicker and pressed as hard as possible. For good measure, I focused on gratitude and positive thinking, with a dash of mindfulness thrown in. To my great relief, the headlights flashed, and the car locked.

As far as I was concerned, that was me mostly redeemed in the eyes of this morning's only witness. Score one for Ollie. Ethereal Being: three billion. The gap was closing.

The girl raised her eyebrows, impressed. "Thank you."

I went to pass the clicker back to her, but her hands were kind of busy with the stack of ten or so books balanced in the crook of her arm.

"Um, do you need a hand with all that?" I asked as we hurried on. The redbrick school building loomed in the distance, all menacing and intimidating. It was three stories high, with practically *acres* of freshly trimmed grass between the parking lot and the entrance, cut through the middle by a steep pathway lined with flagpole after flagpole. Why was Collinswood High so enormous? Collinswood was a teensy little pond, and it had no business boasting a school building that could house an ocean's worth of fish.

The girl laughed. Ouch. Shut down, much? "You wanna carry my books to class?" she asked. "What is this, the fifties?"

"Not all your books," I said. "Just maybe one or two of the light ones." I pointed to the two paperbacks on top. "You could probably manage the rest without me."

"I think I can manage *all* of them without you, thanks all the same."

If it had come from someone else I might've been offended by that, but this girl had a way of half-smiling that made me feel like I was in on a joke with her. I decided I liked her. I hooked her key chain through one finger and held it up. "Guess I'll walk these to your class, then?"

"Actually, that'd be really great." She offered me a brilliant grin, which I caught and threw back to her. Up this close, she smelled like sugary flowers. "So, guessing you're new," she continued. "That, or you're a seriously tall freshman."

"Nope. A regular-sized senior. I'm Ollie. I just moved here from California, I guess. Kind of. Possibly temporarily, possibly for a while. Depends on some family stuff."

*Well, gee, are you sure that was awkward enough, Ollie? If you try really hard, you could sound even* weirder. *Don't settle for halfway, here.*

The girl didn't seem to notice the word-vomit. "I figured you weren't from around here. Your accent and all. Anyway, I'm Juliette. Where's your homeroom? I can take you, if you want."

Hey, *I* wasn't the one with an accent. In fact, Juliette had even more of a Southern drawl than most of the other people I'd met so far. If I had to guess, I'd say Juliette had originated from farther south. So, it seemed someone else wasn't from uh-ree-ound hay-err. I'd have to ask another time, though: Juliette had reminded me how late I was. I racked my brain to access the memory of my homeroom teacher. It had blurred together with the twenty other names I'd tried to memorize. "Um, I'm with Ms. Hurstenwild, I think."

"Oh, snap, you're with us! That makes things easy. Follow me Ollie-oop."

"Ollie-oop?"

"Ollie-oop. Alley-oop. Roll with it, 'kay? It sounds cute."

"For a three-year-old, maybe," I protested, but Juliette didn't seem to hear me. Convenient. She picked up her pace and powered up the path, through the glass sliding doors, and down several empty hallways. I hurried after her, cheeks flushing. Great. Everyone was already in class.

She stopped short somewhere in the maze of classrooms and nodded toward a door. Right. She had no hands.

As expected, a sea of unfamiliar heads turned as I walked in. Awesome. To my relief, Juliette stepped in front of me. "Hey, Ms. H. Sorry I'm late. Ollie was lost, so I stopped to help him."

Way to throw me under the bus, Juliette. Ms. Hurstenwild, a middle-aged woman with an underbite and a neck that was too thick for the high collar of her shirt, didn't seem pissed though. "I'll give you a pass today, Juliette, but you'll have to get creative for me to fall for that for the next hundred and eighty mornings."

Juliette headed straight to an empty desk. How did she know which was hers? How would I know where I was meant to go? "I wouldn't dream of it, Ms. H," she said. "I'll only blame it on Ollie for two weeks, max."

Ms. Hurstenwild turned to me. Self-conscious, I crossed my arms over my chest. Was I supposed to introduce myself here? Was I supposed to insist that Juliette did not represent me?

"Good morning, Oliver. Glad to see you found your way here."

Oh. That wasn't so bad. I managed a smile. I managed to breathe. I even managed to ignore the rest of the students staring at me. For a few seconds, anyway.

Ms. Hurstenwild gestured to the back of the classroom. "You can take that seat. We're going over some housekeeping things to kick off the term."

I scanned the faces at first, then, overwhelmed, I settled for staring at the floor. It wasn't that I was hugely shy or anything. I just . . . I mean, come on. No one relishes feeling like a zoo animal, right?

Luckily, I made it to my desk without anyone throwing popcorn at me, which was a great success as far as I was concerned. Ms. Hurstenwild started talking about hall passes and library access, and I probably should've been paying attention, but my gaze kept wandering around the class. There were thirty or so students. On the surface, they weren't any different from the kids back home. Only your usual distribution of pretty to plain, self-assured to awkward, skinny jeans to boot cut to miniskirts. But while the class might not be any different from the ones back home, I could be. Different, that is. I was a blank slate now. Anything could happen from here on out. Any of these people might become my best friends or worst enemies by the end of the year. I was totally in charge of my destiny. Whatever move I made today might make or break the year.

But no pressure, right? As long as I didn't get tangled

in any more seat belts, and tamed my use of the English language, I should be okay.

"Should" being the key word.

Suddenly, I realized Ms. Hurstenwild had stopped speaking, and people were moving. I froze—was it first period already? There hadn't been a bell? But before I could react, Juliette had plopped her butt on the front of my desk. She had two girls with her. One was tall and curvy, with thick eyelashes straight out of a Covergirl advertisement, and cool brown skin. She was decked out head to toe in brand-name workout gear, from her wool sweater to her three-quarter yoga pants. The other girl, in a *slight* contrast, wore a pale lavender, frilly dress, that shouldn't have worked with her equally pale skin but somehow did, paired with a leather jacket and Converse. That, plus the heavy eyeliner and slumped posture, made her the spitting image of half of my friends back home. Unfortunately, she was the only one of the girls who looked less than impressed to see me.

"Ollie-oop, this is Niamh and Lara," Juliette said, pointing to the L'Oréal model and the punk-looking chick respectively. *Neev?* People had weird names in North Carolina. "Guys, Ollie moved here from California. Apparently he could move back at any time, at the drop of a hat."

Goddamnit, my face was flushing. All right. My turn to speak. Maybe I should take this opportunity to prove my firm grasp on my first language. "Hi. Yeah, we spent the summer here, and my parents figured hey, why bother going home, let's hang out here all year."

Niamh looked puzzled. "Really? That seems like an . . . unusual thing to do."

He shoots, he misses. "Um . . . yeah, no, it was . . . it was a, uh . . . a joke . . . we didn't really . . . um . . . my aunt's sick, so we're staying here for a while to help out."

All three girls stared at me. I stared back at them. Then an enormous black hole opened up in the floor and I happily let it suck me into the depths of the earth.

Lara puffed out her cheeks. "That's a downer." Juliette not-so-subtly elbowed her, and Lara made a show of nursing her rib cage. "Jesus, Jule, the hell was that for?"

"So you spent the summer in town?" Juliette asked, raising her voice over Lara's, clearly trying to smooth over the awkwardness.

"Not right here, no. We were at the lake. This is my first time in Collinswood since I was a little kid."

"Oh cool," Niamh jumped in. "I spent a week over there, too. We probably walked by each other a dozen times without even realizing. How funny."

"Niamh likes to spend as much time there as she can," Juliette said. "She's completely convinced she'll end up in a torrid summer romance one year."

"Closest I got was Grandpa's lawn-bowling buddy," Niamh said, fiddling with her necklace, a simple rose-gold chain with a rose pendant dangling at the end. A rose-gold rose. "But he was more into me than I was into him, unfortunately. I don't mind an older man, but I draw the line at sixty."

I'd seen Niamh's necklace before—on Juliette, I realized, looking between them. Yup, identical. On a hunch, I glanced at Lara. A rose glittered at the base of her throat, too, catching the fluorescent light.

Juliette tapped Niamh's arm good-naturedly. "That's what I keep telling you. If you want adventure, you're gonna have to go a little farther than the lake, don't you think? Scandalous summer romances aren't a thing in North Carolina."

I played my poker face. As far as I was concerned, I'd

nailed it. That is, until Lara narrowed her eyes at me, leaned her elbows on my desk, and said, "Or not? Ollie?"

I blinked. "Hmm?"

But it was too late to play innocent. Lara gave me an evil smile and pointed right at me. "I saw that look! What did *you* get up to over the break? I'm assuming she was younger than sixty."

The flush from before would've been but a soft glow compared to the way I must look now. "Um . . . I, uh . . ."

Juliette jumped on board now. "He *did*, oh my *God*. Niamh, I stand corrected."

Niamh pouted. "Some people get all the luck."

A nervous laugh burst out of my throat like a shaken soda can fizzing over. "Isn't it time for class?"

"Nope," said Juliette. "Didn't you hear Ms. H? She's giving us five minutes to catch up on summer goss. So, please, goss."

Lara grabbed an empty chair from a nearby desk and sat in it back to front, lavender frills bouncing every which way. "Yeah, regale us with all the R-rated details, would you? God knows the rest of us don't have much to report from over the summer."

"You don't?" Juliette asked her. "That's disappointing."

Lara waved a hand in her face. "We're not talking about me right now."

On the one hand, I barely knew these girls, so should I really be sharing so much with them so early? On the other hand, they seemed interested, and I'd barely had the chance to talk about it with my friends back home in the big moving rush. If I didn't tell someone soon, the words were going to overflow right out of my pores.

I swallowed. "Well . . . maybe I did, I guess . . ."

Three heads turned back to me, and the stage person

swiveled the spotlight right on my face. Juliette circled a hand in midair. "Yeesss?"

"I did meet someone," I said. "And . . . yeah, some things did happen. Um . . ."

"Someone? Guy or girl or . . . ?" Juliette interrupted.

Well. So much for tiptoeing around pronouns. I'd known I'd have to "come out" here sooner or later, if you could call it coming out when I'd been out for years. But I'd already *gone* through all that awkwardness back home. I kind of felt like I'd paid my dues, you know? Also, notably, Collinswood, North Carolina, was possibly a *tad* higher difficulty level on the coming-out spectrum than San Jose. I'd hoped it'd happen more organically, like people would kind of figure it out, and we'd all just know and act like it was normal, because it *was* normal for me, and we could skip off into the sunset with zero interrogations.

And yet.

"Guy," I said finally. Weirdly, it was hard to make my mouth form the word. After all these years being comfortable and confident in myself back home, I felt fourteen again. And I did *not* appreciate it.

Juliette nodded like she'd expected it. Niamh raised her eyebrows and tilted her head, as though she'd spotted a rare bird or something. Lara blinked, and made a lemon-sucking face. Well fine. Screw her. I didn't particularly care about her approval anyway, so.

After a slight pause that came close to uncomfortable, Niamh and Juliette spoke up at the same time.

"What's his name?"

"Do you have a picture?"

I hesitated, then figured why not? I flicked through his Instagram—for such a hot guy, his pictures sure didn't do him justice—until I found a photo that was acceptable. I held the phone out to Juliette, and Lara leaned over to peek. I wished she wouldn't, but I couldn't exactly ask her to keep her nose out of it, could I? "His name's Will," I said.

Juliette and Lara made identical taken-aback expressions. "I know," I said. "He's out of my league, right?"

"Don't knock yourself," Niamh chided, holding her hand out to see. Juliette passed it to her silently. Niamh checked the photo, then turned it back around to Juliette. "Wait, Will—"

"He's all right," Lara interrupted, holding up a hand, all traces of lemon lips vanished. "And have you told Prince Charming you're staying south?"

Good question. "Uh . . . well . . . he hasn't posted anything in a while, so I'm not sure he saw," I faltered. No need to go into the painful details of how many texts he'd left unanswered. "The move happened pretty quickly."

"Oh? So he doesn't know you're here?" Lara asked.

I had no idea what her angle was, but it was clear from her tone—and Juliette's sideways glance at her—that she wasn't asking out of empathy. Probably to rub in that I'd been rejected. Which was the case, let's be honest. Who disappears off social media with no warning for two solid weeks? He'd probably blocked me from seeing his new posts. What happens at the lake stays at the lake, right?

"Well . . . no," I said. So much for hiding the "he's ignoring me" thing. "I mean, there could be a good reason he's gone quiet. He didn't really seem like a player, you know? He was really sweet. And I actually . . . kind of . . . don't know where he lives, exactly. He told me once, but I've forgotten."

Juliette and Niamh exchanged glances with Lara, then they offered me weak smiles. "Who knows?" Juliette said. "He could totally have a reason."

She wasn't convincing. Eurgh, was it *that* obvious? And here I'd been holding out some hope it wasn't personal. But of course it was. A guy like that wouldn't go for someone like me in real life. I guess I was probably just the best option he had available at the time.

After watching my face as I got more and more dejected, Lara jumped in and changed the topic. Which was nice of her. Maybe I'd judged her too quickly. "Anyway, Ollie, has anyone told you about the party at Rachel's tonight?"

"I don't even know who Rachel is, so, nope."

"It's our back-to-school-bash thing. You should come with us," Juliette said, clapping once. "We're getting ready at my place after dinner. Can you get there around seven?"

I thought about it. On a Tuesday? I got that it was the first day of school, but *really*? It'd take a lot of bribery on my part to get permission. Assuming no one needed me for babysitting. I could deal with that if it came up, though. I knew what happened if you turned down your first invitation at a new school: you never got a second one. I'd seen it happen a few times to kids back home. If I could help it, it wouldn't happen to me. "Yeah, sure. Text me your address."

With that, we hastily exchanged numbers. Then the bell was ringing, and Juliette was dragging me by the wrist to my first class. It seemed I was adopted into the rose-necklace group. Provisionally at least. I'd far from nailed my first impression, but apparently it hadn't been a total fail.

Good. This was good. Homeroom: achievement unlocked. The hardest part was over. It'd be all downhill from here. I could feel it.

# 3

I buried my toes in the sand while the kids played in the shallows. It was one of those days where it was so warm the horizon seemed wavy and distorted. The sky was a darker, richer blue than usual, contrasting starkly against the fir-covered hills across the lake.

A shadow to my right told me I wasn't alone. Not that I was strictly alone to begin with—there were at least forty others scattered around, bobbing in the water, lounging on beach towels, perched at picnic benches. But none of them noticed me.

Will sat down beside me, staring out at the lake as he did. Today he wore dark denim shorts and a crisp white V-neck that made his warm skin seem even deeper. "Those kids yours?" he asked, without glancing at me. He was being cute. I kind of loved it.

"Nope. Never seen them in my life," I joked.

"Oh. Excellent. Shall we go somewhere a bit more private, then?"

*I bumped my shoulder against his, grinning. "Wish I could. I'm on duty 'til at least two or three, though."*

*He kicked off his shoes and settled in. "Good thing I've cleared my calendar for the day."*

*I brightened. "Yeah? Don't you have that buffet tonight?"*

*"Technically, I do. But I thought about it, and realized I'd rather hang with you. Hope you don't mind me imposing."*

*There they were again. The familiar butterflies. They spent a lot of time fluttering around lately. "Well, it's a bit of an inconvenience."*

*"You'll forgive me for it eventually."*

*Crista noticed him first, and she sprinted out of the water, with Dylan toddling closely behind her. "Will! Will, you missed me before, I did a handstand."*

*"A handstand? Now I'm impressed. Do you think you could do it again?"*

I may have slipped into the dinner conversation that I was super late for school after they forced me to stop for breakfast. Just to amp up the likelihood I'd get a yes and escape the house tonight. I know, I know, I shouldn't have been guilting my parents when they had tried to do something nice for me, but I was desperate. It worked like a charm, too. After graciously forgiving them, I brought up the party in a casual tone, and the next thing I knew they'd said yes— with the caveat that Mom had to drop me off and pick me up. It was a family rule for any event that might have alcohol around somewhere, in case I made Bad Choices.

I ended up at Juliette's at seven-thirty. There was something about this town. Everyone seemed to live in semi-mansions. At least, compared to my suburb back home.

It was like no one here had ever heard of a single-storey house.

Juliette's mom steered me straight upstairs.

"I am so sorry you had to see the house like this. Usually we have it much neater, but Juliette thought she would wait until we got home from work to ask if she could have friends over."

I'd seen messier hotel rooms ready for check-in. I tried hard to locate the "mess" on my way upstairs, like a real-life game of Where's Waldo? One of the trimmed pillows on the couch looked like it was a bit crooked. That might have been it.

Juliette's room, on the other hand, was what you could call messy. Could probably call it trashed, even. The floor—at least, I think there was a floor, it was hard to tell—was covered in no fewer than three layers of clothing. Juliette was wandering around her room in a bra and a denim skirt, digging through the floordrobe. Presumably for a shirt. She didn't seem bothered when she noticed me walk in, either. What *was* it with girls and boundaries when it came to guys they knew were gay? I mean, Jesus, I'd just met her, and now I knew she had a mole sitting right under her left bra cup. Was I the only one who thought that was kind of weird? Really?

Niamh and Lara sat crossed-legged on the king-sized bed. On the bedside table a half-empty bottle of soda stood beside a Minnie Mouse lamp. Lara was still in her outfit from school, but Niamh had changed into a black romper. Significantly more glamorous than the workout gear she'd worn all day. Both girls looked up as I came in; then, with a relieved sigh, Niamh fished a vodka bottle out from beneath Juliette's pillow. I guessed they'd thought I was Juliette's mom.

Niamh patted the bed next to her with one hand, refilling her drink with the other. "Ollie-oop! You made it."

Guess that nickname was sticking. Joy.

Juliette clapped her hands, retrieved a metallic silver shirt from the chaos, and turned to me. "Hey you. I'll grab you a glass. You can share our vodka."

"Or drink it straight," Lara added, swirling her soda around the glass. "You might need a stiff drink before tonight."

What was that supposed to mean? I considered calling her out on it, but I decided to play nice for a while longer. No use making enemies in the only group I had right now. "Actually, I'm okay for now, thanks."

Lara rolled her eyes back so only the whites were visible. "Let me guess. You don't drink?"

"Not often," I said airily. And by that, I meant "never." Back in San Jose, my friends were mostly straight edge. It was cooler *not* to drink in our circle. I couldn't think of a way to say that without sounding like a pretentious douche bag, though, so I left it.

Lara raised her glass. "Then let tonight be one of the special occasions."

I smiled with my lips. "No, thank you."

Niamh looked between us nervously. Lara blinked at me, then took a deep gulp of her own drink. "Whatever, dude. Chill. Take it you, uh, don't smoke, either? What are your views on swearing and premarital sex, pray tell?"

I was saved from responding by Juliette, who shook her head, hopped over the nearest clothing pile, and sprayed perfume all over herself like it was deodorant. If her scent goal for the night was to turn into a walking asthma hazard, she was nailing it. "No smoking tonight, unfortunately," she said. "Mom's been catching on, open windows or not."

Niamh threw herself back on the bed and kicked her legs in the air in a kind of yoga-protest. I watched her, then glanced back to Lara in time to catch her gesturing to me while pulling an "is he for real?" face at Juliette.

Lara didn't realize I noticed her. Juliette did, though. She chewed the inside of her lip, but didn't try to defend me. Which was fair, I guessed. She'd only just met me. Why should she go into battle on my behalf? Still. It didn't do wonders for my comfort levels. I'd better start practicing mindfulness real fast, or I might do something rash, like fake salmonella poisoning and bail. But then I'd have wasted all that emotional blackmail on my parents, and ruined my chances at fitting in with a group. Even if it was a group that was maybe a little too edgy for me. It was better than being alone.

I spent a solid twenty or so seconds thinking over all of the above. And by that, I mean I spent a solid twenty or so seconds sitting in silence, staring ahead mindfully. My brain had officially gone on strike. I think I might have been panicking.

Finally, a topic came to me. "Did you do that on purpose? Rose-gold roses?"

Juliette unclasped her chain and held it out to examine it. "Huh. I didn't even think of that. Rose gold."

"Double the rose power," Niamh said. "Even better."

"What do they stand for?" I asked.

"Female strength," Juliette said. "It was the symbol of Venus."

"Not love?" I asked.

"Who needs love when you can have passion?" Lara

said. She brought the chain up over her jaw and clenched the metal between her teeth.

"I like them," I said.

"Too bad they don't sell them anymore," Lara said. "Limited edition, you know? That's why we don't let new girls into the group. It'd ruin the theme."

Before I spent too long floundering for a response, Juliette jumped in. "Hey, finish your drinks now anyway, guys. We should probably head over soon."

The house was an anthill. Everyone at the party seemed to know each other—everywhere I looked was arm-clapping, and lip-reading from across the room, and people putting silent hexes on each other with angry, narrowed eyes. The temperature soared by at least twenty degrees as soon as we walked into the living room, and the air smelled like warm beer and Axe body spray.

Lara had to shout to make herself heard over the music. "I'm gonna go scout."

With that she was off. To scout for guys, I guessed? Or alcohol? Juliette hesitated, then held a finger up in a "one second" gesture. "I'm going with her. We won't be long."

And then there were two. Niamh and I glanced at each other, basking in the awkwardness. How did you start a conversation again? I was about to settle for *so, you like stuff?* when she saved me the severe embarrassment by speaking first. "I know we're only at the start of the year, but what are your plans for after school? Got any colleges in mind?"

A group of guys pushed past me to get to the front door, and we moved to the wall to get out of the way. "Not really. I'm not even sure if I want to go to college. I was hoping to figure that out sometime this year. How about you?"

Niamh brightened. Something told me she'd had this answer ready for some time. "Actually, college is my backup. Ideally, I'll move to New York and get into modeling."

"Oh, seriously?"

"Yup. There's an agent up there who's pretty interested in some of my pictures, so I'm hoping to build my portfolio a bit and go for it."

"That's awesome. You could have a real shot, too. You're crazy pretty."

Niamh glowed, and shrugged. "Well, obviously we don't have to beat around the bush, I'd be doing plus-sized modeling."

"I'm not beating around any bushes. You *are* crazy pretty."

"Thank you."

"You have the thickest eyelashes I've ever seen. Like, are they false?"

Niamh laughed. "Nope!"

"If I was a girl I would want to look like you. Your *hair*."

"Oh . . . you're laying it on a bit thick, now." Niamh grinned, but it was an uncomfortable one.

"Yeah, no, sorry. That's fair. I, uh . . . I'll stop."

I'd been doing well for a second there, too. A part of me suddenly understood why people drank at parties. It wasn't to have fun. It was to forget how much of an idiot they made of themselves.

Niamh shifted, and then shook her head. "Come on, let's go find the girls. Lara's probably getting into trouble."

"What kind of trouble?" I asked, following after her as

she stalked into the backyard, which was as crowded as the house.

At least the music was muted out here, and there was fresh air.

"Oh, you know. Just trouble. Teasing boys, mostly."

We squeezed past four or five groups, then I caught sight of Juliette's hair through the crowd. Lara was next to her, talking to a group of guys in black-and-white letterman jackets standing in front of a wooden panel fence.

Then one of the letterman guys caught my eye. A letterman guy with dark hair in a deep side part, a freckled nose, and high cheekbones. A letterman guy I knew.

The world fell silent.

It was *him*.

Will.

*Will* Will.

My Will.

We stared at each other in dumb shock. It was hard to tell which of us was the deer, and which was the headlight.

He spoke first. Which was excellent, because I wasn't sure if I should be thrilled or accusatory. "Holy shit, Ollie! What are you *doing* here?" He looked dumbfounded, but it was a happy kind of dumbfounded. That's all it took for all my doubts to disappear. Of *course* he wasn't ignoring me. This was Will we were talking about.

"What are *you* doing here?" I asked, before realizing that at least this was supposed to be his state. It was significantly weirder for me to be here than him. "You didn't say you lived in Collinswood. You said it was something else, starting with M, right? Or L?"

"Napier. I live in Napier. It's twenty minutes out of Collinswood," Will said. "I go to school here. Ollie, *why aren't you in California*? You're so ridiculous!"

He was grinning. Beaming, really. A cheekbone-shattering kind of smile. A viral-epidemic kind of smile. Infectious-as-hell. All of the misery from the last couple of weeks, every bit of it, was gone. Like it'd never been there.

"My parents thought they'd move us over to help out with Aunt Linda. She lives here. In Collinswood."

"You never mentioned that."

"Didn't I? Well, she does. So do I now, I guess."

"Oh my God, Ollie-oop, how awesome is that?" Lara cut in, her voice way too perky to be sincere. Will and I looked at her as one. I'd forgotten she was there until that moment. I'd forgotten *anyone* other than Will was there. "What are the odds? Will, Ollie was telling us *all about* his summer this morning."

Will's smile dropped, and so did my stomach. He wasn't out to his parents. God only knew that meant he probably wasn't out here, either. Or at least, he hadn't been. Until I'd opened my mouth. I didn't know these girls from Abraham Lincoln. For all I knew, they'd already made a group chat for half the grade about Will and me. Uh-oh.

One of the letterman guys sidled up beside Will. He was half a foot taller than Will, with deep brown skin and the kind of jawline people write Tumblr posts about. "By the way, Lara," he said, apparently continuing a conversation that had been underway when I got here, "how come you didn't sit with me in Biology? I saved you a seat and every-thing."

Lara softened. So she *could* be sweet. "You did? I was so tired this morning, I sleepwalked into class."

I tuned the conversation out and stole a glance at Will. His mouth hung slightly open, and his stare was fixed on a spot in the distance. "Will, seriously. I had no *idea* they'd know you. It didn't even occur to me, I—"

He held up a hand. "It's cool. Whatever. Just, uh . . . just keep your voice down, okay?"

"Yeah, of course. So . . . where have you been, anyway? When I didn't hear from you, I figured you were . . . I dunno . . ."

Will's face was still blank. "I was busy. Sorry. Anyway, good to see you. I'll catch you around."

And he turned his back on me to talk to someone else. Just like that. Something deep inside me snagged, like a loose thread catching. I stared at the back of his head with my mouth hanging open. He did *not* just do that. I was imagining this right now. I had to be.

Juliette and Niamh had watched the whole thing. Juliette twisted her mouth, shot Will's back a dirty glare, then led me away by my elbow with Niamh, leaving Lara behind with Matt. "God, he can be a real dick," Juliette said, as quietly as she could, given the music volume. "Ignore him, please. The basketball guys are all a little funny when they're around each other."

"A little funny," I echoed. Every step we took away from them felt like that thread inside of me was unraveling more and more. Like my soul was unspooling.

Time to make an excuse to get out of here, *now*.

I think the girls might've been talking to me, but it was hard to say. The crowd was blurring, and everyone was moving in slow motion. A few people bumped into me as we moved through the living room, or maybe I bumped into them. Who knows if they apologized? Who even knows if I did?

Around the time we got to the refreshments table, I'd convinced myself this was a dream after all, and dug my fingernails hard into my palm to prove it. Unfortunately, the only thing it proved was that I was: a) awake, and

b) still at the damn party. Abort mission. *Now.* Screw the repercussions.

"Come on, I'm sure it's not *that* bad for you," Juliette was saying to Niamh, holding out a ladle. "It's just some punch."

"I'm trying to cut down on carbs. Hence, vodka shots."

"Vodka has carbs. It's *super* carbed-up."

Niamh scoffed. "It's definitely not."

"It's got potatoes in it. What are potatoes made of? Carbs, Niamh."

I cleared my throat, hovering like an awkward stalker behind them.

"Vodka doesn't *have* potatoes in it," Niamh shot back, "it—"

"Hey, I'll be back, okay?" I cut her off.

The only acknowledgment I got was a vague nod from both of them. Guess that was my pass. I broke off and wandered through the living room, pushing past body after body after unfamiliar body.

I had the desperate urge to go outside and call Ryan, or Hayley, or anyone, really. Just to hear a familiar voice. To drown out the fact that I'd screwed up my first day at school, and I'd outed Will, and that if he hadn't wanted to shut me out after all, he *definitely* did now. And it was all my fault.

Out in the front yard, I sucked in a lungful of air and narrowly avoided passing out. That might sound melodramatic, but I hadn't realized how stifling the smoke and body heat and beer fumes were until they contrasted with clean, crisp air. I trotted down the steps and continued around the house until I found a spot where I could slot myself between the shrubs and flower beds to lean against the cool brick wall. Suddenly, I didn't even want to call Ryan.

I had to get out of here. I sent Mom a quick S.O.S. text, and settled back against the wall to wait.

A familiar voice to my right made me start. Will. Of *course* it was. I couldn't have five minutes' reprieve from this absolute bad joke of a day, huh? He must be near the front door, from the sound of his voice. I couldn't let him see me here alone. No way. If we were playing the "I don't care about you" game, the best possible way for me to lose was to be caught friendless and feeling sorry for myself. I'd rather dive into the writhing sea of hormones back inside, thanks all the same.

His voice was getting closer. That left me with two options. One, find a way to climb inside the rosebush and pretend to be a rose. I'd been a bush in a school play once, and, not to brag, but I'd been told I was a natural at it, so option one was solid. Two, flee to the backyard.

I fled. I fled like a bigot dodging the concept of equality.

Luckily, I acted quickly enough to escape undetected. I dove into the crowd in the backyard until I couldn't see anything but the bodies sandwiching me. I clutched onto my phone as if it was a life raft, pinballing between random groups while I killed time until Mom arrived. Then suddenly I spotted someone I knew making out with some willowy redheaded girl. Not Will, thankfully. Someone with long, chestnut brown curls, and a leather jacket, and a lavender dress.

Lara.

I froze, confused as all hell. Then I noticed what I hadn't caught to begin with. Lara's same-sex make-out session was taking place in the middle of a ring of students. Mostly guys, if it needed to be spelled out. They were cheering, and fist-pumping, and generally being gross about it. So, what, Lara was doing this for show? Maybe. Except she looked like she was into it. Like, *super* into it. Not that I was any expert on kissing girls, but that was my layman's opinion. Her hand was on the girl's shoulder, the other wrapped up in her hair, and she hadn't peeked once. Also, I'd been staring for a solid fifteen seconds now and she still hadn't come up for air.

When they finally tore apart, the redhead burst out laughing, throwing her head back. Lara laughed, too, but it was a smaller one, and she bent forward to hide her face. She lifted her chin, watched the other girl for a moment with a pleased smile, then tossed her hair and turned to her audience, as if to say *I kissed a girl, and you liked it.*

Before she saw me, I blended back in with the crowd. It's fairly easy to disappear when barely anyone knows you, it turns out. I walked aimlessly for a bit, dodging spilled drinks and staggering groups, until I found myself in the front yard again. Will was nowhere in sight. Neither was anyone else, for that matter. With a heavy sigh I sat on the curb with my feet in the gutter and settled in for the wait for Mom's rescue chariot.

Way to *utterly* fail, Ollie.

Slow clap. Encore. Et cetera.

# 4

Ollie? Where'd you go?

Are you still here?

Are you mad at us?

Please reply. I'm sorry. Pick up?

Is this Juliette? I don't have your number saved. I'm not mad. Sorry, I went home. I think I have salmonella.

Read Tuesday, 10:25 PM

Even though Juliette and I had sent a few back-and-forth texts on Tuesday night, I still wasn't totally convinced everything was okay with me and the girls until I got into homeroom on Wednesday. On time, I might add. Early, even. I'd barely sat down at my desk when they swarmed. Anyone would think I was Harry Styles.

Juliette spoke first. "Ollie-oop! I didn't think you'd come in. What with the salmonella and all."

Well, from her sarcastic tone it almost sounded like she doubted the validity of my food poisoning. "It was the mild kind of salmonella poisoning. Like, the two-hour-long kind."

Juliette and Niamh nodded like this was completely understandable. Lara watched me like a cat stalking a fly.

"Okie doke," Juliette said, scooting onto my desk again. "First up, the whole Will thing . . . you can trust us to keep it a secret. He knows we wouldn't tell anyone."

I tossed up whether or not to insist they had the wrong idea about Will. Only problem was I couldn't really remember how much I'd told them in the first place, and to be honest, it was probably too late to backtrack now. So I nodded and glanced around to make sure no one had overheard.

"Also," said Niamh, "we found out why he disappeared off Instagram."

"Did you speak to him?" I asked quickly, half-horrified, half-eager.

The girls looked offended. "Please. You're as subtle as a sledgehammer," Lara said.

"We have our ways," Juliette added.

"Lara's close with his friend Matt," Niamh said. "Matt said that apparently Will got his phone confiscated for coming home at four in the morning before his family was supposed to drive home. So, we figured that was probably right around the time you stopped hearing from him, right?"

"Right." Shit, did I look like I was thinking about Will naked? Because I was most definitely thinking about Will naked. I couldn't help it. That night brought back memories. And I knew damn well why he didn't get home until almost dawn that night.

"Apparently he was skinny-dipping with a bunch of girls from the lake houses," Lara added with a smirk. "Did you and Will spend much time with all of those girls?"

Like I said, I knew damn well what he was doing that night, and it wasn't a girl, that was for sure. If Lara was trying to upset me it was working. So this was the story he was telling everyone? I guess it shouldn't have surprised me so much. It's not like he could say what had really happened. But shit. It hurt anyway. I wrung my hands, furrowing my brow.

"Oh, sorry . . . did you not know?" Lara asked, all fake concern.

I plastered a smile on my face and looked back up. "It's fine. How was *your* night? I saw you with a girl before I left the party."

It was petty, but hey. It's not like that was private. She'd done it with thirty-odd people practically munching popcorn in the front row.

Niamh snorted, and Juliette grinned, nudging Lara. "Did you get too drunk again, by any chance, Miss Lara?"

Lara held my gaze. I could read her expression fluently: "challenge accepted." Uh-oh. "Maaaayybbeeee," Lara said to Juliette.

"Lara kisses girls sometimes when she's drunk," Niamh said. "And we *know* it's because the guy she likes gets off on it, but she won't admit which guy it is."

"My bet's on Matt," Juliette said.

Lara scoffed. "*Please,* peasants. Also, I don't kiss 'girls' plural. Just Renee. We have a symbiotic relationship."

Juliette shook her head. "Yeah, well, I hope you've at least disclosed which guy you're trying to impress to her. It'd be awkward if you both had the same conquest in mind, don't you think?"

"Ask me no question, I'll tell you no lie," Lara said, glancing at me as Ms. Hurstenwild gestured for everyone to take their seats. I raised my eyebrow at her. Ever so briefly, she looked rattled. Then she turned away from me without a word.

I had a feeling I knew what she was trying to achieve by kissing Renee.

And I had a feeling I knew why it was such a secret.

Guess the secret was ours, for now.

To my relief, I still hadn't run into Will. I knew it'd happen eventually, inevitably, but I wasn't ready for that encounter yet. It was overwhelming enough trying to navigate my way from class to class. Which, I might add, had so far been distinctly Will-less. So far, our timetables hadn't crossed paths once, and I only had my English and Music Appreciation virginities to go. As of right now, Will was nowhere to be seen in English, and class was due to start any minute. And no way in hell would Will be caught dead in Music Appreciation. He hadn't even known the difference between a piano and a keyboard last time we talked about music. Looked like I was about to hit a home run. No shared classes with Will Tavares.

Question is, was I thankful or disappointed?

Before I decided, the question became redundant. The

teacher, a man who was so young he could've been any of our slightly older brothers, had just gone to close the door when a group of guys skidded through, ducking under his arm like a high-speed game of limbo.

It was Will. Will, and a couple other guys I remembered him standing with last night. He didn't seem to have noticed me yet. He and Matt had spotted a lone desk in the back of the classroom, and they were in the process of racing each other to it, each pulling the other back by their T-shirt to gain distance. God, he looked beautiful. He looked confident. He looked like the kind of guy I'd never, ever, in a million, jillion years think I'd have a chance with.

Matt beat Will to the desk by half a foot, and dove into the chair. Will grabbed his arm and yanked it playfully, offering bribes to convince him to give it up.

"Will, sit down," the teacher said wearily from the front of the classroom.

Will straightened and whirled around. "Hey, Mr. Theo, what's up? I didn't know we were gonna have another year together. Sweet!"

Matt covered up a laugh with an obvious cough, and Will shoved him, smirking.

"I was hoping you might have been kept back a year. I prayed for escape," Mr. Theo said. "But once again, the fates mock me. Take a seat." He indicated a desk in the second row, a few chairs to my right. It was too tight an angle for me to stare at the back of Will's head for long. How disappointing.

Will swung his backpack as he walked, the straps clacking against the metal desks and chair legs. "Anyone would think you weren't happy to see me," Will said in a fake hurt voice, pressing his free hand to his chest.

"I've never been much of a masochist, Will."

The classroom hummed with soft laughter, but it didn't seem to be at Will's expense. There was clearly some sort of inside joke here that I was missing. Which, to be fair, effectively described 90 percent of my "new-kid" experience to date.

"It's an acquired taste, but keep working at it and you might be surprised," Will said, and the class broke up again. He shot a cheeky smile to Mr. Theo, and glanced around the room to bask in the spotlight. That's when he noticed me. All at once, the grin slipped off his face like it'd been glued on with grease. He cut the bravado act short and slumped into the chair, angling himself away from me while Mr. Theo held up his hands for quiet.

Back in California, there was a guy in my class. Pierce, his name was. He was one of *those* guys. The ones who swagger instead of walking, and always have a smartass remark stored for ammo, and photosynthesize attention. Pierce was popular. Like, *super* popular. My crowd didn't have anything to do with him and his friends. Just in case insufferable smugness was contagious, I guess. Besides, we figured Pierce wasn't going to achieve much of anything with his life.

Somewhere up there, the Ethereal Being was smirking down at me from the sky with a handful of popcorn, because Will was Pierce. I'd spent all summer with a guy who was sweet, and thoughtful, and . . . and respectful. Only to find out he was the antithesis in real life. A guy who ignored my texts, and shunned me in front of his friends, and, apparently, had a bit of a superiority complex.

Because the lake wasn't real life. It had felt like a movie, anyway. Everything was suspiciously perfect. How many times had I thought Will seemed too perfect to exist?

Well, joke was on me, in the end.

He *was*.

# 5

A week later, and I was still getting lost more often than the girl in the *Labyrinth* movie, except I didn't even have David Bowie in tights as a reward for my efforts. I was on my way to third period—at least, I *thought* I was on my way, but it might very well turn out I was walking in the exact wrong direction—when I noticed a sign on a bulletin board. BASSIST WANTED.

The words were accompanied by a blurry picture of a bass guitar with a Getty Images watermark printed across the middle, the name Izzy, and a cell number. I forgot all about my class and gave into a thrill of excitement. I usually played guitar, but I had a solid handle on bass. To be quite frank, I'd learn to play the harp if it meant I could get involved in a band again. Riffing with my bedroom wall didn't really cut it for inspiration, and my parents were as reluctant an audience as you could find.

I texted the number.

I play bass. In the right circumstances. What did you guys have in mind?

"You guys" ended up being a rainbow-haired girl called Izzy, a round-faced guy in a hoodie called Emerson, and a mostly-skinny dude with impeccable biceps named Sayid. When I finally found room 13b (which turned out to be a basement, something I felt Izzy could've mentioned in her text to save everyone's time since I had to follow the distant hum of music to find it), they were already rehearsing a cover song I vaguely recognized. The room looked like it was probably a classroom for music students, with a grand piano in the corner, various instrument cases propped up against the wall, and several amps older than I was. It was too bad my Music Appreciation classes weren't held in here. I kind of loved it.

They were playing against the far wall. Izzy was on drums, Sayid had the keyboard and clean vocals, and Emerson took lead guitar and the screamed vocals. They could definitely use more bass, but overall they did a solidly decent job at metalcore. I was instantly impressed. This was worth sacrificing my lunch break for after all.

I didn't have my own bass with me, because I didn't go to school carrying it every morning in case someone asked me to jump in on their impromptu musical number, but Sayid grabbed one of the school ones for me. It was kind of cheap and out of tune, but I was still able to knock out a few lines.

"Not bad," Izzy said, twirling a drumstick. "Can you improv?" Without waiting for me to reply, she hopped onto the drums and jumped straight into a beat. I matched her as tightly as I could, making up the tune as I went along and ignoring the closely watching eyes of Emerson and Sayid. Before long, I stopped noticing them anyway. All I knew was the beat, and the bass under my fingers, and the perfect intermingling of the two instruments. It'd only been a couple of months since I'd played with others, but I'd forgotten how awesome it was. Like blending your soul with someone else's for three and a half minutes. For the first time since I stepped foot in this school, I felt comfortable and calm. I could picture the tension pouring out of my pores like a noxious gas.

Suddenly, Izzy stopped, got up from the drums, and waltzed over. "Can you do Tuesdays and Thursdays after school? That's when we've been catching up so far. Obviously, we'll have some gigs, too, so that'll be a Friday or Saturday usually."

I blinked and put the bass down. "Yeah, sure. I don't really have any standing commitments, other than babysitting, but I can be flexible with that."

"Awesome. So, tomorrow? Three-thirty?"

"Wait, I'm in already?" I asked.

Emerson clapped me on the shoulder, and Sayid grinned while unplugging his keyboard. "Dude," Sayid said, "we weren't expecting anyone to respond. This kind of music isn't exactly big in this school, in case you hadn't noticed. Welcome to Absolution of the Chained. We could've been really big, had we all been born in a town with better music taste."

"Way to make us sound desperate, Sayid." Izzy scowled. "People like us fine. We just usually have to tone down the screaming when we perform."

"A.K.A., put a gag on me," Emerson said. "I only get to have real fun when we're playing around."

"You've got to know your audience, guys, like I keep telling you," Sayid said.

The bell rang then. "Yeah, for sure," I said. "See you tomorrow. Let's do it."

They broke out in grins. It was that easy. So *that's* how you got through a social situation without repelling everyone within ten feet of you. Speak as little as possible, and fill the silence in with music.

Note to self: carry bass around everywhere and break into impromptu solo whenever anyone tries to force you into conversation.

Foolproof.

As soon as we were dismissed the next day, I headed toward the music room. I got about halfway down the hallway when I ran into Juliette and Niamh. Or maybe they ran into me. Juliette did seem quite enthusiastic when she saw me. That appeared pretty normal for her, though.

"Ollie-oop," she said, bounding over. If anyone could be called the human personification of Tigger, Juliette was it. Which made me Piglet, I guess. "Want to come hang with me and Lara? We're gonna grab some fries then hit the mall for a bit."

As tempting as a night with Lara was . . . "I can't, actually. I've got band practice right now in the music room."

"Band?"

"Yeah. It's called Absolution of the Damned. No, wait . . . Apocalypse of Chains, I think. Can you have an Apocalypse of Chains? What would that involve, do you think?"

But, weirdly enough, neither of them was keen on philosophizing about various potential forms of the apocalypse. "Oh, do you mean Izzy's band?" Niamh asked, at the same time Juliette jumped in with, "I didn't know you played!"

"Mm, yeah. Guitar and bass. Do you?"

"Clarinet."

"Slightly different genres, then," I said.

"She's seriously great," Niamh said, and Juliette waved her hands around like she totally-didn't-but-secretly-totally-did agree.

"I'm okay," Juliette said. Which everyone knows is code for *I was better when I was an infant than Mozart was at his peak, but N.B.D.* "More importantly, *you play.* I could really use your help. I have to pick an audition piece for the Conservatory of Music, and I'm stuck between a couple of possibilities. Do you think you might give a girl a hand sometime?"

I was about to say sure. Totally. I know little to nothing about classical music but I'd give it my best shot.

I was *about* to say all of the above. But I ended up staring blankly down the hallway. I probably should've been used to seeing him by now, but I wasn't. I'd seen him in English several times—he was hard to miss, given that he had a smartass remark for every few sentences the teacher spoke—as well as around the hallways and in the cafeteria. And even though I definitely hated him, and he was nothing at all like the guy I'd fallen for, seeing him made my chest tighten. Right now he was walking right toward me, his group of basketball guys flanking their captain, Matt, like disciples in a sea of black and white. It was eighty degrees outside, for God's sake. They always wore those damn jackets, like if they took them off for a second the rest of us might forget their place in the social hierarchy.

Which, to clarify, was: Above Everyone Else.

"Is that a no?" Juliette asked.

I scrambled to catch back up. Oh yeah. Clarinet. "No, no, I'll help for sure. Easy. That's, uh . . . a great, great idea. So great. Awesome."

Niamh was giving me a hesitant look again, like the one she gave me when I over did it with the compliments at the back-to-school party. "All righty guys, well, I've got to run if I'm gonna make it to Spin class, but I'll see you later."

Sometimes being around Niamh exhausted me. This was the seventh time she'd gone straight to the gym after school in as many days. Who knew when she had time for homework.

Juliette folded her arms in the direction of the basketball guys as they disappeared down the hallway. "Will troubles, huh? Have you spoken to him since the party?"

I pulled my best "Will, who's Will?" expression. Which was probably about as convincing as Juliette's "I'm medio-cre at clarinet" face. "Nah, but it's fine. What happens over summer stays over summer, right? It's not like we're enemies. We just . . ."

Just what?

Juliette nodded, like I'd made total sense. "Yeah, got it. We hang out with the basketball guys at lunch sometimes, you know. Mostly because of Lara and Matt being tight. We sat together yesterday. I forgot to tell you."

My stomach spun and flipped and nailed a triple Sal-chow. So, if I hadn't ditched to meet Izzy and the others, I would've ended up sitting with Will? I wasn't sure if the idea was horrifying, or something I'd trade my guitar for. "Oh," I said. "Great. That is *so* great."

"I'll hit you up about the audition thing, yeah? See you tomorrow. Have fun at practice."

She headed off down the hall. Well, at least I was

prepared now. Likely, in the near future, I'd be stuck in close vicinity with Will. Will, who'd spent all day every day with me this summer. Will, who now seemed to have developed an acute allergic reaction to me. That was fine. This was *fine*. I definitely had the tools in my vast and nuanced social tool kit to deal with this without making it uncomfortable for everyone.

Really, the only option I had right now was to stop liking him. Obviously, nothing was going to happen, so cut that cord as quickly as possible. Step one: delete his number from my phone.

There. Done. That was only 95 percent agony. It was getting easier by the day to move on from him. With any luck, it wouldn't take too long for him to feel like a scar instead of an open wound.

I strutted the rest of the way to the music room wearing a self-satisfied smirk. *Here walks Ollie Di Fiore. Master of his feelings, expert detacher, only mostly devastated.*

Now *there* was something to put on my tombstone.

# 6

"You're trying to play me," Will said, darting forward to take the basketball from me. "You can't be this bad."

Said the vice-captain of the basketball team. I hoped he was more encouraging to his team members on their off days.

I stepped back, trying to dribble the ball, but hitting the air instead as the ball lost its height. "I swear I'm not," I said. "These skills are all innate. Couldn't fake them if I tried." Will lunged for the ball and I threw myself onto it, burying it under my body. "It's still my turn. Time out!"

"You've lost your privileges."

"You can't discriminate against me because I suck, Will."

"I can do whatever I want, it's my house. Come here, come on." Will clapped his hands, and I got up, still clutching the ball. "All right, okay. We can revisit dribbling later. Can you handle a pass?"

"Are you asking me if I can handle balls, Will?" I grinned, and he darted forward to wrench it from my grip. "Okay, okay,

*I'm sorry! That was bad. I'll focus. Please, explain how one passes a ball."*

Before Will could figure out if my deadpanning was serious, his father poked his head around the side of the house. "Hey, you two. I'm heading to the store. Any requests for the grill tonight?"

Will took the distraction as an opportunity to reclaim the ball. Right out of my hands. This guy's parents had never taught him to play nice. "Mm, yeah, can we do hamburgers, Dad?" he asked.

"Sure thing. How 'bout you, Ollie?"

Will shot me a sideways warning look. I knew what it meant. *Don't even think about saying sausages.* I almost did it, just to see his reaction. But I opted not to. Double entendres were funny when we were alone, but it'd be significantly less funny if his dad got suspicious and banned him from seeing me for the rest of the summer. "Hamburgers sound great to me, Mr. Tavares."

Mr. Tavares made a super-uncool clicking noise and gave us finger guns as he left.

I turned to Will, shaking my head with a grin. "You always expect the worst from me."

"Because I know you."

"Details, minor details."

Will shrugged, glanced behind him, and threw the ball backward over his shoulders. It went straight through the hoop. I couldn't stop myself from cheering, legitimately impressed. "Holy shit! That was actually awesome."

"Wait, did it go in?"

"Straight in."

"No shit? Total fluke." He spun around, pumping his fist. "Check the modesty on this guy."

———

"My fingers aren't big enough," Crista complained, spreading her hand like a starfish over the fret board.

I rolled back on my haunches to see for myself. On the one hand, she kind of had a point. Her fingers were skinny and short, little spidery things. At best, she'd end up with killer cramps after a few chord progressions. Then on the other hand (no pun intended) I'd seen a four-year-old on *Ellen* nail Santana, so, *really*, she was years behind already.

I couldn't quite bring myself to explain to my little cousin that her weak will was bringing shame on the family, and that Ellen would never want her at this rate. Instead, I grabbed the neck alongside her. "Here. Put one finger here on the fifth string. Remember which one that is? Perfect. And then this one"—I grabbed her middle finger and raised it—"up here on the sixth string. I'll hold this one down here. Remember which string this is?"

"First."

"Great job, right. Now, do you think you can give it a strum as well?"

"That's too far, Ollie. You do it."

"I do it," Dylan interrupted. Up until now he'd been playing some pig-based game on his iPad near his bed like a good twenty-first-century toddler. I should've known he was following along with what Crista and I were doing on the guitar. If Crista was doing it, Dylan wanted to do it, too. Luckily for the sanity of everyone in the family, Crista didn't mind indulging him. Once or twice, I'd actually caught her staring at him while he slept with a slightly deranged expression, while whispering, "Sleep well, Anna," to him. I assumed Crista was probably *Frozen* role-playing, so I didn't ask. Well, that and because I was secretly terrified she'd come out with something horrifying, like, "Anna was the girl who lived here a hundred years ago, and is currently sleeping next to Dylan right now."

All I'm saying is, I've seen enough horror movies to have a healthy mistrust of kids.

"Pinch your hand like this and play it, Dyl," Crista instructed. Dylan did as he was told, and honestly it wasn't half bad. Maybe I was putting my *Ellen* hopes on the wrong cousin, here.

"Awesome, guys. That's what a G-seven sounds like."

Crista's grin was so big you'd think she'd wrapped up a performance in a sold-out amphitheater. "Can you play the song again, please?"

"Which one?"

"The one that goes daa-da-daa-da-da-da."

Unfortunately, Crista's singing abilities were questionable, so I remained lost. I shrugged, while Dylan absentmindedly strummed the guitar. "I've, uh . . . forgotten that one."

Crista sighed, like I was *the* biggest idiot she'd ever met. Oh no, not her, too. "The one with all the chords."

Right, that one. That *really* narrowed it down.

"Because you showed me the C, and the A minor, and then I couldn't do the G one, and you said you'd show me that tonight."

Suddenly it clicked. She wasn't talking about an actual song I knew, just a progression I'd made up on the fly the other night while I was keeping an eye on the kids in the tub. I grabbed the guitar and played what I could remember, narrating as I went. "So it's C . . . A minor . . . F . . . and G-seven, like you guys just played."

Crista jumped up and started spinning in circles, her

tight curls splaying out behind her. "It sounds like 'Let It Go'!"

I mean, not really. No. "Oh yeah, I can see that."

Why do we lie to children?

I kept playing the progression, and Crista pretended to fling off an imaginary glove, with Dylan twirling around behind her now. Before Crista could burst into song, like I was 90 percent sure she wanted to, Aunt Linda pushed open the door. I hadn't even heard everyone come home. It was impossible to predict how long I'd be babysitting when Aunt Linda had appointments in oncology. Sometimes she and Uncle Roy would be home in half an hour, sometimes I'd get a text with her credit card details asking me to order Chinese for delivery. Hence, why I'd started leaving a guitar here. Figured I might as well give myself something productive to do if my shift got extended.

"Hey, munchkins," she said as she scooped Dylan into a hug. "What are you still doing up?"

"Well, funny story," I said, letting Crista take over the guitar. "I went to the bathroom for one second, I swear, *ten* seconds at most. Then when I came out, a quarter of the Nutella jar was magically gone."

"*Magically gone?*" Aunt Linda repeated, raising her eyebrows. Neither Dylan nor Crista met her eye.

"Magically," I confirmed. "I know it had nothing to do with these two, because they told me it didn't, and I know they'd never lie. Then, Aunt Linda, the *funniest* thing, after I'd cleaned all the Nutella off their faces and hands, they had all this *energy*. Almost like they'd had a whole heap of sugar."

"How mysterious," Aunt Linda said, putting Dylan back down. She seemed out of breath, just from holding him for that long. "And I'm sure the Nutella on their faces was a coincidence, too?"

"Total coincidence."

Aunt Linda shared a conspiratorial glance with me. I could tell she wasn't pissed, but looking at her, I felt guilty for not trying harder to get the kids to sleep on time. Her eyes were all puffy and red, and the wrinkles on her face seemed more obvious than usual.

"Okay, guys, time for bed," I said, getting up. "For real."

"It's okay, Ollie, I'll take it from here," Aunt Linda said. "Roy's ready to drive you home. You've been here for too long already."

"I don't mind, really," I said. "It'll take me five minutes. You haven't even taken your jacket off yet."

That was another thing. It was eighty degrees today. No one in their right minds needed to wear a jacket in this kind of weather, but Aunt Linda always seemed to need a jacket or coat these days. The sundresses she used to live in when I was little were banished to the back of the closet.

Aunt Linda hesitated. She totally wanted to take me up on the offer. So I launched into the bedtime routine, which was pretty familiar to me these days. "Hey, Crista, finish getting into your jammies. You're not sleeping in that shirt. Dyl, go grab your chi chi." His chi chi was some raggedy, woolly, bacteria-filled *thing* he carried around for comfort. I think it was supposed to resemble an animal, but mostly, it resembled my nightmares. To each his own.

The kids did what they were told. Like I said, they were pretty much saints. Aunt Linda told me once they weren't always so well behaved. They seemed to sense that she needed a break.

Aunt Linda hovered, then cracked. "All right, well, I

might go put on some tea, then. Thank you, Ollie. You've been such a help."

"It's cool, really."

She smiled and rested her head against the door frame. "I heard you playing. I'm so glad you kept it up. You've always been so talented."

"Not really. I just like it. But thanks." Even as I said it, I knew I sounded like Juliette.

"Mama, Ollie taught me how to play 'Let It Go' on guitar," Crista piped up in a muffled voice as she pulled her pajama shirt over her head.

Aunt Linda shot me a look that was half sheer terror, half witch hunt. The face of someone at peak *Frozen* saturation.

*I didn't, I swear,* I mouthed, making chopping motions by my neck.

I was saved by Dylan returning with his chi chi, which he'd apparently found in the pantry, next to the Nutella jar. Aunt Linda retreated to the kitchen, and I worked through the bedtime routine of checking under the bed for monsters (while making *zero* jokes about the chi chi being the real threat) and reading the same fifty-word picture book approximately fifty times.

Dylan was out first. Crista had her eyes closed, and I thought I was ready to clock out. I'd almost made it to the door, when, "Ollie?"

So close, and yet . . . "Yeah?"

"When is Will going to come over again?"

Damn. Hearing his name was like being lightly shoved onto the edge of a cliff. If you're ready for it, no harm done. If it catches you off guard, bam, over you go. Suddenly, ridiculously, I wanted to spill my heart out. To someone who'd get it. Who knew how close we'd been all summer.

So I didn't feel like I'd imagined the whole freaking thing. Even I knew that a seven-year-old didn't make the ideal confidante for romantic issues, though, so instead I shut it down. Right down. "Will was from the lake, remember? He doesn't live here. We can't see him anymore."

"Oh." Crista rolled onto her side. "Are you sad?"

I forced a smile. "Sometimes we only get to be friends for a little while. That's why you've always gotta make it count, right?"

"Right. 'Night, Ollie."

"'Night."

# 7

He looked at me.

No, I'm sure of it. There had definitely been times when I'd thought Will was looking at me, when actually it was at something behind me, or on top of me, or below me, or through me, but this time it was *super-certainly at me*. Not a drill.

Sure, it only lasted a second, but still. He'd turned away when I saw him. Way too suspicious for an accident. Plus, his table was on the opposite side of the cafeteria. If he hadn't been staring right at me, there's no way he would've even noticed me glancing back.

*Breathe. Breathe, Ollie. You don't care about Will anymore, remember? Just because it's finally occurred to him that you've been existing in his vicinity for the past couple weeks does not erase his doucheyness. And it is most certainly not a marriage proposal.*

"Wow, Jules, I've heard chewing helps," Lara said, her fork hovering halfway to her mouth as she stared at Juliette.

Juliette shrugged, wide eyed and chipmunk cheeked. "Ree ung Awrry—"

"No, no, stop," Niamh interrupted, holding a hand up. "Swallow. Breathe. Proceed."

Juliette complied. When she'd finished coming up for air, she continued. "Me and Ollie are going to pick my audition song. We need as much time in the music room as we can get."

I'd actually forgotten about that, but hey, sure, I was down. It'd be cool to—oh, hell no, he did it *again*. What was he looking at me for? Had someone said something? Was I hot today? I glanced down at my outfit. I pretty much lived in these jeans, so it wasn't them. The shirt made my arms seem bigger than they were, so it might be that? Or—maybe it was my hair? Whatever I'd done with it, I'd just have to make sure to exactly replicate it every day from here on out until I died. Easy.

"Come on, Ollie," Juliette said. "You've barely eaten."

I somehow snapped my attention back to our own table. "Sorry. I think I'm full, anyway."

Lara turned behind her. To see what I'd been distracted by, I guess. When she flipped back she had on her Disney villain smile. Which, in the short time I'd known her, had never led to anything too fun. For me, anyway. "It's been so long since the guys sat with us," she said.

And there it was. Cue the trap. I shoved a forkful of potato salad into my mouth so I'd have an excuse not to fall into it.

Niamh did the honors for me. "Yeah, it really has. Do you think it's because of Ollie?"

Juliette side-eyed the hell out of her. Like the thought would've never occurred to me without Niamh pointing it out.

Lara's laugh was a touch too loud. I braced myself. "No, oh, no way. Matt told me why. It's because of Jess."

Niamh and Juliette shared twin confused expressions. "Jess Rigor?" Juliette asked.

"Yeah. Apparently she was getting all jealous that Will was hanging with us, and asked him to stop. Even though he was with the guys, too. Pretty girls are so easily threatened, have you noticed?"

*Potato salad. Potato salad. Don't take your eyes off the damn potato salad.*

Lara must have been disappointed at my non-reaction, because she pushed harder. "Did Will ever mention Jess to you, Ollie? She's his ex. They used to be joined at the hip, didn't they, Niamh?"

I cracked and resurfaced to join the conversation. Even Niamh seemed to have caught on to what Lara was doing. At least, she looked pretty unimpressed. "I guess," she said. "Until she cheated on him. That was a while ago. I'm surprised he still talks to her."

"Oh, all the time," Lara said. She crossed her legs underneath her to prop herself higher.

"Well, I've never seen her," Juliette said airily, standing up. "Anyway, come on, Ollie. We've really got to go if we're gonna do this."

I scrambled to follow her. As I did, I checked Will's table one last time.

Will ripped his gaze away, pretending to be all absorbed in whatever Darnell was saying. He burst out laughing, and a couple of the guys slapped him on his back and arms. Whatever they were laughing about, it seemed to be with Will, not at Will. Probably a super-hetero joke about his super-hetero past relationship with this Jess girl. A vicious part of me wanted to ask the girls to point her out in the crowd so I could find flaws with her. Maybe she was duller than vanilla ice cream. Or, even better, one of those people with an obnoxious laugh that makes you want to fill your ear canals with gasoline and light it. Or she might be an earnest flat-earther. As long as I could cheerfully hate her, I'd take any of the above.

As the guys stopped laughing, Will's eyes were aimed toward me again. We looked away from each other at the same time. Him to turn back to his group. Me to the back wall. Half because I didn't have anywhere else to look, half because I could still check Will out in my peripheral at this angle.

Suddenly, I desperately didn't want to go off with Juliette. Why did he have to pick today to remember I existed? Why couldn't I sit in that seat for the next twelve hours, counting how many times we locked eyes?

"I really don't know what's up with Lara," Juliette said as we dumped our trays. "She's doing that on purpose. Don't think me and Niamh haven't noticed."

"I don't think she likes me very much," I admitted.

Juliette made a show of shaking her head, all wide-eyed horror. "No, of course she does! It's not that at all."

She didn't offer any alternative explanations. I didn't push it, though. Even two weeks in, these girls were my best options for friends. Actually, that wasn't fair. I really, genuinely liked Juliette and Niamh. It was just Lara. I got along with the others in Absolution of the Chained okay, but they didn't hang out together, so I didn't have an easy in. Basically, if I wanted to keep the peace with the two people I could call proper friends in this school, I had to put up with Miss Malice Personified. Small sacrifices, right?

In the music room, Juliette set herself up on a chair,

with about three novels' worth of music stacked on the sheet stand. "All right, so, these are the four pieces I have to choose from. I think I have it down to two final ones, but I'd really, *really* appreciate your feedback. See, I have to balance it between the ones I perform better and the ones that are technically harder. I *think* it's better to be awesome at an easier song than less awesome at a tricky song, but . . . what do you think?"

I sat on the piano bench and played a couple of notes. "Can you just, like, get really awesome at a complex song?"

I got a scrunched-up piece of sheet music lobbed at me for that one. Apparently not.

One by one, Juliette played the pieces. I was no expert judge of the clarinet, but she was obviously good. Really good. She tripped up once or twice during the first song, but after that she was pretty much flawless. Either that one was the "tricky" piece, or she'd had nerves. I wasn't sure how much help I'd be, because they all sounded the same to me.

I was starting to imagine how the clarinet would sound covering Nightwish or something—epic, probably—when she started on her last song. And, finally, something sounded different. From the expression on her face, it was obvious this was her favorite. Something about the piece made me think of crying, and emptiness, and death. Frankly, it was awful. I spent half the song staring at the wall, thinking about Aunt Linda, and how sunken her cheeks were looking, and what would happen if she didn't make it. Then I thought about my friends back home, and how they probably barely missed me, and they'd have all these memories together that I wouldn't be a part of. All I wanted to do suddenly was go home, climb into bed, and sleep until everything was all better.

The second Juliette stopped, I said, "Play that one."

That might sound weird, but even if that song made me feel horrible, it made me *feel*. And that was the point with music, wasn't it?

"Really? Why that one?" But she looked pleased. Clearly I'd told her what she wanted to hear.

"I could tell you meant it."

"I did. But it's not as hard as the second one."

"Doesn't matter. Anyone can play a note. Talent's what you do with the notes. Don't you think?"

Juliette rested her clarinet between her knees and flushed. "You think I'm talented?"

"Nah. You suck. I was being nice."

She laughed, then gave me that little half-smile of hers. "I'm so glad I met you, Ollie-oop. You know, you're not this funny around the others. Have you noticed?"

Well, that was because every sentence I spoke around Lara was like pulling the trigger in a game of bitchy Russian roulette. Kind of puts a damper on attempts at humor. "I'm not great in groups," I said. "I'm socially awkward."

"You're *not* socially awkward." Said the girl who insisted Lara didn't dislike me. Super credible. "But you should try to relax more. Don't be afraid to talk with us, okay? We love having you around."

*Love.* That was a strong word. But it perked me up, anyway. I shuffled around to face the piano. It was easier to speak to an instrument, even one I couldn't really play beyond the basics. "Maybe if we ate lunch in here I'd be more relaxed."

Juliette started packing up her clarinet. "Oh my God, I *know*. There's something about music, don't you think? It makes everything feel so much easier, and nicer."

I played a C chord on the piano and nodded. "All my friendships were based on music back home. We all listened to similar stuff, we all played together . . . It doesn't seem to be as big here."

"I guess it depends what groups you hang around with. You're right, though. You're the first person I've been able to talk about playing with."

"It's an honor." I grinned.

"My parents don't take it seriously. Apparently I get everything from my grandpa. It skipped a generation."

"Their loss, I guess."

"Try my loss. I mean, they're not horrible about it. They sprang for private lessons. As a hobby, though, not a career."

"So, what do they think about this audition?"

"They don't. Think. They don't know about it."

I gaped. "You rebel!"

"Easier to say sorry than ask permission, Ollie-oop. Needs do as needs must."

"You can quote as many clichéd sayings at me as you want, but I'm still impressed."

I couldn't imagine going behind my parents' backs with something that big. The most rebellious thing I'd ever done to date had been sneaking out to see Will his last night at the lake, and I could blame that on irrational hormones.

I'd been *pumped full* of those irrational hormones. Like Romeo and Juliet, but a teensy bit less stupid.

I grabbed my phone as Juliette gathered her music, and only then noticed I had a new text. The tone must have been drowned out by the clarinet. I unlocked it, expecting it to be Ryan or Hayley through some weird, telepathic connection, telling me they missed me or something.

But it was way weirder than that.

It was Will. I recognized the last few digits.

Can we talk?

Shit.

Shit shit shit shit oh God shit fuck crap. I was not pre-pared for this, oh Jesus.

My first instinct was to text him back, begging him to meet me right this second.

The next was to delete this message thread so I wouldn't be tempted to ever reply. I actually got halfway through doing that, then chickened out. I wasn't quite *that* strong. Alas and alack and whatever.

I went with door number three. Don't reply, for now. I'd wait until I came up with the perfect response. If experi-ence was anything to go by, the perfect response was never the first one that came to mind. Let him think I was busy. I was, after all. Busy putting together a life here. A life that didn't need to revolve around Will "Who?" Tavares.

As soon as I made that decision, a rush of power coursed through me. Finally, after all these weeks, I had the op-portunity to be the one ignoring *him*. I could get used to being on this side of the power balance.

I didn't reply throughout the rest of the school day. Played it totally cool, if I do say so myself. I was 90 percent sure it was because of all Mom's mindfulness training. When I realized that, I did some visualization. Of Will checking his phone every five minutes with his heart in his throat, like I'd been doing the whole last couple weeks of summer. And that felt so good, it was *sure* to manifest. It turned out I got most of my positive energy from the thought of kar-mic schadenfreude.

At home, Crista and Dylan were over. Aunt Linda had taken a "bad turn" during the day, according to Mom, and was back in the hospital overnight. The kids seemed pretty down—and so did the adults, to be perfectly honest—so we decided to go out for cheeseburgers. It was one of those places with entertainers wearing creepy, anthropomorphic costumes of chipmunks, ducks, and bears that have crazy eyes like they've taken a strong hit of something. The animals, I mean, not the entertainers. Although, *their* eyes were hidden, so it was hard to make that call either way, I guess.

Anyway, Crista and Dylan loved it, and spent more time following around one of the chipmunks than they did eating. It seemed ridiculous to me that they could be so scared of things like the dark, or trees rustling outside, and not the slightest bit terrified of the chipmunk costumes. Those wide, staring eyes and creepily stretched-out, half-open mouths . . . Nothing has ever said "I eat children" more than the face of Chipmunk Charlie, put it that way.

Even though I was still ignoring Will, I kept opening the message thread, like something would've somehow changed since I looked at it thirty seconds before. A part of me wondered if Will had noticed the seen receipt. If he was maybe even obsessing over it a little, internally rationalizing why I hadn't replied.

Can we talk?

Talk about what, Will? About how you've ignored me since . . . well, since *that night*? Or about your reaction at the party? Or do you want to discuss why you were basically Jesus at the lake and are now in the running to be the Antichrist? Because as interesting as those conversation topics all sound, I'd rather invite Chipmunk Charlie into my room to watch me sleep every night than hear you explain how little I mean to you.

Every time I took my phone out, my parents started talking in low voices, like I would somehow miss what they were saying from the other side of the rounded booth. I was distracted, but not *that* distracted. They were talking about Aunt Linda. The topic of the times, these days. I picked up enough snippets to get a feel for it. *Not responding to treatment . . . Changing medication . . . Demand some better pain meds . . . Says she doesn't want to be foggy, but . . .*

My phone buzzed in my hand, and I jumped a full mile. Then I saw who was calling, and my parents' conversation was officially tuned out.

Will. Will was calling me. Will was out there somewhere, right now, calling me. Thinking about me. Wanting me to pick up.

Maybe Mom was onto something with this "manifesting" theory after all.

I almost answered it, too. Almost. But there was that tingling power again. And honestly, it was more than that. The more I'd been thinking about his message, the more I suspected that he wanted to beg me not to out him. Or to tell me the summer meant nothing, and he'd see me around. Goddamnit, I didn't want to hear him say that. It'd cheapen the whole thing. As if the second I heard him discount it, it'd erase all that happiness. With everything going on with Aunt Linda, and being away from my friends, and having to deal with Lara, those memories were all I had. I needed them for a little longer.

So I watched my phone in silence until the call ended.

Sorry, Will.

Too busy.

Just like you've been.

# 8

He ambushed me.

I was running more than ten minutes late the next morning. I'd finished up at my locker, mentally rehearsing my excuse to Ms. Hurstenwild, when I got that creepy, ominous feeling. The one that says *there's someone, possibly-slash-probably a serial killer, right behind you.* I turned around to find Will all up in my personal space, staring me down like he was a freaking matador or something.

"Didn't get my text, I guess?" he said in this airy way, like he couldn't really care. Which would be believable if he wasn't in the process of cornering me in an empty hallway about it.

I was rattled, but I did my best not to make it obvious. "Pot, kettle," I said, even airier. So airy it was approaching helium. Okay, maybe it was obvious after all.

He shoved one hand into the pocket of his chinos and stuck one finger of the other in his mouth to chew a cuticle. I got déjà vu seeing that. It's what he did whenever I caught him off guard in the summer. Cuticle nibbling, faraway look, shifting his weight. He was so familiar. I knew him. Probably better than someone had any business knowing someone they'd only met a few months ago.

He removed his finger from his mouth. Here we go. Considered, thoughtful response time. "You're right. I'm a total hypocrite."

Again. Not what I'd expected. And there I'd been bracing myself for a gentle lecture about how he didn't owe me anything, or how I'd been reading into the summer too much. It was a surprisingly mature response for someone who'd spent a solid two weeks refusing to look me in the eye.

It made me relax a little. "Yup. Do I get an explanation, or . . . ?"

"That's what I wanted to talk about."

"Well, I'm here. So, let's talk, I guess."

We faced each other down. Will's finger had wandered into his mouth again. Procrastinator. Ms. Hurstenwild was going to genuinely murder me.

I closed my locker and started walking backward. "Look, Will, if you don't have anything to—"

At that moment, two things happened.

A little farther down the hall, a door opened, and a student stepped halfway out of the classroom. Only the back of the head was visible—the student had paused to speak to the teacher on the way out—but the close-trimmed Afro and black-and-white letterman jacket looked a lot like it belonged to Will's friend Matt.

Lo and behold, I was right on the money with that one. With a small yelp, Will lunged forward, opened a nearby door, and shoved me into the room.

Before I could get my bearings, Will had joined me and slammed the door closed, plunging us into darkness.

I tried to back away and stepped right into what felt like a mop bucket. Or at least, it *was* a mop bucket, I figured from the crunch of snapping plastic. I shot a hand out to steady myself and smacked straight into a shelf of some sort. A bunch of unidentified items clattered onto the concrete floor—and onto my feet. I swore in pain as a particularly heavy bottle all but shattered my toes. Mother*fucker*.

"Jesus Christ, Ollie, hold still," Will's voice hissed through the darkness.

"What are you *doing*? Is this an assault? Should I scream?"

"I didn't want Matt to see us."

"Ah. Getting rid of witnesses. So it *is* an assault?"

"Come on, Ollie, be serious."

I kind of was, to be honest. "And why does it matter if Matt sees us?"

Even though I couldn't see a thing, my third eye clearly made out some cuticle-chewing action. "Do you have to ask?"

And what the hell was that supposed to mean? "Uh, given that I did ask . . . yes?"

A long pause. Long pauses are never good. One day, I would write a thesis on the history of long pauses, and the hurt feelings that followed them 200 percent of the time. This was *just* like the time in tenth grade, when I shaved one side of my head and asked Ryan how it looked at school the next day. Except this long pause was lasting longer, and oh God, this was going to really stab, wasn't it? Fuck long pauses. Motion to ban them from social interactions, please.

"Well . . . you know . . ."

Nope. But I was about to, wasn't I?

"Like . . . most of the school has figured out you're gay."

"Oh. Interesting. I haven't met most of the school, so don't know how they managed that."

"Yeah, but . . ."

I knew what he was getting at. It was fine. Whatever. It's not like it was a state secret or anything. And hey, if people guessed, it saved me having to have a discussion about my sexual preferences with people who didn't even know if I preferred ham or peanut butter on my sandwiches. For reference, the answer was, "both, simultaneously."

"And so what?" I asked. "So what if they know I'm gay? Why, exactly, does that mean you can't be seen with me? Am I contagious? Because I guess that'd explain a lot." As far as explanations went, that'd win an award for creativity. *Sorry, I stopped texting you because my precise strain of "gay" was only temporary. Kind of like salmonella.*

Will's sigh was particularly loud and scathing in the small space. Claustrophobia does that. "The guys are being dicks about it. It's like a running joke. They keep trying to 'set each other up' with you at lunch."

Well. I'd like to say that after years of being out and coming to terms with myself, and homophobia, and the rest of it all, that I'd be able to brush that one off. But it hurt. It always hurt a little, at least, to know people were talking about you in a less than flattering way. Being so new at the school, though, and people already having an opinion about me? And *Will* being involved in it? Had he even tried to defend me? Or had he laughed along with them?

"Uh-huh." My tone was flat.

"I don't join in," he added quickly.

*But do you stop them?*

Suddenly, I laughed. It spilled like blood from a fresh wound. Out and out and out.

"What's so funny?"

"We're in a closet."

"I told you, I didn't want—"

"You dragged me *into a closet* to have this conversation. Did you do this on purpose, or what? Unbelievable."

"I don't . . ." Will started, then it must've clicked. "Really, Ollie? Super mature."

"*I'm* immature? You're too afraid to be seen *talking* to me. Are we done?" It was funny. All this time, I'd been through so many emotions. Hurt. Betrayal. Sadness. Acceptance. Maybe a bit—okay, maybe a *lot*—of longing. But I hadn't been angry. At least, I hadn't realized I was so angry. Here I was, however, bubbling right up and over. Pissed off as all hell.

"We haven't even started. Can you give me a chance to explain?"

A chance? We'd been talking for at least five minutes now.

". . . Ollie?"

"*Yes,* I'm listening, whatever. Go."

"I wasn't ignoring you, I swear. My parents caught me coming home that night and went nuts. They confiscated my phone, I wasn't allowed to touch my laptop, nothing. For three weeks. It was ridiculous."

Yeah, yeah, I knew all this. I considered pointing out that he'd told people he was with girls that night, but I couldn't even be bothered going down that road with him. It'd only conflate things. "It's cool. Really. I'm more concerned with how you acted at the party. What was that? The conversation with your friend must have been *really* riveting for you to forget I was there so quickly."

My eyes had started adjusting to the darkness. There he was. Leaning against the door, one hand draped across his stomach, the finger of the other in his mouth. He was looking right at me, at least. Suddenly, I was self-conscious. How did I look today? Had I put enough effort in getting ready this morning? Had I checked my teeth before I left the house?

"You told the girls about me. I freaked out, okay?"

"I'm sorry. Really, I—"

"I know you are! I'm not mad. I know you didn't do it on purpose. You had no idea. But that doesn't mean it's all fine, you know? I mean, what if they tell someone?"

"They haven't yet."

"Yet. If my parents found out . . . Ollie . . ."

I didn't reply. Because what could I say to that? My whole face flushed with shame, the anger temporarily forgotten. It was all my fault he'd been put in this situation. Whether I meant to or not. Why hadn't I kept my damn mouth shut? I hadn't even *known* those girls and I'd spilled out my life story. Or at least my summer story. Which was more torrid than the rest of my life combined, to be fair.

Will hugged himself with both arms and stared at the ground. "I wasn't good enough to get a basketball scholarship, so I'm relying on them to support me. I can't fuck anything up this year, or I'm done."

And a fuckup would include . . . right.

"I see."

"I didn't know what to do. I mean, Jesus, it's not like I expected you to be here. It's so ridiculous."

That was another thing with Will. Everything was "ridiculous," from minor anomalies to life-altering events. I had to fight a smile hearing that word again. Even if it did kind of apply in this situation.

"I was scared, okay? What I did over the summer . . . like, what *we* did, isn't something I would've done with anyone from around here. I thought it was safe."

Right. So he'd been counting on never having to see me again. Bam. Ouch.

"Then it's like, oh, hey, Ollie is right fucking there, and now some people *know*, and for a second I thought that was it. Like well, here we go, now everyone's about to find out everything." He paused to let me speak. When I didn't, he went on. "I had to see you, though. I haven't thought about anything else since the party. I was just scared. I mean, you're *here*."

He touched my arm. Even though it made me shiver, and my blood heat up by several degrees, and my stomach kick up, I yanked away. The anger was well and truly back, and it wasn't having any of my body's romance bullshit.

Will blinked at me, hurt. "I'm so glad to see you," he tried.

"Yeah, I can tell," I said, gesturing at the walls. So glad to see me he couldn't even be seen speaking to me. So glad he'd taken two weeks to text me after getting his phone back. Clearly he was *rapturous*.

"I have to get to class," I said, trying to push past him.

He blocked me. "Wait."

"I have claustrophobia."

"You do *not*."

"As romantic as I find chatting around dustpans and rags, Will, I think I'm going to have to decline. Let me know if you ever want to talk somewhere with oxygen, but until then, good luck with college."

"Don't be mad at me."

"I'm not mad." The lie was so blatant that Will scoffed at me. I didn't care. "We're late. Come on."

"No."

"Fine. Suit yourself." I squeezed past him and opened the door. Sweet air and light.

Will hesitated. Like he expected me to go back in and join him for a bit longer. To do what? Have another somewhat heartbreaking conversation? Kiss him? In a goddamnit-I-can't-believe-I'm-even-saying-this *closet*? No way.

When he didn't follow, I gave him a sweet smile, and shut the door on him. Right in his face. I stared at the door, surprised at my own gall. I didn't know I had that much sass dwelling under the surface. I felt a little guilty, but mostly I was impressed with myself.

With a tiny laugh that sounded suspiciously like a sob—except it couldn't be, because I'd promised not to cry anymore—I turned on my heel and hurried to class without turning back to see if Will had let himself out.

I'd won that round. The spiteful side of me was polishing a trophy with a smug grin.

So why was the rest of me so hollow?

# 9

"Who are these guys again?"

Will's cheek was barely an inch from mine. We lay side by side on my bed, sharing headphones. It was one of those rare afternoons where I'd managed to score the house to myself. Our fingertips were spidering around each other's, our hands resting on my thigh.

I bumped my phone to light it up for him. "Letlive. Good, right?"

"Surprisingly, yes."

"Surprising because you're a music snob?"

Will smiled, and touched his temple to mine. "Shut up." His tone was all warm and tender. The way a guy talks to someone he really likes. I knew that tone. It was the first time I'd heard him use it. A part of me died with happiness. Straight-up curled into a ball and died. "I guess whenever I hear the word 'punk,' I think, like, Blink-182 or Fall Out Boy."

"Both solid bands. You'd better not be knocking them."

"I am a bit."

"We can agree to disagree."

"They're a bit more . . . simple than this."

"I guess. They're pop punk junk food."

Will laughed. "I love that. That's perfect. Pop punk junk food."

Rejuvenated, I started flicking through my albums. "If you like them, you should check out these guys. They have this thing they do with harmonies that's just argh, and the drummer, God, I could listen to a whole album of just his solos. Hold on, I'll find them—what?"

Will was staring at me with a funny little smile. "Nothing. It's cute how passionate you get about music. I feel like you could convince Bach all he was missing was some heavy bass guitar."

"I really like music, I guess. So sue me."

"Yeah, well, I really like you. So sue me."

Tuesday, 4:02 PM

I'm sorry.

I didn't speak to Will again after that morning in the closet. He did try to text me, once, later that day, but I forced myself to ignore it. I knew myself, and I wasn't much of a "let's stay friends" kind of person. If I didn't cut Will off cold-turkey, I'd end up pining over him, all hopelessly devoted, and hurt, and unrequited. Well, like, more than I was currently.

I did spend quite a chunk of the week replaying my reaction in my head. Depending on my mood, I interpreted the memory differently. Sometimes I internally congratulated myself for having the strength to storm out and slam that door. All I'd needed was a Destiny's Child song playing as an overture, and it would've been the greatest "screw you" since Rhett Butler in *Gone with the Wind*.

Then other times, I convinced myself Will still had feelings for me, and that I'd ruined a beautiful future—culminating in marriage and three adopted children—with a five-second tantrum. Those times were way less fun.

One night, in the middle of one of these fits of despair, I asked Mom if she had any huge regrets from when she was a teenager. She apparently thought the appropriate response to that question was to break out into an off-key rendition of "Let It Be" by the Beatles. Word for word. From beginning to end. A performance I was expected to watch in full. I made a mental note never to ask Mom for relationship advice again.

At school, I was settling into a rhythm. Juliette and I often escaped to the music room during lunch. With band practice on Tuesdays and Thursdays, the music room was fast becoming my favorite place in the school. Everything about it, from the cheesy inspirational posters lining the walls, to the collection of crappy-quality guitars and violins, to the microphones and amplifiers stored in the nook at the far end of the room, was familiar. Comforting. Music was music, whether in California or North Carolina.

Thursdays, I had Music Appreciation right before lunch. When the bell chimed, I packed up my stuff and wandered to my locker, all dreamy and happy. I was too busy dwelling in my own little world of melodies and advanced beats to notice anything different when I first made it into the cafeteria. But you can bet I sure as hell noticed when I got to the lunch table and found Will sitting in my seat.

Sitting in my damn seat like a smug, seat-stealing, little . . .

Oh, no, wait, the other guys were there, too. They'd dragged over extra seats and crammed around the perimeter of the table, shoulder to shoulder to fit everyone in. My first thought was that Will had made them come here so he could talk to me. My second thought was, holy shit, you are the poster child for narcissism, Oliver Di Fiore. Not everything revolves around you, get all the way up and over yourself. Juliette had said some of the basketball guys sat with us from time to time. Well, here was one of those times. No stress. Be cool.

Please, for the love of God, be cool.

Then, oh yeah, silly me, I remembered I hated these guys for making homophobic jokes with me as a punch line. So, basically, fuck every single one of them.

"Ollie-oop, I saved you a seat." Juliette waved me down and gestured to the empty seat next to her. Just in case I thought she was referring to one of the taken seats, I guess.

As soon as Juliette said my name, Will's head cocked to the side, and he glanced up in a not-very-subtle way. Without looking at him, I breezed past and Tetris'd my lunch tray into a tight gap between Juliette's and Niamh's.

Matt sat directly across from me, with Will on his left side. On Matt's other side, Darnell, one of Will's other friends, was leaning his elbows on the table to speak to Niamh. Darnell wasn't a short guy by any means, but compared to his friends, he was practically a pixie. He had warm, medium-brown skin with a smattering of freckles over a wide nose, and tilted eyebrows that gave him a permanently concerned, kind sort of look. From the way he had zeroed in on Niamh, you could tell he'd forgotten anyone else was sitting at the table. ". . . You basically don't eat a thing for almost two days," he was saying. "Last year I raised two hundred bucks. It's not that hard."

Niamh tossed her hair and simpered in a very un-Niamh-like way. I was used to the Niamh that mostly looked pleasant, and a little vacant. This was Niamh on a mission. A mission involving a hot guy. "It kind of sounds like that fasting diet you see all over Instagram. Doesn't it mess with practice, though?"

"Nah," the guy said.

"*Yes,*" Matt spoke over him. "He was useless the whole week after the famine last year."

That earned him a hard glare from Niamh's Prince Charming. The message was clear: *you are actively cock-blocking me, and have precisely one second to stop that.* "It's for charity, man."

"Yeah, well, if you could help the poor when we *don't* have a game against Williamstown, that'd be *sweet.*"

Will stayed quiet, watching the exchange. He kept glancing up at me, like a pigeon that feels mostly safe, but also wants to check that it isn't about to be ambushed. Is that what he thought? That I'd do something to out him in front of his friends? Although to be fair, he'd made it pretty clear that acting like I knew him at all would doom him forever. Because he might catch the gay, after all. He probably hadn't even told the guys we'd ever met. Aaaand this was supposed to be *my* Prince Charming. I kind of felt like Niamh had gotten the better deal here.

Niamh swirled her mashed potatoes with a fork. She'd spent more time playing with her food than eating it. Did she not want to eat in front of the guys? Or had she lost interest? "I think it's really selfless," she said. "I might have to try it one year."

"You could time it with a casting," Lara suggested through a mouthful of bread.

Niamh frowned. Juliette and the guys seemed to miss it, but I knew too well what it was like to be on the receiving end of Lara's jabs. Time it with a casting so Niamh could lose a bit of weight. That's what she meant. Even if she said it innocently. This was the first time I'd noticed Lara directing her nastiness at someone other than me. She *must* have woken up on the wrong side of the bed. Or maybe she didn't like the attention Matt was giving Niamh right now.

The conversation went on around me. I didn't join in. It wasn't super unusual for me to be quiet at lunch, and there was no way I felt comfortable enough to speak up with *this* audience. The weird thing was that Will didn't speak, either. This was the first time I'd really seen him around the basketball guys up close, so I had no way of knowing if that was out of character for him or not at first. Then Matt asked him twice why he was so spaced out and I had my answer.

We both did really terrible jobs of sneaking glances at each other. I caught him almost as many times as he caught me. As for those butterflies in my stomach, I was going to have to get myself some DDT pretty soon, because this was getting old. It didn't matter if I could see the crazy-soft skin beneath his neck in that shirt, or that his lashes looked thicker than normal, or that the crook of his arm was distractingly beautiful. He was a dick. So he had to be dead to me. Book the damn funeral, *please*.

Finally, the guys left to grab seconds, or dessert, or both. The moment they were gone, I calmed down. I hadn't practiced nearly enough mindfulness today, apparently, because I'd been a *little* highly strung for a few minutes there.

A brief pause hung in the air, then Juliette and Lara turned on Niamh like hyenas.

"Oh my God, Darnell *likes* you," Juliette said.

Niamh blinked. "No way."

"Niamh, come on," Lara said, tapping her lunch tray for emphasis. "The pheromones were so thick I could taste them seasoning my sandwich. Don't play dumb. Ollie, Darnell was drooling, yes or no?"

Wow. Lara speaking to me like I was a fellow human being for once. Maybe I was growing on her. "I'm gonna go with a hard yes," I said apologetically to Niamh.

"Guys, don't. We're friends."

"What's the problem?" Lara asked. "He's hot as a soldering iron. If you don't want him, I'll take him."

"You've already got Matt, let Niamh have a turn," Juliette said.

Lara smirked. "I may have Matt, but Matt doesn't have me. Although now you mention it, he and Darnell do have a bit of a spark. Think they'd be up for a ménage à trois?"

"Darnell might, if Niamh was the trois."

Niamh moaned and tipped her head back. "They'll be back soon. Don't let them hear you."

"Right, we need a plan of attack," Juliette said.

Lara sniffed. "No, *no* we do not. We do *not* chase men. Men come to us, and we deign to pay them attention if we so choose."

"Um, Lara, these aren't men. These are boys. Different species, remember?"

"Same same, just smaller muscles."

"And brains."

I mean, I was sitting right here.

Niamh slammed her hands on the table, making the rest of us jump. "Stop. Don't try to set me and Darnell up. I don't want to get tied down here, okay? I can't afford to get serious with anyone if I'm moving to New York."

"Who said anything about getting serious?" Lara asked with a wicked smile. "And besides. You can't put all your eggs in one basket. If New York doesn't work out, you'll regret not keeping Darnell on your little line here."

Niamh's face went hard. I was pretty sure I knew why. She was remembering Lara's comment about fasting from earlier. "And why wouldn't New York work out?"

Juliette cleared her throat. I was with her. Could we make an excuse to escape before all hell broke loose? I tried to run through a list of possible reasons, but my mind inconveniently blanked.

"Not saying it won't. It's competitive, though, you know? The standards are high. Even perfect girls struggle to get casted."

"Not that you're not perfect," Juliette jumped in hastily.

Lara shrugged. "Niamh's gorgeous. Obviously. But it isn't always enough, is it?"

"What else is there?" Niamh asked.

"Well, like I said, it's competitive. For some of those girls, it's, like, their lives. They devote everything to it."

"*I* devote everything to it."

"Kind of," Lara said. "But, you know . . ."

"No."

"Well, like, the kind of girls you're competing with . . . they wouldn't be eating mashed potatoes at lunch, put it that way."

*Damn.* There it was. Juliette and I cringed. I felt the sting of that one like Lara had slapped me personally.

Niamh's face reddened, and I wasn't sure if she was going to cry. I got ready to rise up to hug her, or touch her arm, or shove Lara off her chair, I didn't know. Then Niamh stood. "Just because you're so insecure with yourself that you need to hook up with anything that moves for *your* validation, doesn't mean you can take it out on me. There are more important things in life than guys, okay, Lara? And if you think you're better than me because you can strut around in size-two jeans and make out with Renee for a group of immature guys to give them all blue balls over a faux-lesbian fantasy, then please. Don't. It's trashy, and me and Juliette are embarrassed for you."

With that, Niamh stormed away, leaving her lunch tray behind. Juliette gave Lara a stricken glance. Lara waved a hand, bored. "Someone's on her period," she said.

"Jesus Christ," Juliette muttered. She stacked Niamh's lunch tray on top of her own and stood up. "I'm gonna go after her."

"Walk, don't run," Lara said.

Part of me wanted to go after Niamh, too. God knew she hadn't deserved those digs, and I wanted her to know I had her back. But something stopped me from leaving Lara. A little voice that said maybe Lara needed someone here, too. And that maybe, with all her thorns and brambles, Lara didn't get much in the way of comfort.

I watched her closely as Juliette left us alone. It was like she'd forgotten I was still here. As she stared after Juliette, her stoic expression crumpled so quickly I thought I'd imagined it. Then she was back to looking amused and detached. She caught me staring at her, and raised her eyebrows at me in a challenge. *"What?"*

"Nothing," I said. Actually, that wasn't true. I'd been about to say something, but she looked like she wanted to make me her next victim, and the courage had faded fast.

"Good." She sat in silence for a moment, poking at her food with a fork, then grabbed her tray and left.

The guys returned looking bewildered. "Where'd everyone go?" Darnell asked.

Will wore a concerned expression, and held his lunch tray out toward the doorway Lara had stalked through. "Is she okay?" he asked.

And all at once, we were back at the lake. There, Will was always the first one to tell if someone wasn't quite right, as well as the first one to try to fix it. That was how we'd met. It was one of the things I'd liked most about him. Where had that sweetness gone, and why was it coming out now, and over *Lara* of all things? Who was the real Will? He had so many masks I had no idea what his damn face looked like anymore.

"Actually, I'm going to check on her," I said. "Can you get my tray for me? I need to try and catch up with her."

Will nodded and gestured for me to go, and it was like we were on the same team again. Despite my best intentions re: switching off all affection, a little burst of happiness popped somewhere inside my chest. I kept it firmly off my face.

I found Lara near the lockers. She'd grabbed her books, and was hovering around in front of the classrooms, too early to go in. She saw me approaching from a mile away, and she shook her head in annoyance, turning her back on me to lean against the wall with her books clutched to her chest.

"Hey," I said, slowing as I reached her.

"*What?*" she snapped.

I ignored the fact that she clearly didn't want me here and joined her at the wall. We didn't speak for a while, until I got the courage back up. "You can kiss whoever the fuck you want," I said finally. "And it's no one's business but yours."

She turned around, surprised. "You don't think she actually got to me, do you?" she asked with a scoff. "Please. Like I give a crap what anyone thinks about what I do."

The show was convincing. Except . . . "I think everyone cares what people think, a little. Even if they don't want to."

Suddenly, I was staring at her back again. "Well, you don't know me very well, then."

"Guess not. If you really don't care, then I envy you."

"Good. You should."

"If you ever need to talk, though . . ."

"I don't."

"Good," I said. Well, at least I tried. Maybe I was wrong. For all I knew, Lara hadn't liked kissing that Renee girl the way I thought she had. It was possible I'd misread her expression at the lunch table just now. But if I hadn't, then, well . . . if I'd had no one to talk to when I was thinking about coming out, I would've gone crazy. I didn't want anyone to go through that if I could help it. Not even Medusa's distant relative over here.

I got halfway down the hallway when I looked back at Lara. Just in time to see her peeking right back at me.

# 10

Aunt Linda was taking bad turn after bad turn these days. She seemed to be living in a permanent bad turn, if you asked me. Not that anyone did. They'd stopped telling me things, too. Mostly, I just got ordered to babysit Crista and Dylan while the adults went to sort out adult things. I guessed they thought I couldn't handle hearing what was going on. Or maybe they thought the less I knew, the less chance I'd accidentally let on to the kids how serious things were. Who knows? Either way, it didn't matter how much I pressed my parents, they kept me firmly in the dark.

In a weird way, it was a good thing. If no one told me how bad things were, I could still kid myself it was temporary. Just a blip.

Anyway, with my newly contracted role as Crista and Dylan's guardian from after school until bedtime, I didn't have much chance to practice bass. Not seriously, anyway. And the guys in Absolution of the Chained were as serious as it came. The others didn't *make* mistakes. They didn't shame me if I slipped up in practice and threw everyone else off, but it was pretty obvious I was the only one who ever did. So I started ditching lunch altogether and holing up in the music room instead, repeating the trickier lines over and over until they became second nature.

One of these lunches in early October, I was so focused on what I was doing that I didn't hear the door open. It wasn't until I caught something move out of the corner of my eye that I noticed Will. Seeing someone at all, let alone Will, when I didn't expect it gave me such a shock I jumped in my seat and swore.

Will raised his eyebrows, amused. "Sorry. I thought you heard me come in."

Eurgh. He looked particularly good today, and the bar was set high to begin with. He wore this figure-hugging long-sleeved shirt that was somewhere between maroon and plum, with equally tight khaki chinos. On top of that, the sweet, musky smell of his cologne reached me from across the room. The same one he'd worn all summer. If only smells didn't trigger memories, I might've been able to keep my feelings off my face.

I gave my head a little shake like I was an Etch A Sketch and—my face a blank slate again—returned to my bass playing. "What are you doing here?" I asked.

"Juliette told me you were here."

That traitor. "I can't imagine why she thought that's something you should know."

"I asked her where you've been. You disappeared."

*Just keep playing. The instrument is way more interesting than Will could ever be.*

He cleared his throat. "I wasn't sure if it had something to do with me. I can ask the guys to stay away from your table, if it helps."

I stopped playing. "It has nothing to do with you," I snapped. "I haven't been able to practice at home, so I had to get it in somewhere."

Will dragged over a chair from the wall and sat on it backward, folding his arms on the back. Right. He was settling in, then. Good thing he hadn't asked for an invitation, because I wouldn't have given one.

"How come you can't practice at home?" he asked.

"Crista and Dylan are around every night. Don't get a chance."

His face went all soft. "How are they? I miss those kids."

"They're fine." I started playing again. If anything would make it clear I was too busy to talk, this would.

"How's your aunt?" he asked gently.

I didn't expect it, but my throat closed over, and my heart started thudding like it was trying to break out of my chest. I could taste bile. My fingers stopped moving on the bass.

Will looked stricken. "Is she . . . ?"

"She's alive," I croaked.

Will studied me. He tended to hold stares a bit longer than most people to begin with, but now it was like he was afraid to blink. He seemed to be cataloguing every one of my skin cells. Like they were telling him what I wouldn't. "I'm sorry," he said. He sounded like he meant it.

For a second I thought he was going to get up. To come over to me? Or to leave? He didn't, though.

I wanted to thank him for caring. I wanted to tell him I hadn't really told anyone else here about Aunt Linda, because I didn't want them to feel uncomfortable. I wanted to ask him to hug me and convince me it'd be okay. "Be careful," I said instead. "Someone might see you in here alone with me. Who knows what they'd think."

Will shrugged one shoulder. "I doubt it. No one ever comes down here. We'll be fine."

Wrong answer. My skin prickled cold again, and I returned to the guitar.

Will sighed. "I can't stand how things have been between us. I'm sorry for how I acted at the party that night. I *am*. Tell me how I can make it up to you and I'll do it."

Honestly, if he thought I was still angry about the party, he was too far behind to get why I was pissed now. Besides, I shouldn't have to ask him to stop being ashamed of me. If I had to beg for him to acknowledge me in the hallways, it wouldn't mean shit if he eventually did. It had to come from him, or else what was the point?

"Everything's fine," I said. "Whatever. I came here to practice, so I'm trying to focus on that."

Will nodded carefully, and all at once I wanted to take it back. *No. Don't leave. Say something that'll make me cave. Say something to convince me I shouldn't be hurt anymore.* "I'll leave you to practice, then," he said instead. My shoulders slumped. I shouldn't have expected anything different. I'd insisted he go away, after all. "If you wanna practice at night anytime, though, bring the kids over. Kane still remembers them, and I'm sure he'd love to play with them. You can use our basement, or my room. You can be alone, if you want."

That was surprising. "Thanks. Maybe."

He offered me a sheepish smile, and closed the door behind him.


The next Monday, he showed up in Music Appreciation. As casual as anything, like he belonged in there.

Then he settled himself into a spare desk a couple of rows over from me, and, oh crap, he *did* belong in there.

He must have transferred. What in the hell? Since when was he the type of guy to take a music class? My first reaction was to glower. How dare he come in here to ruin my class? If he acted up, I was going to corner him after the lesson and force him to transfer right back out again. This class was important to me. I wasn't going to let him make it a joke.

I kept trying to catch his eye through the whole class, but he didn't glance at me once. He kept his attention on the teacher and the textbook. No comments, no laughing, no wry looks around the classroom.

This was exactly the kind of joke the Great, Ethereal Being liked to play on me to keep things interesting. I could picture it up there with dozens of other mystical figures from every religion in existence, watching this on a magical television in the clouds, laughing themselves silly at the bewildered look on my face.

After an eternity the bell rang. I knew Will didn't want me to speak to him where people could see, but I did not give one crap. I headed straight over to him and put a hand on his desk. "What's going on?" I asked.

He blinked innocently. "Oh, hey, Ollie. I forgot you took this class."

"You did *not*."

Will grinned at me. Well, glad he found this so amusing. "The career counselor said I needed to ditch peer tutoring for a class with credit. I figured why not this? It'll make me an all-rounder for college applications."

I folded my arms, exasperated. "This class isn't an easy ride, you know. Can you even name one music period?"

He shook his head, sliding his textbook into his bag. "I figured if I got confused, I had a friend who's pretty good at music who could help."

"Oh, really? Who is it? I assume it's someone you can be seen with?" I said coolly.

Will took a second to reply. "That's right. Speaking of, Darnell wants to sit with you guys in the cafeteria today. He's totally into Niamh, have you noticed? Are you hanging here to practice, or are you eating?"

"I was gonna eat, today." Actually, I'd been planning on practicing, but surely that's what he'd been hoping to hear. And I didn't want to give him that. I glared at him, silently daring him to ask me to skip lunch so he didn't have to worry about me addressing him at the table.

"Awesome. Let's head over together, then." He stood up, ready to go.

I paused. I understood what he'd said, but I didn't trust it. A wild, paranoid part of me even wondered if there was a hidden camera somewhere. Before I remembered this was real life. "Um . . ."

"What?"

*What*, he asked. Like he hadn't been so terrified of being seen near me last week he'd shoved me into a mop bucket.

Sure. I'd play along. "Okay. Let's go," I said.

The whole time I expected him to make an excuse to leave. Or tell me he was only kidding. Or inexplicably produce a mop bucket from thin air and throw it in front of me to slow me down while he escaped.

But he didn't. He just walked with me all the way to the cafeteria, talking about his family, and the basketball team, and my friends back home. No one accused us of being in love. No black holes materialized to tear apart the fabric of the universe. We didn't even trigger a natural disaster.

What the hell had sparked this sudden change?

"Ollie, your phone made a noise," Crista called out from the living room.

I was in the middle of making three mugs of hot chocolate in the kitchen a few days after Will's sudden class transfer. More specifically, I was holding Dylan up to the counter so he could stir the powder into the milk. Aunt Linda and Uncle Roy had come home from the hospital earlier than we'd anticipated, right after I'd promised the kids some warm drinks. Uncle Roy offered to take me home, but I wasn't in any particular rush. I'd gotten my homework done during a rousing *Paw Patrol* marathon. So he dove straight into the shower. Probably his first in a few days, given how run off their feet he and Aunt Linda were.

"Can I try to read the message to you?" Crista continued when I didn't respond.

Earlier that evening I'd been messaging Ryan about my new band, so I figured it was a reply from him. "Go ahead," I called back.

"'Hey . . . wanna sit . . . next . . . to me . . . tomorrow in . . . music? I p-prow . . . m-eyes'? 'Prow-mies'? Mama, what does this word say?"

My life flashed before my eyes, and I detached Dylan from the hot chocolates with a jiggle so I could sprint into the living room, still holding him. "D-don't, don't read the rest, it's okay, I'll read it."

Crista was already in the process of passing the phone to Aunt Linda, who sat stretched out on her recliner under a bright blue Snuggie. Aunt Linda raised an eyebrow mischievously and held out the phone. "And who's *this* from?" she asked.

"No one." I jostled Dylan onto my hip and reached for my phone.

"Is it a *boy*?"

"Come on."

"Please, Ollie, let me be the cool aunt," Aunt Linda said. "You used to tell me everything. I want to gush."

"No gushing."

"I'm going to play the cancer card."

I snatched the phone back. "Eurgh, *no*, that's not fair."

"Neither is cancer."

I stared her down, and Dylan struggled to the floor to join Crista on her iPad. I lowered my voice so Crista didn't overhear. The last thing I wanted was a re-formation of the Will fan club right now. "Fine. It's Will."

"Will from the lake?"

"Bingo."

"Oh my *gosh*," Aunt Linda squealed. "You didn't tell me he lives in Collinswood."

"He lives in Napier, but he goes to Collinswood High."

"Is he your boyfriend?"

My grin felt a little pained. Probably not as award winning as my musical debut as a bush, put it that way. "Nah. He's not out, so we don't have that much to do with each other."

"Sounds like he wants to sit next to you in class. That doesn't sound like nothing."

Wednesday, 6:47 PM

Hey, wanna sit next to me tomorrow
in music? I promise I won't distract
you. Finding it hard to keep up! I'm
dumb : (

No wonder he was finding it hard to keep up. He knew nothing about music. It made zero sense for him to have transferred into the class at all.

"Yeah, well, not serious enough for him to risk being seen alone with me," I said, exiting the message app. "So, whatever."

Aunt Linda turned the television down with the remote. She meant business. D and M time, so it would seem. "I remember when you were in eighth grade, and you had that crush on the older boy. What was his name again?"

"Ben."

"*Ben*. You were crazy about him."

Damn right I was. Ben with the perfect singing voice and bright green eyes. Who wouldn't have been crazy about Ben? Too bad Ben was straighter than a curtain rod. "So?"

"So, even though you told me all about Ben, you didn't tell everyone."

Of course I hadn't. Barely anyone even knew I was gay back then. I hadn't come out properly until tenth grade. "Yeah, I wasn't out yet. I get your point, but it's different. I could never have had Ben anyway. If he'd told me he liked me, I would've done anything."

"Well, maybe you were ready a little earlier than some. You also had a supportive family, and great friends. Not everyone has it so easy."

I was unmoved. "If Will liked me the way I liked Ben, he'd at *least* speak to me in public."

"Is music class not public?"

"Sure, but he ignored me for *weeks* up until just recently. In the halls, and in the cafeteria, and in English . . ."

"But not music class anymore. Seems like progress to me. It's small, but it's something. Sounds like he's trying."

Eurgh. I hated it when adults made sense.

"Try not to take it personally if he's not going as quickly as you'd like him to," Aunt Linda said. "If friendship is all he's able to give you right now, don't knock it because you were hoping for more. Maybe, if you're lucky, he'll be ready for something else one day. If not, at worst you'll have yourself a good friend in a new school."

I thought about it, trying to find the holes in her argument. It didn't appeal to me, the idea that Will might only ever be a friend. Was that because deep down, I was hoping he'd magically turn back into the old Will overnight?

Aunt Linda might be right. Maybe I'd been unfair to pin that kind of expectation on Will. Now that I thought about it, he had been trying. Sure, he hadn't done the thing I wanted him to do most of all—declare his love for me publicly on the bleachers in a grand musical number—but that didn't mean I had to knock the baby steps, did it?

I bit my lip, then sent him a text back.

You're definitely not dumb. We can sit together if you want. I'll even give you a distraction hall pass or two, if you're lucky.

Aunt Linda gave me a tired, but genuine, smile.

## 11

"Stop, stop, stop. That sucked."

I stopped the recording dutifully, but shook my head. "That was *fine*. What's the problem?"

Juliette lowered her clarinet and stared at me like she was doubting the legitimacy of my ears. "Um. All of it. All of it was the problem. One more time, okay?"

We were holed up in her bedroom, taking advantage of the natural late-October light to film her audition for the Conservatory. A task that was taking longer than I'd expected. Like, a *lot* longer. She'd played the piece so many times I knew it inside and out. I'd had to stop myself from humming along the last five or so takes.

"Sure, but seriously, we need to wrap it up soon. I have to be at the Lost and Found by five-thirty for sound check." It was my first gig with Absolution of the Chained that night. Sure, it was in a bar that was usually emptier than a college student's refrigerator, but it was still important. I didn't want to mess anything up, and that included being late. Also, I had good reason to expect there would be at least a handful of people in our audience that night. Juliette and the girls had a few connections around the school they were dragging along, and Will had even promised to bring the basketball guys. Sure, he'd said it was so Darnell could get a shot to speak to Niamh alone, but I appreciated it either way.

"Okay, one more time," Juliette said, waving to get my attention. "Count me in."

I did, and she took it again from the top. Her fingers flew over the holes and keys, her gaze distant as her chest rose and fell in a steady rhythm. She was somewhere else. Which was promising. The last few takes, she'd been stealing glances at the camera, until I'd promised her it wasn't likely to explode without notice.

I sang along in my head until I realized I didn't know this part. She'd gotten further than before. I held my breath, willing her to keep it going, to hold on to the streak. She made it another second. Then another. Surely the piece was almost over now. Surely.

Then she played a final note, and breathed out. I waited for her confirmation, hopeful.

"Switch it off, Ollie." She laughed. "Okay. That was okay. I got through it all, anyway."

"We are victorious," I said, switching off the camera with a flourish. "That is a *wrap*. Well done, Valentina Lisitsa." Valentina Lisitsa was a piano player Juliette showed me on YouTube a couple weeks earlier, whose fingers moved so fast it looked like her videos were sped up to double time. Juliette had brought the channel up somewhat defiantly, telling me it was proof that someone from North Carolina could become a famous musician. Let the record show that I'd actually never implied otherwise. Something told me a little voice inside Juliette's head might have once or twice, though.

"Valentina's a pianist."

"All right, be pedantic then. Well done, Valentina Lisitsa's clarinet equivalent. You're halfway to college!"

Juliette came over to grab the camera. "Not so fast. I'll have to make sure it's okay before I send it off. I need it to be perfect."

"Have a look at it tomorrow. If you don't like it, shoot me a text and I'll come for round two. I don't have plans."

Juliette climbed onto the bed beside me, standing up on the unmade covers. "You're the best, Ollie-oop. *Thank you,* so much."

I got up and jumped on the spot, grabbing her hands. "You've got this. You did awesome."

She jumped a few times, too, bursting into nervous laughter. "I hope so. God, I hope so." She let out a small scream, then threw her hands up. "Now let's get you to sound check, Bon Jovi."

"Bon Jovi, really?"

"Closer comparison than Valentina. Come on, Ollie-oop, go, go, go. The night's all about you, starting from . . . right . . . now."

I took a dramatic leap from her bed and bowed to her as I landed. "I'm happy to share the spotlight. But only with you."

Juliette applauded me, then grabbed my arm to swing it back and forth. "Will's coming tonight. Are you nervous?"

"About Will coming?" I asked. "No."

*Yes.*

"He's been talking about you at lunch a lot."

I blinked. "Really?"

"Yeah. Just casual stuff. Like, 'Oh, Ollie thinks this,'

or, 'Ollie told me a story about that once.' Well, he was, anyway. Then Matt asked when the wedding date is. He hasn't really brought you up since, now that I think about it."

The unhappy pang that accompanied the gay joke was, for once, outshined by a warmer feeling. Will was talking about me. When I wasn't even there.

We'd been sitting next to each other in Music Appreciation since his message two weeks before. Five lessons in total. It was easy to get along with him in class, but a part of me figured that was because his friends weren't around. I'd been low-key terrified all day that he might give me the cold shoulder tonight. Even with Aunt Linda's pep talk, there was no way I could overlook it if he completely ignored me. But if he was acknowledging me in front of the basketball guys, that was different.

Maybe we'd be able to manage being friends after all.

So, a "few" people turned out to be closer to a hundred or so. Apparently it'd spread around the grade that the Lost and Found was the place to be that Friday night. I had more than a slight inkling it was down to the basketball guys. I wondered what it'd be like to have that kind of power? To be able to decide what people you barely knew did with their lives, just by doing it yourself?

Sayid and Emerson were a tiny bit nervous when they saw the crowd. And by that I mean Sayid had made a genuine attempt at backing out due to homework commitments he'd forgotten about until that very second, and Emerson was shaking so hard he spilled half his water bottle down his front when taking a drink. Izzy was loving every second of it, though. She spent the half hour before the set running back and forth to report back on how much the audience had grown, her eyes alight. She had good reason to be excited. Being able to draw a crowd would do wonders for the band's rep. We were unlikely to struggle finding a host for the next gig now. The Lost and Found would probably make more on soda and bar snacks tonight than they'd bring in the rest of the week combined.

Before I knew it, it was time to begin our set. Thankfully, Emerson and Sayid got over their nerves once we were onstage. Actually, that's not even giving Sayid enough credit. For all his freaking out, he belonged on the stage in a way I never saw in practice. He moved around seamlessly between the keyboard and the center mic, jumping about the place, joining me and Emerson, and engaging the crowd. I was pretty sure the music was the opposite of what 99 percent of the crowd would choose to listen to, but it was hard not to be entertained by Sayid.

As for me, I didn't mess up. Much. Maybe a note or two, but nothing noticeable. At any rate, I threw zero people off, so I considered it a resounding success. Thankfully, Mom and Dad raised me to aim low, to encourage a healthy contentment in hitting par.

Then, suddenly, it was over. A few minutes of packing up our instruments, and we were walking out to join the growing crowd while a DJ set himself up.

Juliette flung her arms around me as soon as I came out. "Ollie-oop, that was *so good.* Holy shit! You're like a freaking rock star, you know that, right?"

"That was really great, Ollie," Niamh chimed in, touching my upper arm. Her voice was softer than usual, and her eyes seemed heavy and tired. The problem with going out on a school night, I guessed.

"Spectacular," Lara deadpanned, hanging back. As

usual, I had no idea if she was being sincere or not. Probably not.

The girls all had glasses of soda, and Juliette passed me one. Lara glanced at the bartender, and turned aside to let me see her pocket. I saw a flash of a silver bottle. "Want a little something to celebrate?" she asked.

Of course. I wondered if they were all drinking, or if it was just Lara. Not that she was likely to be the only one in here with a flask. "No, thanks," I said tightly. Tightly, because I knew what her reaction would be.

She rolled her eyes without even trying to hide it. "Why do I bother?" she muttered to herself.

"Take it slow, all right?" Juliette said to Lara. "They'll kick us out if you get messy."

"Yes, Mom."

Matt and Darnell came over to talk at that point, and while Lara greeted Matt, Niamh shook her head at Juliette and me. "It must be nice to be able to eat and drink whatever you want, without *ever* exercising, and never have to justify your lifestyle to anyone."

Juliette shrugged, but it was a sympathetic one. She and Niamh joined the rest of the others in a conversation about next week's game, while I scanned the crowd curiously. And . . . yep, there she was, hanging out near the bathrooms with a group of senior girls. The redhead Lara had hooked up with at the start of the school year. Renee. I wondered if Lara was hoping to kiss her tonight. If that was why she was already drinking at seven-thirty.

Then I noticed Will had joined us, and I was suddenly interested in the conversation again. Lara gave him a mischievous look and poured something in his and Matt's drinks, keeping things below waist height to dodge wandering bartender eyes. This would be interesting. Would

ONLY MOSTLY DEVASTATED 105

Will be as eager to make up with me now that his whole letterman-wearing crew were active witnesses?

"Hey, man," Matt said to Will, slapping him on the shoulder. "Help us settle this. If you had to choose between making out with a Labrador that turned into a chick after you stopped, or making out with a chick who then turned into a Labrador, what would you go with?"

Will leaned against the bar and crossed one foot over the other, pushing his hair back off his forehead. If I did that, I'd look like I was trying and failing to emulate James Dean. Will made it work, though. "What the hell kind of conversation did I just walk into?"

"Answer the question."

"Um . . . well, where's the consciousness? Is the idea that you're kissing a Labrador in a girl's body, and then it turns into its true form? Or is it a girl who just shape-shifts?"

"The first one. It's actually a Labrador the whole time and it's like, *whaaat*, surprise!"

"Yeah, got it. How hot is the girl?"

"How hot is . . . What is the *relevance*?"

"Well, if I'm gonna frog-prince a Labrador, I'd better be saving a girl I'd wanna date."

Darnell cut in here. "Wait, so if it's not a hot girl, you'd just let her stay in a dog's body, forever? That's fucked up."

"What, so you'd make out with the Labrador?"

"Fuck no, I'm not making out with any Labradors, what kind of bestiality fetish do you think I've got?"

The same mischievous, playful, fist-bumping kind of attitude that'd pissed me off coming from Will in class was way more palatable outside of it. I still found the cocky posture and wry eyebrow raise a bit of a turnoff, but a part of me liked how much the other guys admired Will, and the way they pounced on him the second he joined a group. It even made me jealous, in a way. It didn't seem to matter what he said, or how terrible his jokes were, or whether he put his foot in it, they drank it up. It was just his energy. He was ineffably charismatic. Life came so easily to him.

Suddenly, the guys drifted away, the Labrador paradox apparently resolved to everyone's satisfaction. Matt to speak to Lara, Darnell to moon over a slightly perked-up Niamh, and the others to head outside. All at once, Will and I were alone in a crowded room. I swallowed, turning red. Was he going to pretend he didn't know me? Back away so he wouldn't be seen with me? If he did, I decided, that was it. No more second chances.

Instead, he shoved his hands in his pockets and drew closer. "You're full of surprises, aren't you?"

"How so?"

"You looked very . . . different up there. Like, relaxed and confident."

I couldn't help it, I flushed with a little spark of pleasure. "Did I? I guess I'm comfortable performing. I've been doing it for years."

He took a sip of his spiked Coke, then held the glass ahead of us. "Hey, who do you ship more? Darnell and Niamh or Lara and Matt?"

I let out a scornful noise, relaxing into the conversation. This was like talking to music class Will. Or the lake Will. "Lara and Matt? No way. She's into someone else."

"Really? Who?"

Why was he so interested? I shrugged. "That's her business. I'd put money on it, though. I notice things."

"Yeah. I know you do."

Matt was leaning against the bar, all attention on Lara.

He definitely liked her, anyone could see that. She was giving him a little bit back, sure. Giggling, hair tossing, et cetera. But she kept looking around the room, like she was keeping tabs on someone.

Darnell and Niamh, on the other hand, had pulled away from the group. He gave a shocked-sounding laugh at something and nudged her shoulder. She rubbed the spot he'd touched with a wide grin, then curled the tips of her glorious, long hair around one finger.

"Definitely Darniamh," I decided. "They're an inevitability."

"Darniamh," Will repeated. "That's perfect, isn't it?"

"Another reason Lara and Matt don't fit. What can you do with those names?"

"Latt? Mara?"

"Larmatt?" I tried, and Will choked on his drink.

"That's ridiculous. It sounds like a cleaning product," he said, wiping his chin.

"You think? I thought it was more like a ground surface. Like, hey, I'll meet you out on the Larmatt."

"Let's go shoot some hoops on the Larmatt court."

It wasn't even that funny, but we started giggling until we were helpless anyway. Half of it was me laughing at the stupidity of it. The other half was because it felt so damn good to be talking to Will out in the open.

When I'd calmed myself—which took an embarrassingly long time, because every time me and Will caught each other's eyes we cracked up again, despite the weird looks we were getting—I straightened and noticed something.

Over near the stage, red-haired Renee—Lara's Renee—was standing beside a guy I didn't recognize. Not that that was unusual. What *was* unusual was how close she stood to him. With her hand in his. And her cheek leaning against his shoulder.

That wasn't the body language of someone who was flirting, or even someone who was about to hook up with someone. Nope, ladies and gentlemen of the jury, that was unmistakably the body language of someone in a relationship with someone.

Lara was nowhere to be seen. I did a quick sweep of the bar. Niamh and Juliette didn't seem to have noticed she was gone. Although, to be fair, Niamh looked like she'd forgotten anyone other than Darnell was in the room at all.

Maybe Lara was in the bathroom or something. But maybe not. "Hey, I'll be back in a minute," I said to Will. An apparently naive part of me wanted to check that Lara was all right. For some unexplainable reason, I gave a shit.

Well, she definitely wasn't in the crowd anywhere. She wasn't backstage, or hanging out on the sidewalk outside like a few others were. I stood outside, crossing my arms and looking around, then decided to head back in. Just before I did, though, I wandered around the side to peek down the alley. There was Lara. She was sitting on the edge of the curb, her soft pink, tulle skirt haloing around her on the dirty concrete and her stockinged legs stretched out in front of her. She was clutching her leather jacket across her chest for warmth, staring ahead at nothing.

Without a word, I sat next to her, plonking myself right above the storm drain.

She didn't even look at me. "Yes?"

"I saw Renee in there. Wanted to see if you're doing okay."

She laughed shortly. "Why wouldn't I be?"

"Do you want me to spell it out?"

There was a long silence. Then she waved a hand, her silver bracelets jingling. "Screw her. It doesn't matter."

"Nah. You can totally do better than that. But it still sucks. So."

Lara drew one leg up and picked at her boot. Her face twisted up, like she was trying to scratch her nose without touching it.

"How long were you two hooking up for?" I asked.

She sighed, clearly resigning herself to the fact that I wasn't going to leave this alone. "Like, a year, I guess? It was only at parties. It didn't mean anything."

I figured. Hence, the drinking. Because if you could blame it on alcohol, then you didn't have to deal with any awkward conversations. Like, "me, gay, *what*? Nah, that's just a side effect of alcohol. Blurry vision, inability to walk straight, sudden insatiable desire to undress other girls. Wait, that doesn't happen to everyone? Weird."

"Do you think it meant anything to her, or . . . ?"

"We never talked about it. Probably not. Why do you care anyway? *Oh,*" she said, slapping her forehead with so much exaggeration she might as well have been a Looney Tunes character, "it's because of Will, isn't it?"

I studied her, then shrugged. "Maybe. That, and I figured you wouldn't have many other people to talk to about this."

She actually relaxed at this, and made a taken-aback face. It kind of felt like a trap, but I decided to give her the benefit of the doubt. "So what's his deal, anyway?" she asked. "Is he pretending nothing ever happened, or is he just playing straight?"

"Not sure right now. You said he's been spending time with his ex, didn't you?" I asked.

Lara let her hands fall in her lap. ". . . I made that up. They haven't been talking. Not that I know of, anyway."

"Oh, thank God." I grinned. To my surprise, she grinned back, and it didn't even have the slightest hint of Evil Queen to it. I hadn't realized she was capable of that when it came to me.

"Do you think he still likes you?" she asked.

"Will? I don't know. No clue."

"Ugh. Don't be that person. Figure it the hell *out*, okay? I can't stand people who float around, wringing their hands and hoping someone sees how goddamn *special* they are. If you want him, go after him. If you don't, find someone else, and make sure you flaunt it in his face for good measure. It's sure as hell what I'm gonna do."

Now this was the Lara I recognized. Even though she was snapping, however, she was snapping *with* me, not at me. She shook her head, but half-smiled at the same time. By God, we were making progress! At this rate, with a little positive manifestation and a sprinkle of mindfulness, we'd be making friendship bracelets and inventing handshakes by New Year's.

Footsteps at the entry to the alley made us both look up. Juliette and Niamh had found us, their heels clattering on the concrete.

"I was texting both of you," Juliette said. "Where'd you go?"

Lara stood up and folded her arms. "Wasn't feeling the vibe in there. Call me old fashioned, but I'd take a house party over a group of schoolkids getting high off sugar. Kind of juvenile, don't you think?"

"Lara, in case you haven't noticed, this night isn't about you. We're here for Ollie. Can't you pretend to have a good time for an hour or so?" Niamh snapped.

Juliette blinked, looking shocked. Even I was a bit taken aback. Niamh had been pretty quiet toward Lara ever since the great mashed potato incident of 2019, but I hadn't expected her to openly confront her

Lara and Niamh faced off. It seemed like they might throw down. That, or Lara might even apologize. Instead, Lara pulled her flask out of her pocket, took a deep swig, then handed it to Niamh. I guess it was a gesture of peace, even if it wasn't exactly an apology. "Why pretend?" Lara asked.

Niamh studied the flask, her face stony.

"Come on, you two," I said in a quiet voice. "Talk it through, or let it go. Holding grudges isn't going to solve anything."

Lara folded her arms. "I'm not the one who—"

Juliette and I both gave her a sharp look, and she cut off midsentence.

Niamh sighed, turned the flask around in her fingers a couple of times, then brought it to her lips and tipped her head back.

Juliette and I glanced at each other with relief. A temporary truce, sealed with a vodka shot. I didn't even have to break into a solo performance of "Give Peace a Chance." I counted this as a win, if there ever was one.

# 12

"Dylan, come out of the water right now," I said, in what was supposed to be a "firm parent" voice. It had a tinge of panic in it, though, and was probably a touch too high-pitched to strike fear into anyone's heart. I was torn between not wanting to take my eyes off him in case he drowned, and trying to watch what I was doing with Crista. It's hard to delicately clean approximately twenty pints of blood from a mystery wound without glancing at your hands every now and then.

"No."

"Dylan!" So help me God.

"Wanna play! Wanna swim!"

"Ouch, Ollie," Crista yelped through her tears, pushing my hand away. "Stop."

"I have to get the blood off."

"You're hurting me."

"It's only gonna sting for a second, I promise."

"You're not cleaning it right. You can't clean blood with a napkin. It's going to get sepsis."

*Well, a napkin was all I had. And how the hell did she even know what sepsis was? I ignored her, and turned back to the lake.* "Dylan Thomson, if you don't come here in the next five seconds . . ." *I didn't finish the threat, because I didn't know what an appropriate punishment for someone who wasn't even three years old was. This was only my third day here, and my first day looking after my cousins without an adult nearby. Usually I'd threaten to grab Aunt Linda or Uncle Roy. But they were out God-knew-where with my parents. So here I was, trying to run a dictatorship while my two citizens were staging a coup.*

*The napkin began to fall apart. It was dark red, and so were my hands, and I was starting to think I might vomit. What the hell had Crista done? Should I take her to a clinic? Would she lose her leg? Should I call Aunt Linda? Or 911?*

*A shadow fell over us, and out of nowhere, someone was kneeling by my side.* "Hey," *the someone said.* "Do you need a hand? It doesn't look like the napkin's gonna cut it."

*Crista and I glanced up as one. Our Guardian Angel was a guy about my age, with thick dark hair that curled a little at the ends, light brown skin, and a first-aid kit.*

*I said something that didn't even slightly resemble English.*

"Dad forces me to bring the kit every time I take Kane here," *the guy said, unzipping the bag and fishing through various wipes and bandages.* "That's my little brother. He's right over there, in the water. This is the first time the kit's come in handy, though."

*Speaking of firsts, this was the first time I'd ever seen Crista shut up. She was staring at the guy like he'd ridden in on the back of a unicorn. I had a nasty feeling I was looking at him in the same way.*

*The guy held up a pack of disinfectant wipes.* "Is this okay?" *he asked.*

*Was water wet? Was the day hot? Were his freckles perfect? Of course it was okay. Nothing had ever been more okay in all of human history. Someone needed to write a ballad about how okay this was. I needed a picture of this, to submit to the* Oxford English Dictionary, *to substitute in for the definition of "okay."*

*I think I managed a faint nod.*

*"What's your name?"*

*He wasn't asking me, unfortunately.*

*Crista was totally solemn. "Crista."*

*"Isn't that a pretty name? I'm Will. Crista, is it okay if I clean off your leg? It looks like it must hurt a lot."*

*Crista also managed a faint nod.*

*Will glanced up at me. "If you wanted to go and grab Dylan, I can hold the fort here for a sec."*

*Wait, did he know Dylan? Did he know me? Had we always known each other? Suddenly, I remembered how many times I'd screamed Dylan's name across the shore. Right. That made sense.*

*"Yeah," I choked out. "Thank you."*

*Then we really looked at each other, and it was like being locked into place. Like I couldn't have blinked if someone was offering me a winning lottery ticket to. It wasn't the first time I'd felt like this looking at a guy. But it was maybe the first time a guy had stared at me in the same sort of way.*

*"Anytime," he said. And smiled.*

"I still don't get what the difference between major and minor is supposed to be."

I kept my eyes on my bass without pausing in the plucking. "I'm not listening to you."

Will made a point of turning his textbook upside down,

and tipped his head at a 90-degree angle. He was sitting backward on one of the metal chairs, crossing his legs at the ankle in front of him. His hair was a little too long, hanging in his face in dark, wavy tendrils.

"Seriously, Ollie. How do you decide one note is sad and another is happy?"

I paused in disbelief. "You don't have minor notes. You have minor scales and *chords*."

"But aren't the minor notes the black ones?"

Now I felt as baffled as he looked. "Black notes? Do you have synesthesia or something?"

"Huh?"

"Like hearing and tasting color?"

"Don't be ridiculous," Will said, jumping to his feet and striding over to the piano. He played several notes in ascending order. "Black note. Black note. Black note."

Suddenly, it clicked. He was talking about piano keys. He was even more screwed than I'd thought. I burst out laughing and dropped my bass to join him at the piano. "No, hold on. Okay, *these*, all of these, are keys. Piano keys."

Will threw his hands up, frustrated. "Well, *I* don't know!"

"Clearly not." I smirked. "Multiple notes make up chords. You can play a chord in one hit, or rolling, like this . . ." I played a C, E, and G with a quick wrist movement, "and it's the notes in the chords that make it major or minor. So this is a major chord. You can hear it, see? It sounds happy?"

"Are you sure *you* aren't the synthetic one?" Will asked. "Synesthesia."

"Po-tay-to po-tah-to. I don't see how that sounds happy. It just sounds . . . I don't know. Blah."

Will hadn't exactly made a habit of joining me in the

music room at lunch—that probably wouldn't go unnoticed by the basketball guys—but he'd followed after me occasionally over the last few weeks. Today being one of those occasions. He always told the others it was to get one-on-one tutoring from me, and no one seemed too suspicious.

In our defense, it wasn't exactly the scene of a depraved porno when we shut the music room door. Or, unfortunately, even a regular, nondepraved porno. He never made any attempt to touch me, or sit too close, or throw me a loaded compliment. We just hung out, chatting about music, or life, or nothing at all. Even though I couldn't forget the fact that he wouldn't admit he liked spending time with me to his friends, I gave in and let him join me every time he flashed that smile. Aunt Linda would be proud.

Between these lunchtime visits, Music Appreciation, and the occasional conversation after English—always ostensibly so he could ask a question about an assignment or something until his friends left the classroom—it was getting easier to adjust to the idea of going at his pace. I didn't have the energy to resist his endless olive branches. Even if they resembled olive twigs more than branches, sometimes. Plus, it felt so much better to let him melt me than to fight to stay frozen.

Despite our fragile truce, though, a part of me wanted to at least clarify if we were supposed to be totally platonic now, to address the elephant—and ringmaster—and whole freaking *circus*—in the room, but I was too self-conscious to bring it up without an opening. Like, what if he said I imagined everything at the lake, and I had to deal with the inescapable knowledge that I was going slowly mad? Call me dramatic, but it was starting to feel like I *had* imagined the whole thing.

Maybe Will found this normal, but for me it was super

weird. Like, how do you handle being just friends with someone when you have in-depth knowledge of what their tongue tastes like? Among other things.

Also, I didn't want to freak him out. Clearly, as far as he was concerned, everything that happened at the lake was in the past. Including his entire sexual orientation, apparently. At least we had a rhythm going in our new little friends-without-benefits pantomime. He hadn't pushed me into a single mop bucket since we started this dance.

Will dragged his finger across the piano keys, from high to low. Stunning. This guy was such a natural talent. "What are you doing for Thanksgiving?" he asked.

"My house. We're having Aunt Linda and the kids over. Probably gonna be kind of quiet, but as long as I get to eat my body weight in Brussels sprouts, I'm happy."

Will slammed his hand on the piano, clunking the keys. "Wait, you what?"

"What?"

"Brussels sprouts? Is this a sick joke?"

"I'd never joke about Brussels sprouts. They're the *best* all roasted, with bacon bits and some syrup . . ." I trailed off, dreamy. It occurred to me that my feelings for Brussels sprouts bordered on sexual.

He blinked at me. "Ollie, that's foul. Yuck. If I'd known your taste was that bad I never would've—" He caught himself, then became suddenly interested in the piano again. Oh, *there* it was. The opening to acknowledge summer. He was kidding himself if he thought I wasn't gonna take this for all it was worth.

"Never would've what?"

"You know what."

"Done my taxes?"

"No."

"Gone paragliding with me?"

"We never went paragliding."

"It's on my list. And to be fair, you never did my taxes, either. Was that an option?"

"You're ridiculous."

"*Oh*," I said, dropping my mouth open, and then whispering, "*you meant you would've never let me dribble your basketballs?*"

Will let out a noise that wouldn't have sounded out of place coming from a surprised dog. He drove his elbow backward and into my side. "Shhh!"

I'd gone to laugh, but the smile dropped right off my face. Seriously? We couldn't even discuss it in private? Wasn't that a tad dramatic? "What?" I asked loudly. "Afraid all the people in the room might think you're gay if they found out you hooked up with me?"

"Ollie, seriously."

I stepped back and threw my arms out, spinning in a circle. "There's no one here, Will. I get that you don't wanna advertise that you knew me before school, but do we have to keep pretending we don't have a history when we're alone, too? It's making me feel kind of uncomfortable. I don't know where we stand."

Will closed the lid of the piano and swiveled around on the bench. I had a sudden flashback to an evening at the lake. I didn't remember exactly when, or what we'd done that day. Only the sunset casting a lavender glow over the water, and dragonflies zipping past my head while I stood on the edge of the jetty. And Will had been treading water, his head and shoulders sticking out of the lake. Only in my memory he was smiling. In real life, right here and now, he looked apprehensive. Like he was worried I was going to hurt him. If the truth was a weapon, then maybe I was.

"I didn't want to make it weird," he said finally. "Why bring it up if it's going to be awkward?"

Um, fucking ouch? Yep. The truth was *definitely* a weapon. Man down. "Why should it be awkward? Do you regret it?"

We had a sort of standoff then. Both of us stared each other down, like whoever blinked was the one who actually had feelings. The one who could be hurt. Will caved first. "No. I don't regret it."

"Then can we acknowledge it, please?" I jumped in, almost on top of his words.

"Um, sure."

"Say you kissed me," I said.

Honest to God, he scanned the room like he was worried someone had snaked their way into it in the last thirty seconds without either of us noticing. "I kissed you."

"He whispers reluctantly," I said.

"I kissed you," Will said, loudly this time.

"Multiple times."

"Not as many times as you kissed me," Will said, and I felt the tension shatter. There. *This* was the Will I knew. He was supposed to be the confident one out of us, not me.

"I wasn't keeping a record," I said.

"Take my word for it."

"I'm gonna have to."

He stood up and came over to me, without breaking eye contact. "I remember more than just kissing, by the way."

"Is that so?"

Dear God, I sounded like a forty-five-year-old cougar.

*Is that so?* Really? Send help, I could not flirt. Woah, wait, he'd taken another step closer, and another, and he was looking at my mouth. Blatantly staring at it. Suddenly all I could do was stare at him staring at my mouth.

Then I was certain. He was going to kiss me.

People say when you die your life flashes before your eyes. Well, in that very moment, my future flashed before mine. Will was firmly, firmly in the closet, and obviously not comfortable with this, or us, or what we'd had. Even if he was trying to kiss me right now, a minute ago he'd definitely checked an empty room for spies. He couldn't *be* less chill about this.

Argh, but right now I could smell him. So strongly. And even that made me dizzy, and weak, and honestly, I'd have traded my own grandma for the chance to kiss him now. If I kissed him, though, I'd taste him again, and I'd be right back at square one. I'd go home tonight floating and spinning out and squeaking, and I'd wait for him to text me. But he maybe—*probably*—wouldn't. And he'd maybe—*probably*—be all weird at school tomorrow. Then there'd be me. Basking in the putrid glow of unrequited hell.

For the last month I'd had control over things. We had a rhythm. It was *calm*. I couldn't give that up. I couldn't go back to desperately pining and hoping, only to be let down. Not even for a kiss from Will.

Not even if I really, really, really, really, oh-fuck-am-I-actually-going-to-turn-this-down, *really* wanted it.

So, actively kicking myself the whole time, I sprang backward. "You're right," I said. "I remember a lot of basketball. Anyway, can you give me a few minutes? I almost had this line."

I scrambled to pick up my bass and held it up between

ONLY MOSTLY DEVASTATED  121

us, like it was garlic and Will was a heartthrob vampire. Keeping my stare fixed on my hands, I returned to playing like the last five minutes hadn't happened at all. I did not look at Will. Nope, I did not.

Until I did. Alas, he'd gone back to his chair, reading his textbook like nothing had happened.

Except it was the right-way up this time. And he'd angled his body away from me.

It's an indisputable truth that one of the best things about holidays is getting to sleep in. Waiting until the sun rays drag you out of your coma, tossing around in bed a few times, maybe falling back asleep once or twice. Then rolling out of bed and down the hall to plonk in front of the television, phone in hand, cereal bowl in lap, with English class all but a faraway dream.

The night before Thanksgiving I burrowed into bed all satisfied and eager, knowing I didn't have an alarm clock the next morning. My biggest problem was deciding if I'd go for Cheerios or Cinnamon Toast Crunch. The last thing I remembered before drifting off was deciding I'd combine them both into a monster bowl, maybe with chocolate milk instead of regular.

Three hours later, I was very rudely awakened. I peeked through bleary eyes into the pitch-black room, trying to piece together what was going on. Hand on my shoulder. Voice telling me to wake up. A voice that was not an alarm clock. Why did I have to wake before the sun, though? Wasn't it Thanksgiving? Had I overslept somehow?

". . . hospital. Come on, grab a change of clothes. You don't need to get dressed, you can sleep in Roy and Linda's bed. Quick, Ollie, come on."

It was Dad. I staggered out of bed, and he thrust a shirt and jeans against my chest. I felt around for my shoes, trying to form a coherent picture of the situation in silence. Dad was muttering to himself in a panic, digging through my underwear drawer. "Jesus, Ollie, why don't you pair your socks?"

"Grab any two. It doesn't matter."

"It *does* matter. You should fold your socks together. How lazy do you have to be to just shove socks in a drawer? You don't even do the washing, or the drying. All we ask is for you to keep your room neat. *One* small request—"

I rubbed the crust out of my eyes while I tried to catch up. Dad barely ever even came in my room. He'd never cared what it looked like before. "So what? They're just socks."

"You're *eighteen years old now, Ollie.*"

"I'm seventeen."

He slammed the drawer shut so hard the pencil tin sitting on the bureau tipped over. *"For fuck's sake, Oliver."*

Dad never swore. Never, ever, ever. I shut my mouth and sat back down on the bed, my cheeks burning. It didn't take a rocket scientist to figure out something was going on with Aunt Linda. Something probably worse than usual. "Who's with the kids?" I asked.

"Roy is. He needs to go to the hospital. We need to get you over there now."

"Wait, we're not going?"

"Use your brain, Oliver. It's three A.M. in the morning. Crista and Dylan are asleep."

But I wanted to go with the adults. I didn't want to be at home, not sure what was happening. Waiting for the worst. But arguing with Dad in this mood was like asking a wasp for a handshake. With some effort I forced my head to clear and collected the things I figured I might need for the day. At the last second, I turned back and grabbed my phone charger before following Dad downstairs.

Mom was bustling around with puffy, bloodshot eyes, collecting magazines, fresh wipes, and blankets under her arm.

"Get in the car," Dad barked at me. Like I'd somehow done this to Aunt Linda. I started toward the garage, then hesitated. *"What?"* he demanded.

"Um . . . uh . . . if I drive my own car, I'll be able to bring Crista and Dylan to the hospital tomorrow if we need."

Dad stared me down like I'd said the stupidest thing in the world. I racked my memory to figure out if I'd done something to piss him off. Nothing came to mind.

Thankfully, Mom came to the rescue. "Great idea, honey," she said, pushing past me to throw her load into the backseat of the Honda. "You can follow us."

I trailed after her, still carrying my own small collection of stuff. Dad made a beeline for the Honda, telling me to hurry up.

Mom shut the back door and flipped around, wrapping me in a fierce hug out of nowhere. "It's gonna be okay," she whispered. "Think positive thoughts for me. We need to combine our energy. We're stronger together."

"Okay," I said. But it was a lie. My brain was already preparing the show reel of horrors it liked to deliver in moments of crisis. Aunt Linda was already dead. Aunt Linda was alone in the hospital, crying for Uncle Roy with no one around. Aunt Linda's body was under the ground with bugs burrowing under her fingernails to lay eggs.

The drive to Linda and Roy's house went by in a hazy fog. My body drove on autopilot while my mind floated somewhere near the car ceiling, chanting "doom, doom, doom" like it was in a trance. I guess I was. In a trance.

Mom and Dad stayed in their car, and I swapped batons with Uncle Roy. Him to the hospital. Me with the kids. Team break.

I felt super weird sleeping in Aunt Linda and Uncle Roy's bed, so I dug through their linen closet until I found a blanket. I cocooned myself on the sofa, fluffing up the hard cushions as best as I could. Then I proceeded to stare at the ceiling. Like I was going to get any damn sleep now.

It's funny how you can spend weeks, or months, or sometimes even years preparing yourself for a nightmare that's more "when" than "if." Then just when you're fooling yourself that you've accepted the world's end, and you'll roll with the impact when it hits . . . suddenly, it might be hitting, and you're not rolling. You're collapsing, sitting where you stood, totally overwhelmed by a loss you were never really ready for.

How could I have thought I'd cope with losing Aunt Linda? The reality of it all made me feel helpless. My life stretched out in front of me, made up of hundreds of thousands of hours, which were made out of millions of minutes, which were made up of billions of seconds. And right now, each second pinned me down like rubble. I'd have to somehow get through all those billions of seconds without Aunt Linda being alive anymore.

Tick.

Tick.

Tick.

# 13

I woke up to three missed calls and a text. My stomach plummeted, and I steeled myself to open the message.

**Thursday, 7:16 AM**

Linda's doing okay. Bring the kids
when you can.

Okay.
Okay was good.
I moved through a bubble, getting the kids up, dressed, and fed. Neither of them had a clue their mom was in the hospital, it turned out, and I didn't know how I was supposed to frame this. In the end I just kind of minimized it, passing it off as a minor blip, sounding as chirpy as I could. Which was a hell of an effort, considering I'd had about four hours' sleep by my estimate. Luckily for me, the kids didn't seem suspicious. They were too busy chattering about what they wanted to have for Thanksgiving

dinner. How Aunt Linda had promised she'd do the potato gratin with bacon pieces, and that they could have a glass of Coke if they were well-behaved.

Shit. I hadn't even thought about dinner. Someone was going to have to break it to the kids that Thanksgiving dinner wasn't likely to happen today. That someone was not going to be me, though. I'd been the bearer of enough bad holiday news. In fact, I decided then and there that I wasn't going to contribute to making this day suck any more than it had to for them. So when Crista wanted to put on her Elsa costume, complete with teeny little kitten heels, even though it was forty freaking degrees outside, I let her. And when Dylan wanted a banana smoothie as a "special" breakfast, he damn well got a banana smoothie. Who cared, at the end of the day? Life was short.

At the hospital, Aunt Linda was lying in bed, propped up by stiff white hospital pillows and the bed itself, which was raised at one end. She was missing her headscarf. Even though she'd been going through chemo for a while now, her scalp wasn't totally bald. Instead, a few short wisps of the curls that used to tumble down her neck were left behind. Also, her face was totally clean. She never, and I mean *never*, went without makeup. Even if it was just eyebrows and eyeliner. Bare like this, she looked capital-S Sick.

My parents were side by side on the ugly floral love seat, and Uncle Roy slumped in the chair by Aunt Linda's head. When he noticed us come in, he gave the kids a tired smile and held out a hand.

Crista and Dylan went straight to the bed. "I thought you were doing chemo?" Crista asked in a voice so small I died a little.

Aunt Linda's smile was even more exhausted than Uncle Roy's. "Happy Thanksgiving to you, too, Elsa. I felt a little sick while you were sleeping, so we came here to get me better. Don't you worry a bit."

"Does it hurt?" Crista pressed.

Aunt Linda and Uncle Roy exchanged a quick look, then Aunt Linda shrugged. "Nothing I can't handle. But, Little Miss Munchkin, excuse me. Where is your coat? It's freezing out."

I held up the kid's carryall. "Got it. Sneakers, too."

"I don't *want* sneakers."

"Elsa wears sneakers after she's done parading in those heels," Aunt Linda said.

"She does *not*."

"Believe me, she does. Elsa would need to take a Tylenol on the hour to wear those things all day. The blisters alone . . . And don't get me started on the practicalities of walking on ice in pumps. Aunt Catherine tried it once. Ask her how *that* turned out." Aunt Linda winked at Mom, who burst out laughing.

"That's a story for when you're older," Mom said to Crista. "Much older."

The rest of the morning was relatively quiet. The kids took their iPads off by the wall and sat on the ground, tearing through movies and games without complaining. I couldn't imagine myself being that well-behaved when I was little, but then, these two weren't regular kids. Dylan probably couldn't remember a time when Aunt Linda wasn't sick, and if Crista could, it'd be hazy. The hospital was like an extension of their home these days.

The adults rotated between trying to keep Aunt Linda company and going on their own phones while Aunt Linda napped. Her naps weren't really deep sleeps as much as they were an inability to hold her eyes open for more than ten-minute stints. A part of me wondered if she wouldn't prefer for the rest of us to leave her the hell alone so she could really rest for once. But then, it was Thanksgiving. You couldn't abandon your family on Thanksgiving, even if they really, really wanted to be abandoned.

At around eleven, the kids started whining a little—which, in their defense, was an impressive stretch of good behavior. After some not-so-subtle pleading looks from my parents, I led the kids downstairs to run in the hospital gardens. I set myself up on an ornate wooden bench underneath a shockingly red sugar maple so I could keep an eye on them, and hopped back on my phone.

Snapchat was pretty much an endless stream of people cooking and showing off about it. Yay, pumpkin pie ready to go, hashtag blessed, hashtag clean eating, hashtag loljks. To be honest, it was weird to see people going about their day like normal. Like, because my Thanksgiving had gone to hell, it should somehow grind to a halt for everyone else, too.

Nothing from Will. Which was fine. He had his own life. He was probably busy with his family, and his friends, and music, and laughing, and corny games.

Totally, totally fine.

"Ollie, can we have a selfie?" Crista popped up out of swear-to-God nowhere, peeking at my phone over my shoulder. Dylan, as usual, stood on tiptoes at her side. Crista bounced backward. "Can you show everyone my dress?" As she spoke, she shucked off her thick overcoat. Beauty was pain, after all. "Hold on, hold on. I'll tell you when to take it. Get ready."

I brought Snapchat up and switched it to front facing, holding the phone as high as I could to get the other two in. Crista was crouching on the ground. "I'm ready."

"Okay, go." Crista shot up at that moment, flinging

sunset-colored leaves in the air. I took the picture just as
the leaves started showering us. Dylan cackled in the background, swatting at the leaves as they fell, and Crista threw
a handful at his face, shrieking.

I captioned the picture "better than pumpkin pie,"
which was maybe a lie and definitely petty, and sent it
out to everyone but Will. If Will spoke to me, I wanted
it to be because he was thinking of me, not because I
prompted him. Apparently, despite how platonic we'd
become, I still cared about being chased. Hashtag pa-
thetic.

My phone buzzed. Will? Be Will, be Will, be Will.

It wasn't Will. It was a message from Lara. Hah. I think
I know those kids.

Even though Lara and I had reached a kind of truce, talking outside of group situations still wasn't a normal thing
for us. I'd added her to the Snapchat list, yeah, but I'd also
sent it to about a hundred other people. After a moment
trying to figure out if she was trying to set me up somehow,
I sent back, They're my cousins. A minute passed, then she
replied. No shit? They used to go to my church.

"Ollie, I'm hungry." Dylan appeared at my side again,
his puppy-dog eyes gazing up at me.

Right. Yeah. It was lunchtime, wasn't it? I considered
offering to take the kids to McDonald's or something, then
I remembered Aunt Linda might not still be awake by dinner. Whatever we did for lunch was probably going to be
the Thanksgiving meal for the day. We'd have to make do.
I grabbed Crista and Dylan and hit up the hospital cafeteria, as well as a hallway vending machine. By the time
we got back to Aunt Linda's room we were armed with
french fries, hot dogs, hash browns, lasagna, Hershey's
chocolate, a few peanut butter cups, a real slice of pumpkin

pie (the last one the cafeteria had left) and bottles of Coke (Dylan insisted).

Luckily, Aunt Linda was awake, so we were able to pool the haul in the center of the bed. Crista and Dylan clearly thought the lunch's contents were the biggest stroke of luck they'd ever come across.

Mom raised her eyebrow at me. "No vegetables?" she asked as she reached for a hot dog.

"Good luck finding any." I shrugged. "I think this is the hospital's profitability plan. Don't provide anything with vitamins, so visitors get sick and need to come to the hospital. Then their visitors get sick, too. It's a vicious cycle."

"Why aren't you eating, Mama?" Crista asked through a mouthful of peanut butter and chocolate.

Aunt Linda lifted her head off the pillow. It looked like it weighed fifty pounds. "I ate earlier, honey. I didn't know we were all doing lunch. Now I'm jealous!"

I didn't think for a second that she'd eaten earlier. But she looked a little green, so I didn't push it.

As far as Thanksgiving meals went, it was modest, but still nice. No one complained, in any case. Mom, Dad, and Uncle Roy talked and joked like normal. Even if Aunt Linda was too tired to join in, she smiled the whole time. She barely took her eyes off Crista and Dylan, though.

After we finished eating, my parents decided to take the kids for another walk. They were bounding around like fleas riding pogo sticks in a jumping castle. My bad. I forgot about the downside to sugar indulgences.

We were plunged into an eerie silence as the kids' voices faded down the hallway. Linda closed her eyes, and I assumed she was angling for another nap. Then I realized with a shock she was crying.

"Are you okay?" I asked, as Uncle Roy jumped to grab her hand.

"What hurts, baby?" he asked, but she flapped him away.

"Nothing. Nothing, I'm sorry. It's just . . . I just . . ." She wiped her eyes with the back of her hand, and sucked in a breath. "This is the oldest I'm ever going to see them. I'm never going to see Dyl grow bigger than a baby. And Crissy in her dress . . . she'll have a prom dress one day. And I'll never see it. I won't be there. It'll happen without me."

Uncle Roy looked stricken. I desperately wished I'd gone with Mom and Dad. This felt like a private moment. But there was no way for me to excuse myself now without looking like a massive dick.

"Not necessarily, baby. There's a chance—"

She scoffed. "Roy, don't."

"There is."

"Four percent isn't a chance. It's a sentence." Her eyes welled up again, and then she shook her head like a dog drying itself. Like she could shake off her tears. "I need you to promise me something. Promise me you won't let anyone tell them they aren't beautiful. You, too, Ollie."

I nodded mutely.

Her voice choked. "I was told I wasn't beautiful when I was little. But they're the most beautiful children in the world. They're smart, and funny, and creative. I won't be here to remind them, so you have to. Both of you. Daily. Okay?"

We nodded. Uncle Roy kept squeezing her hand, like if he let go of it something terrible might happen. He looked more than a bit emotional himself.

Before long, my parents returned with a worn-out Crista,

and Dylan out cold in Dad's arms. They settled both kids on the couch to nap, and gathered single chairs from around the room.

"You don't all need to be here," Aunt Linda said finally. "Really. I'm fine, and I just want to sleep."

"You can sleep," Uncle Roy said. "We'll be here when you wake up."

"No, honestly. If you go now you can do at least part of dinner. Maybe not a turkey, but the rest? And you could bring some sweet potato pie for me tomorrow?"

She had the same kind of look I'm pretty sure I get when I'm aiming for a long shot, like leftover pizza for breakfast or an advance in my pocket money. Earnestly hopeful, but weirdly resigned at the same time.

"Not happening."

"Roy, the *kids*."

"They don't know the difference."

"They've been looking forward to this all week."

"We can do a makeup when you're home."

"I'll be too tired to cook, you know I will—"

"I'll cook."

"You can't cook. You don't even know what paprika is! Catherine needs to do it. Cathy, sweetie, will you—"

"No, Catherine isn't doing it, because the kids and I are staying right the hell here. It's Thanksgiving. They should be with their family."

"They've been here all *day*, Roy. They've *been* with me. When they're here I feel like I have to smile, and be energetic, and make sure they don't worry, and I've been doing it all *day*. I am *tired*. I just want to nap, and watch a bad movie, and complain and moan without ruining their day. It's a special day for them. Please."

Uncle Roy hesitated. "I'm not leaving."

"Cathy?"

Mom looked at Aunt Linda, then me, then Dad, then the kids. "I . . . Linda, I don't think I can. If I wasn't here, I'd just be worried and distracted. I feel better here."

Three . . . two . . . one. On cue, the adults all turned to me.

I didn't really want to leave the hospital, either, but I had the least right to be selfish out of everyone here. "I . . . Look, if it helps, I'm more than happy to take the kids to McDonald's. Then I can bring them back here, or we can go home and play some games or something."

Aunt Linda broke into her first full-faced smile of the day. "Ollie, you are the best thing that ever happened to me. I'll give you some money, and you let them eat whatever they want, okay? *Whatever*. I don't care if they want a Big Mac with hot fudge sauce, they can have it. No rules today."

Goddamn, kids get excited about McDonald's. Got to give that clown one thing, he knows how to target a vulnerable audience. Any other middle-aged man wearing a clown costume and luring kids in with toys and music and sugar would be arrested, but not good old Ronald.

As we pulled into the parking lot, Crista and Dylan were literally bouncing out of their seats. Well, Crista was anyway, because she knew how to unlatch her seat belt.

I noticed my phone flashing as I switched off the ignition. At first I figured it was Mom or Aunt Linda but—but! It was Will! Finally, finally, finally. How are the Brussels sprouts?

I checked the time stamp. The message came through fifteen minutes ago. It was a reasonable time lapse. I took a quick snap of the McDonald's sign and sent it to him, along with the text, Wouldn't know :(

Before I'd even gotten to the back door to let Dylan out, my phone started buzzing.

"Where are you?" Will asked as soon as I answered.

"Uh, McDonald's. Nice family restaurant. Have you never heard of it?"

"*Why* are you at McDonald's? Did your house burn down or something?"

"Ooh, close. Actually, we had a bit of an incident with Aunt Linda. Everyone's at the hospital."

"Shit. Is she okay?"

"Yeah, for now. Just we've been there since the crack of dawn, and the kids were hungry, so . . . we ditched for food."

There was a brief pause, then: "Come here."

"What do you mean? Where are you?" The first, wild thought that came into my head was that Will was also at McDonald's somehow.

"My house. Seriously, it's overflowing here, all my cousins came up. We've had to move things outside with, like, three tables. But our back porch is enclosed, and we've got heaters, so you wouldn't even be cold. Kane would love to see Crista. I told him she lives nearby and he's always asking to see her. We have so much food, just *so* much, it's ridiculous, you have no . . . am I babbling?"

I grinned to myself and leaned against the car door. From the inside, Crista banged against the window with a closed fist. "Kind of."

"Yeah, I thought I might be. I'm a bit nervous. Because I'm not sure if you still hate me a little." He laughed. "But if you don't . . . seriously. Please don't say you're busy now that I've asked you to come over, because that'd be really embarrassing for me. Sorry to put you on the spot, but, for real."

There was no way this was real. Never in a million years had I expected this. I tipped my head back and let it hit the car. I wanted to say yes. So badly. "The kids really wanted McDonald's."

"So tell them you forgot it's illegal to eat McDonald's on Thanksgiving. You'd barely be lying. It should be illegal."

Eurgh. He was making it so easy. Way too easy. "Don't you live out of town?"

"Twenty minutes, max. I'll text you the address."

"I'd have to check with their parents."

"They remember me, don't they? It's not like I'm a stranger."

"Still."

"Yeah, still. Look, ask them, then if you're out of excuses send me a text to give me an E.T.A., okay?"

"Okay."

"It sounds like you're smiling."

"I'm not." I smiled.

"I'll see you soon, then."

He hung up on me before I had time to change my mind.

I looked inside the car. Crista shrugged up at me, splaying her hands out like a sassy thirteen-year-old. Dylan was still wriggling in his car seat, tapping his hands on his knees.

Maybe if I bribed them with an order of fries to share and the promise of seeing Will, they'd be down.

My chances seemed good.

# 14

"Ollie, why aren't we driving anymore?"

Breathe in. Breathe out. Don't die. That last one was particularly important. *Don't die.*

"Ollie?"

"Yeah, uh. We're here, that's why."

"Oh. Why aren't you getting out, then?"

Excellent question, Crista. Kids were full of excellent questions. How could I explain to a seven- and three-year-old that I was afraid to get out into this too-dark street, walk up that too-long driveway, and ring the too-loud doorbell?

Maybe I could put it in a way that was accessible to them? Like, this is the cortisol that's flooding the blood, that flows in the veins, that leads to the heart, that's pumping too fast in the chest of the guy, who's too scared to knock on the door of the house where Will lives.

I only had three options. Option one, turn back and drive all the way home with two cranky, hungry kids rightfully complaining in the backseat. Ruin their night, let Aunt Linda down, *but* avoid having to knock on Will's door. Pros, cons.

Option two, get out and knock on Will's door.

Option three, sit here for a while longer, and explain calmly to Crista and Dylan all about the cortisol that's flooding the blood that flows in the—

*Okay,* fine. Fine. I'd do it.

Dylan, who was still squirming in his car seat, reached up as I unbuckled him and hoisted him out. Crista had no such issues, unclipping herself and quite literally leaping around on the road. Part of me wondered if she'd smuggled some of the leftover vending machine loot into her pockets and eaten it on the drive. I'd seen her do craftier things in my time—she was capable.

Will's house was pretty much a clone of the houses in Collinswood, with a large, green front lawn that met stairs leading up to a spacious front porch. The house was two stories (of course), and covered in navy weatherboards, with white trimming on the Victorian-style arch windows.

He'd said everyone was outside eating. What if they'd already started? They might not hear a doorbell or knock. Then how would I know how long to wait before trying again? What if Will hadn't asked permission for us to come, and his parents answered the door and sent us away? Or, worse, what if *Will* decided he didn't want us there after all?

I stopped under a streetlight and placed Dylan down to stand. "Let's wait here," I said. "I'll just send Will a text, then he'll come to get us."

At least, I hoped he would. If he was allowed his phone at the dinner table, that was. I sent a quick plea to the Great, Ethereal Being that he'd see the message quickly. It was freaking freezing, even for late November, and our breath was opaque enough to reflect the streetlight. By my knee, Dylan started grumbling before I'd even finished the text.

Apparently frigid air was a good prayer conductor, because Will flew open the front door and trotted down the steps within seconds. "What are you doing all the way out here?" he asked. "Come on. It's ridiculously cold."

Will looked even colder than I felt, actually. Even in a hoodie *and* a denim jacket he had his bare hands tucked under his armpits. Dylan grabbed my hand as we started toward the house, but Crista planted herself by Will's side. She was as determined to claim him as ever.

"Ollie said we have to eat outside," Crista hiss-whispered to Will.

"Well, he's right, but we have *heaters* in the backyard. You'll be toasty, I promise."

As soon as we entered Will's house we were hit by a wave of heat, accompanied by the tantalizing smell of meat and spices, and upbeat Latin music playing at about a billion decibels.

The rooms were buzzing with people ferrying plates and trays from the kitchen to the backyard. Will hadn't been kidding about the turnout—altogether there had to be about fifty people here, what with aunts and uncles and grandparents, along with kids running around between it all, clutching fist-sized snacks they'd managed to swipe from the kitchen. Among the din, I could make out an even mixture of Spanish and English.

Mrs. Tavares, a tall woman who had Will's freckles and large brown eyes, burst out of the kitchen carrying a tray with a hunk of delicious-looking slow-cooked meat on it, bopping from side to side in time with the music. *"Ollie,"* she cried, lifting the tray up a little to greet me. "It's so good to see you again! Thank you so much for coming by tonight."

"No, thank *you*," I said. "I'm so sorry we didn't bring anything, it was kind of short notice."

"Ah, I *think* we're going to be okay," she said, nodding at the platter in her hands. "We could feed half the neighborhood with just the side dishes."

"Should we go help bring stuff out?" I asked Will.

"Under no circumstances. It's mayhem in there, honestly. We just try not to get in anyone's way for the next five minutes. You got here at the perfect time, it's almost dinner."

"I'm surprised you haven't eaten yet."

Will pursed his lips together in a silent laugh. "We don't eat 'til late. The first few hours of Thanksgiving are for dancing, ponche crema, and explaining to thirteen great-aunts why you don't have a girlfriend."

"Ponche crema?"

"It's kind of like a Venezuelan eggnog, but it's way better."

"Alcohol?"

Will rolled his eyes at me. "I'm not drunk. I only had a little bit."

"My parents would literally kill me if I drank."

Will led me outside, Crista and Dylan in tow. "I've been having wine at dinner since I was a kid. It's normal."

Outside, several tables were lined up on the porch, with chairs squeezed in wherever possible. Straightaway, I saw what Will meant about the cold. The sides of the porch were enclosed by detachable clear vinyl sheeting, so while some frigid air blew through under the gap at the bottom, for the most part we were protected from the wind and chill.

A whole bunch of the seats were taken already—mostly by men—with other seats saved with half-drunk glasses of wine, or a white liquid I guessed was the fabled ponche crema, or a well-placed handbag. Fairy lights twinkled above us, glittering and snaking around the rafters and poles, and the standing outdoor heaters gave off a welcome blast of heat to counteract the frozen air that did sneak in. A bunch of the people sitting at the table had a Will-like vibe to them. Whether they shared his well-defined lips, or the delicate shape of his jaw, or his long fingers, you could tell they were blood relatives.

It was like a peek into the future, in an oh-God-Ollie-it's-too-early-to-think-about-the-future-please-stop kind of way.

Will squatted down to meet Crista and Dylan at eye level. "So, at my house we have a special table for the kids. Kane will be sitting there, and some of my little cousins, too. Do you feel comfortable sitting with Kane?"

Crista gave a shy nod, and Dylan copied her.

"Excellent. Come on, I'll get you set up. Would you like a drink?"

While Will looked after the kids, I hung back, giving an awkward smile to the people sitting at the table. Were they wondering who the hell these random people strolling into their family dinner were? Should I introduce myself? Should I wait for Will to do that for me?

Will reappeared beside me. "So, the bad news is, there are only single seats left. How would you feel about getting to know some of my family?" I raised an eyebrow at him, and he scoffed. "You know what I *mean*."

To be honest, the thought made my heart drum nervously until it reverberated in my throat. My appetite almost disappeared. "For sure," I forced out, casual, casual, casual. "Whatever works."

The tables were quickly filling up with piles and piles of food, some familiar, some I'd never seen in my life. On one end of the table was a fat turkey, and on the other end, a plate held an enormous chunk of some type of meat that looked sticky and crispy on top—likely slow roasted, from the way the meat was falling off the bone. Mashed potatoes, rice with peas and olives, glazed yams, little parcels wrapped in plantain leaves, plates of beans, cranberry sauce, salsa, and dozens of salads.

I was starting to form a mental game plan—one bite of everything until I figured out my favorites, and then concentrating on that—when Mrs. Tavares rolled up one of the plastic sheets to provide a clear view into the yard, then stepped out onto the lawn with Kane and two young girls. This seemed to be a sign that things were getting serious, because there was a quick flurry of movement while everyone found their seats.

"We have an announcement," Mrs. Tavares said, hugging herself to protect against the night's chill. "Tonight, in their first ever performance as a group, Kane, Camila, and Nayeli will be demonstrating a new cheerleading routine for our entertainment."

I shot Will an amused look across the table as a Taylor Swift song started blaring through the speakers. The family cheered and whistled as the kids launched into a basic-but-adorable cheerleading routine that was composed of mostly box steps, low kicks, and running around in circles. But, in their defense, it was all highly coordinated.

"Kane's having more fun than the girls are," one of the men said in a low voice to Mr. Tavares. From the passive-aggressive tone of his voice, it seemed like a dig. "Maybe he should start spending more time with his brother? On the right side of the court?"

Because a boy's role was to play the game, and it was the girls who were meant to cheer them on. Right?

Mr. Tavares held a finger to his lips. "He's just a kid," he hissed. "He'll grow out of it."

And what if he didn't? I wondered. Would he still be as much of a man in their eyes? Or, what if Kane didn't identify as a guy at all? What *then*?

Not to mention, what if they found out that Will, for all his time spent on the "right side of the court," wasn't straight?

Where did this idea of the "right" way to be a guy or girl fit into real life?

Tearing my eyes away from them, I forced myself to wipe the frown off my face, and joined in on a standing ovation.

I half-expected everyone to go around the table listing things they were grateful for like my family had always done, but, as Will told me later in the night, it was apparently a Tavares family tradition to have a group gratitude discussion over ponche crema not long after everyone had arrived. It was probably for the best, I reasoned—with a family this big, it could get rowdy real fast trying to do a serious activity later in the night.

While the adults jumped into serving themselves, the kids were instructed to bring their plates up to the main table. I started to rise to help Crista and Dylan, but one of Will's aunts took over the role, generously filling both of their plates with the best cuts of meat she could find.

Crista skipped over to me with a look of urgency while her plate was being filled. She patted my shoulder then leaned in to speak right into my eardrum. "Please, Ollie, can you make sure I get some turkey?"

"You'll get some turkey."

"I don't want all that other stuff. Just the turkey."

It was kind of a little late for that. Crista's plate already had a selection of meat, rice, and beans, as well as some other extremely delicious-looking things I didn't know the names of. "Just give it all a try, and if you don't like something, you don't have to eat it. You can have more turkey later if you're still hungry."

She screwed up her face, and I gave her a *look*. "Don't be rude."

As for me, I was more than happy to explore the various foods in front of me. Only I didn't have a helpful aunt picking out the best bits, so I just guessed when it came to loading up my plate. After much experimentation, I came to the conclusion that I had a particular fondness for a kind of potato salad–type thing with chicken, peas, beans, and carrots, all tied together with the most delicious, creamy sauce that ever caused a guy to salivate at the thought of seconds. Will's older cousin Josephina helpfully explained that it was called ensalada de gallina, and I made a note of the name in my phone so I could find it and eat it again every night for the rest of my life.

"Ollie?"

"Hmm?"

Crista was back at my side, holding up a mostly empty plate. "Can I please have another one of those yellow things?"

Yellow things, yellow things . . . there was so much food in front of us it took me a full two table scans to figure out what she was talking about. That's right, those tamale-like things in plantain leaves were bright yellow once un-wrapped. But the plate was out of my reach. I went to ask Josephina but faltered when I realized I didn't know what they were called. I mean, I doubted she'd judge me, but I'd still feel pretty stupid asking if she could pass the plate of "yellow things."

Will noticed my lost look right away. "What's up?"

No one seemed to be listening in, at least. "Crista wanted to grab another of those . . . tamales?"

Luckily, he seemed to know exactly what she wanted. "Oh, yeah, for sure. Come over here, Crista." He took her plate and piled a couple plantain-parcels onto it. "They're called hallacas. Seems like you didn't mind the food so much after all, huh?"

He said it good-naturedly, but I died inside anyway. I'd hoped he hadn't heard Crista's whining.

"Well, these things are really yummy. And the turkey, and the other turkey. The shredded one."

"That's not a turkey. That one's called pernil. It's pork."

"Oh. I don't like pork, though."

"Do you like ham and bacon? That's pork."

"Oh."

"Would you like any more pernil?"

"Yes, please."

While he served her, Will caught my eye across the table and gave me a soft smile.

My stomach flipped.

After dinner was finally over—and I do mean finally, because after that gigantic spread was done, a dessert course of flan and pecan pie was brought out and it was on for plate number five—the kids started playing together in the backyard. I stayed and watched over them for a little bit, until Will suggested I have a tour of the house. I was reluctant to leave Crista and Dylan alone, but it wasn't like they didn't have supervision. Plus, I had to admit, I was curious to check out the room Will slept in every night.

"It's so *clean*," I said in wonder once I was inside.

Will hovered by the door. "Is that surprising?"

"Honestly, yeah," I said, crossing to the far wall to examine his shelving.

"Why? Do I seem like a pig?"

"Not necessarily. But I saw your room at the lake. For a basketballer, your laundry basket aim wasn't so great."

There was a gentle click as he closed the door behind us. My whole body tightened, and I kept my body angled toward the wall so he wouldn't catch my expression.

"Wait, so you were judging me the whole summer?" he asked.

"Yeah, unfortunately. I didn't wanna say anything 'cause I was totally into you."

"'Was'?" Will said. I couldn't tell if it was a joke or a genuine question. Maybe he didn't want me to be able to tell.

"Hey, count yourself lucky. Earlier today you thought I might hate you, remember?"

He didn't reply, so I glanced behind me to check on him. He was staring into space, but put on a forced-looking smile as soon as he noticed me.

"Mom made me practically scrub it down with disinfectant this morning," he said, and it took me a moment to realize he was talking about his room. "You know. Just in case all the visitors wanted to gather in my room to inspect it."

"And aren't you glad she made you now?" I asked, running a finger along one shelf. Spotless as Juliette's complexion.

"*So* glad. Not that I expected you to end up in it, of all people."

"Yeah. Thank you so much for inviting us. It made a shit day . . . less shit. Especially for the kids."

"Of course. I'm really glad you came. So, how's your aunt, anyway?"

"She's okay. She was awake, and talking, and stuff. But she's pretty sick right now. It's hard, you know?"

"I know. I can imagine."

We fell into an awkward silence. I felt like I was supposed to be doing or saying something, but I had no idea what that might be. Why had he closed the door? Did he want to talk about us? Or was I imagining things?

I cleared my throat and walked along the length of the wall, where about fifty-billion trophies and medals lined the shelves. "So you've had a good game or two in your time," I said.

"I guess."

"I feel inferior right now."

"What? Don't be ridiculous. You have your band."

"Like, yeah? I don't get trophies for playing, though, I just get, you know, tolerated. But this . . . you must be good, huh?"

Will's voice was tight. "Not good enough for a scholarship."

I picked up one of the taller awards, a towering gold figurine of Michael Jordan landing a slam dunk. Well, at least, it might have been Michael Jordan. It was hard to tell because it was faceless and a little misshapen. "So, do you want to try to go pro?"

The creaking of bedsprings told me Will had sat down. "That's what everyone wants me to do."

"Okay. But is that what you want to do?"

I turned around to find Will shrugging at the ground. "Basketball is fun, but I can't help feeling like I should be more passionate about it if I were gonna try to go pro. Can't something you do as a hobby just be that? A hobby? Does it have to be your entire life?"

Why did I get the feeling he wasn't aiming that last part at me?

"It can," I said. "What do *you* want?"

When he finally replied, his voice was small. "Honestly? I've always really wanted to be a nurse."

"Yeah?"

"Yeah. I thought about being a doctor, but the grades to get in are ridiculous, and what I really like is the hands-on stuff. Like, being able to comfort people, and to be the first person there when they're in pain or if they need something. I wanna be *that* person."

I sat down next to him, the mattress sinking. Our shoulders bumped. "You'd be so great at that."

He looked surprised. "Really?"

"Of course. You're always there when people are upset or hurt, and you're the one trying to make it better. Every time. It's basically that, but in job form."

Suddenly, Will was staring at me, and my stomach lurched. "You're the first person to say that," he said, taking the trophy from me.

"Yeah?"

"Yeah. Everyone else just says basketball, basketball, basketball." Curling his lip, he put the trophy down on the bed behind us like he didn't want to look at it anymore.

"No," I said. My chest was tight, and my fingertips were buzzing with something. "Not if you don't want to."

He didn't speak. He just kept watching me. His breathing had gotten louder. Or maybe I'd just tuned in to him. If I wanted to stop this I had to break eye contact now. *Now.*

But I didn't want to stop this.

He leaned closer, and closer, and then he kissed me. The second our lips touched his hands flew up and around me, pulling me in as tight as he could. His fingers ran through the hair on the nape of my neck, sending me damn near into a frenzy, and I gripped his waist under his sweater in response. It'd been so long since I'd touched him, I'd forgotten how unreasonably warm and soft the skin there was. No one in history had ever had a softer waist than Will Tavares.

He tasted like sweetened condensed milk. He must have been sneaking some of that rum drink the adults were passing around.

How could I have gone all these months without kissing him? How had I gone without him?

I never wanted to again. Never, never, never.

"I missed you," he whispered. He grabbed my hand and laced our fingers together, and when he went in to kiss me again his grip tightened.

"Do—" I started, but broke off at the sound of a floorboard creaking. Will launched himself back and snatched up Michael Jordan, holding the trophy like it was *way* more inexplicably interesting than anything I could've been saying. I didn't have any nearby prop—he'd stolen mine—so I just sat up as straight as I could and focused on looking calm and not-at-all turned on. Just in time, too, because

Will's dad flung the door wide open without stopping to knock.

In hindsight, I can see how opening a closed door to see his son closely examining a trophy he'd had for years, while his son's friend sat awkwardly on the bed with perfect posture and tousled hair, could've raised an alarm bell for Mr. Tavares. To his credit, if he did suspect something, he stayed pretty neutral. "Ollie, the little guy's asking after you."

*Way to cock-block, Dylan.*

"Thank you, Mr. Tavares," I said. "We'll come right down."

Will nodded and placed the trophy back on the shelf.

As soon as his dad was gone, Will turned back to me. For a moment I thought he meant to kiss me again, but it was just to nod over at the doorway. "Guess the kids need to get to bed soon, huh?"

"Yeah. It's a long drive back at this time of night for them."

"Got it. Well, thank you so much for coming."

It seemed like I was being unceremoniously kicked out. I stood up, and hesitated. "Hey, Will?"

"Yeah?"

"That definitely just happened, right? Like, we're not going to pretend it didn't?"

He took a second to reply, but when he did, his expression was mischievous.

"Oh, it definitely happened. Don't worry about that."

# 15

We'd wandered for a while, following the edge of the lake, just talking, before we settled down in front of a tree to finish our ice cream. The crowds had thinned and then I virtually disappeared about five minutes before, giving us some privacy.

Rivulets of melted mint ice cream ran down Will's cone and over his fingers. He didn't try to lick them off, not even as they started to drip onto his knees. I stirred my spoon around my own cup until it made a chocolate soup, while Will finished off the last bite of his cone. How anyone could eat that fast without brain freeze was a mystery. "You're covered in ice cream," I said.

He looked down at himself and tried to wipe it off his leg. All he managed to do was spread it in a sticky mess around his thigh. "Shit. One second."

With that, he pulled his shirt off, took off for the lake, and jumped straight in, spraying water all over me.

He popped back above the surface and shook his head to dry himself off.

"You drenched me," I complained. Not to mention the rest of my ice cream, which was half lake water now.

"Well, you're wet now," he said. "You might as well get in."

Something about the thought of stripping down to my shorts and jumping into the lake with this guy I barely knew seemed illicit and thrilling to me. Even though I knew it was stupid, and he would probably freak out if he knew I was thinking about him like that. Chances were pretty strong that this was completely innocent. Still, it was fun to pretend. And with a guy this hot, who could blame me for fantasizing a little?

But then, when my head emerged from taking my shirt off, I swore I saw Will stare at me. Only for a second, though.

I jumped in.

"You know, a lot of people back home can't swim," Will said, his head bobbing up and down. "I asked my friend Matt to come up with us but he bailed because of that."

"I don't think I've ever met someone who can't swim," I said. "What if your plane crashed into the ocean?"

Will burst out laughing. "That's your main concern?"

"Well, it's true! I mean, I guess you could just float."

He shook his head. "No way, floating's way harder than swimming. I can't do it at all."

"Seriously?"

"Yeah. I never learned how."

"It's easy. You just kind of . . ." I launched myself onto my back to demonstrate.

He tried to mimic me, and ended up flopping backward into the water like a finless whale. "I told you!" he said, snorting water out his nose.

"No, just try and . . . yeah, a bit more arched, though—no, more arched, Wi—here." I put my hands at the top and bottom of his back and moved him into position. "Like that."

*His skin was warm to the touch. "Oh," he whispered, before swallowing. "Like that."*

*Then he rolled over to return to a paddling position. Which brought him about three inches away from my face.*

*He didn't move back, though.*

*Our legs collided a few times underwater. My hands were still burning from where they had touched his skin. He looked at me with an intensity that took me by surprise.*

*All at once, I realized he had been staring at me before.*

*With exactly this expression on his face.*

*I was just starting to hope when one of his hands found my waist, and he kissed me.*

Another Thursday, another band practice.

This one was running particularly late, too. The band had a new set of songs Izzy wanted us to learn as soon as possible, and we couldn't get Sayid and Emerson to agree on anything, from the tempo to the harmonies to the lyrics.

It didn't matter too much to me if we went overtime, though. The girls were at a basketball game. I would've totally gone, but the thing is, I'd rather floss with barbed wire than watch a live sports match, so I declined with regrets. Besides, I'd had to skip the last band practice to play emergency babysitter when Aunt Linda developed a sudden pain in her side. It didn't turn out to be anything major—thank God—but I couldn't guarantee it wouldn't happen again, so I couldn't afford to play hooky from practice on top of that.

We'd been practicing for about an hour when Sayid and Emerson called a time-out to argue over a line in the song—Sayid thought the original "you throw your arms around me, while all the lights surround me" was better, while Emerson was pushing for the obviously superior, "when darkness seeks to blind us, a fire ignites inside us." Izzy, who thought lyrics were only there to complement an epic drum track, decided to mostly ignore them while she experimented with different beats, humming the chorus to herself. I wasn't able to focus—I'd been a ditzy, gooey mess since Thanksgiving—so I perched myself on a stool and watched the others with a vague smile. So vague, even, I didn't notice Izzy had stopped drumming. Until she threw a Skittle at my head.

"What are you all smiley about?" she asked. "You look like a Disney princess; stop it."

I hunted for the Skittle on the carpet then popped it in my mouth.

"Ew, I *touched* that," Izzy said. "My hands are all sweaty."

"It was a red Skittle. A sweaty red Skittle is worth three green Skittles."

"What kind of bodily fluid would bring a single red Skittle below the net worth of a green Skittle?"

"It's less about the bodily fluid, and more about who the bodily fluid comes from."

She cackled. "Touché."

Emerson paused in his argument long enough to give us a withering glance. "You guys are really killing the mood."

"Your lyrics killed the mood," Sayid muttered. "You took it from a love song to a song about overthrowing the establishment."

"Ooh, I think you just sold Emerson's version to me," Izzy said, stroking her chin like a supervillain. "I do love overthrowing establishments."

Sayid held his hands up. "Seriously?"

"My vote's with Emerson, too," I said. "Sorry, man."

Sayid scowled and went to pack up the keyboard. "You guys never side with me," he said.

"They can't help it if I'm a lyrical genius," Emerson said.

"Oh *yeah,* we got a regular Lin-Manuel Miranda over here."

I grabbed my phone just as a text came in from Juliette.

Hey, the game just finished. We're heading to You Got Soft-Served over on Hamilton Street if you want to come grab a shake?

Wait, so I could go consume some sugar, see Will again, *and* support a local pun-appreciating business? It's not like I could say no to that, now, was it?

Everyone was already there when I arrived. Five basketball guys formed a row of black-and-white varsity jackets, crowded around a booth against the wall. They all had damp hair from their post-game showers. Will's hair was the longest out of all of them, and he kept sweeping it back off his forehead with an impatient hand. He paused when he noticed me coming, his hand midsweep, and then ducked his head with a shy grin.

Across from them, Lara, Niamh, and Juliette sat, already sipping on milkshakes. Juliette beckoned me to sit next to her on the light blue pleather. "The guys haven't ordered yet," she said. "We've been waiting here a while."

"We had to get ready, didn't we?" Matt asked. "Do you think looking this good happens by accident?"

Lara raised an eyebrow. "Oh, God, girls, I think this is what they look like when they're *trying.* How tragic." She looked down at her phone and smiled at something on the screen. I tried to catch a peek of it but she was too far away.

"So, uh, how did we do?" I asked in a small voice. I wasn't used to talking in front of the basketball guys. Honestly, they intimidated me a bit. They always seemed so confident, and loud, and judgmental. Not really the best mix with people who weren't also confident, and loud, and judgmental.

One of the guys I'd never spoken to before, Ethan, started thumping his hands on the table. The other guys joined him, in a four-by-four beat that got louder by the second. Except for Will. Will just folded his arms and leaned back in his chair, looking damned pleased with himself.

Darnell jumped out of his seat and grabbed Will's shoulders. "This man right here, *this man*, won us the game."

"We're even footing the whole way," Matt added, holding his arms up in front of him, "then in the last quarter we start dropping. We have, like, two minutes to go, Will's one-on-one on the wing, he makes the shot, then he steals the inbound pass and hits another contested shot absolutely out of nowhere, and suddenly we're in the lead."

Will was grinning, but it wasn't gentle like his usual one. It was the harder, smug smile that kept crossing his face whenever he was around these guys. I'd seen him look like this across the cafeteria a few times. So self-satisfied. It didn't suit him.

"That's the kind of play I'm used to seeing from you, man," Matt said. He had what must've been his "captain" voice going on. Like a teacher congratulating an apprentice. It had such a warm tone to it, I could imagine guys busting their asses to have Matt talk to him with that kind of appreciation in his voice.

Darnell nodded. "Yeah, we worried you might've gone soft on us, with all those music lessons," he said, nudging Will. Will's eyes flickered toward me. He wasn't smiling anymore.

Matt nodded. "Yeah, man. No offense, Ollie, but we thought you were turning him into a freaking goth or something."

Right. Because I was totally a goth.

"Try emo pussy," Darnell added, then wilted at Niamh's fierce glare.

"Do you *need* to be a sexist pig?" she asked, before sucking on her straw like it'd done her some great wrong. "That's foul."

Will snickered—*snickered*—and hit Darnell with a rolled-up menu. "Yeah, don't be a sexist pig, Darnell. The proper terminology is emo genitalia."

Darnell swatted at him. "That doesn't even make sense."

"And do I *look* fuckin' emo to you, smartass? Give me some credit."

Well, *this* was uncomfortable. And not that I exactly identified with being emo—come on, it wasn't 2007—but obviously Will didn't see any difference. And the way he'd scrunched up his nose at the idea told me a lot about what he thought of seeming anything like me. I glared at the table.

"To be honest, Will, it's a good thing you're not," said Lara in a hard voice. "You don't have the ass to pull off jeans that tight."

The guys broke out into laughter, high-fiving each other. "*Damn*, Lara," Matt said, looking half-impressed, half-delighted.

Wait, had Lara just stood up for me? That seemed very unlike her. But then she caught my eye, raised her eyebrows, and ran her tongue over her teeth. She had the air of someone who'd won a battle with the patriarchy. Holy shit, she *had* said that to stand up for me.

I almost would've grinned, if I didn't feel so empty all of a sudden.

A waiter came over. The rest of the guys all competed with each other over ordering the best freak-shake—the shake with the most brownies, Nutella, strawberries, Oreos, peanut butter, whipped cream, shaving cream, laundry detergent, and whatever-the-hell-else they added on top.

When he came to take my order, though, I just shook my head and asked for a water. Will seemed to notice, but he didn't say anything.

Juliette had leaned over to whisper with Niamh, then as soon as the waiter left, she turned back to the guys. "So, Darnell," she said, while an alarmed Niamh shook her head at her. "Has anyone asked you to the Snowflake dance yet?"

His eyes went straight to Niamh, who was turning an interesting shade of burgundy. "Not . . . *yet*. It's a little early for that, right?"

"It's never too early," Juliette said.

"What's the Snowflake dance?" I asked, trying to keep quiet enough that the conversation didn't become about me. But, of course, the whole table turned to look at me. Maybe if I talked more, I'd get less attention when I *did* speak up.

"It's a dance we have right after Christmas break," Juliette said.

"The catch is, girls have to ask guys," Matt added.

Huh. Seemed pretty heteronormative. And what if a girl wanted to ask a girl? Or otherwise.

What if no one asked me?

Oh, God, what if someone *did*?

"Yeah, right, and how about you, Juliette?" Darnell asked. "You gone and asked someone already?"

"Oh, I can't go," she said airily. "I have an audition with the Conservatory that weekend."

"*What?*" I screeched. For once it didn't even occur to me to feel shy in front of the group. "Holy *shit*, you do *not*!"

"I do!" She beamed and grabbed my hands. "I just found out."

"Oh my *God*! I'm so proud of you."

We bounced up and down in our seats while the girls squealed their congratulations and the guys tried to figure out what the big deal was.

I noticed Will was watching me with a funny smile. My excitement evaporated, and fire started shooting up from the ground, and my fingernails turned into talons so I could rip that smile off his face. How dare he look at me like that after talking shit about me, *right in front of me*?

When they brought out the rest of the shakes, I admittedly felt a little twinge of regret that I'd passed them up. They were works of art made out of chocolate, some of them towering several inches above the Mason jars they were served in, covered in whipped cream, candy, edible glitter, gold flakes, mint chips, and most of them drizzled with three months' worth of melted Nutella.

And here I was with my water.

Eurgh. This was all Will's fault.

My phone buzzed. I tuned out of the conversation and checked my phone.

Will.

I'm heading to the parking lot. Meet me there in 1.75 minutes?

His chair squeaked as he hopped up and clapped Matt on the back. "Hey, I'll be back, bro."

"Your milkshake just got here."

"I can't help it. And don't you *dare* touch it while I'm gone."

Matt grinned. "You know I can't promise that."

I tracked Will out of the corner of my eye. He headed over toward the restrooms, but then, casual as anything, veered left to go out the back door.

All right. Time to count down. One-point-five-three minutes until I had to pull the same maneuver.

I leaned in to whisper to Juliette. "I'll be back in a sec."

"Where are you going?"

Really? *Really?* "You know. Just over, ah, to the . . ."

"Oh, bathroom?"

"Yeah."

She lowered her voice even more. "It's just, I thought you might be going to meet Will like he asked you to."

Oh my God she totally eavesdropped on my text. Or, like . . . eyesdropped. What was the visual equivalent of eavesdropping? Actually, no. Irrelevant. With as much dignity as I could muster, I rose to my feet, gave her a pointed look, and headed over to the restrooms. Super casual, just like Will had.

Then when I got there, I turned around to check if anyone was watching me. Juliette caught my eye and smiled, and I paused, frozen, terrified someone might notice her glancing at me. Super not casual, the exact opposite of Will.

But what else was new.

I *think* I made it outside without anyone other than Juliette catching on. In fact, I was so distracted by the whole mission that I briefly forgot I was kind of pissed at Will. But then I saw him, leaning against the wall near the edge of the building with his hands stuffed into his jacket pockets, and oh boy I remembered.

I stalked toward him, arms folded. "Yes?"

He lit up when he saw me like the way he used to at the lake when I'd torn him away from his thoughts. Somehow, this annoyed me even more. He could at least acknowledge that I was annoyed. He didn't have to look so happy to see me.

"Hey," he said.

"Hi."

"You're not eating?"

What an icebreaker. "Not hungry."

He nodded, then opened his mouth. Then closed it, opened it, then closed it again. He folded his arms against the cold and stepped from side to side. He looked like an unusually melancholy square dancer. Well, at least he wasn't acting all cheerful anymore. "I feel really stupid," he said.

"Uh-huh."

"God, I don't even know what to say. It just slipped out. I'm so used to acting a certain way around the guys, you know? It's not me, I know it's not me, but I always joke with them, and they expect me to say things, so I don't even think."

I didn't say anything.

He sighed, and tipped his head back. "I'm really sorry." He peeked at me, but I still didn't reply. I mean, what *could* I say? That it was okay? Because it really wasn't. "I'm a dick because I've always been a dick around my friends" wasn't really an excuse.

"I like your jeans," he tried. "And your music. And you in general, really. So much it's ridiculous. I haven't been able to stop thinking about you since Thanksgiving."

Since Thanksgiving? I hadn't been able to stop thinking about him since summer. Honestly, it was starting to feel like maybe since birth. I couldn't remember a time when I'd been able to brush my teeth, or make toast, or play guitar without Will's face popping into my mind like a jump-scare in a viral video.

But. Still.

He hadn't been able to stop thinking about our kiss.

Did that mean the idea of us—being with me, properly, for everyone to see—wasn't so scary to him anymore? Could our kiss have reminded him of what it was like when we were together? It had definitely reminded me. Maybe he'd decided I was worth the risk.

I softened the tiniest bit.

Suddenly, he shrugged out of his varsity jacket and held it out to me. "Will you wear this?" he asked. "Just for a few seconds or whatever?"

I didn't mean to look at it so suspiciously, but my mind couldn't help but race to see if there was a trap or a catch here. "Why?"

He shifted his weight from one leg to another, giving the jacket a small shake. "I wanna see how it looks."

For once, I didn't have a sassy comeback. I crossed my arms over my chest to barricade my insides, which had melted like butter. Peak softness reached. "Really?"

Deep inside my chest, my heart was beating as though it was trying to tear free of bondage. With an embarrassingly giddy grin I took the jacket and slipped it on. I mean, it definitely couldn't look any good on me—like a Chihuahua trying to pull off a Great Dane's collar, I imagined—but . . . okay, admittedly, it made me feel good. So good. Special, even. Like, it didn't matter that I'd had a breakout that week, or that my cowlick wouldn't behave itself, or that I'd never gotten braces when by all means I should have.

None of it mattered, because Will wanted me to wear his jacket, and Will thought I was beautiful.

I lifted my hands awkwardly, the cuffs of the sleeves drowning my fingertips. "Sexy, am I right?" I joked.

He didn't laugh when he nodded. "It looks great on you." He glanced around us to make sure there were no basketballers lurking in the shadows waiting to catch us out. It ruined the moment for me for half a second, but then, with this affectionate little smile that made me seriously worry about spontaneous combustion, he held out his hand to search for mine inside the left sleeve. He looped his pinky finger around mine. "I wish you could wear it at school."

"Me, too."

I waited for him. This was an in. He could say "wear it inside now." He could say "maybe you'll wear it some-day." If he'd just given me something to hold on to, I'd take it. But he didn't.

Suddenly, the jacket felt too heavy. I started to shuck it off but Will stopped me.

"Can I get a picture?" he asked.

I shrugged, and waited sullenly while he took his phone out. He held it up, then lowered it again. "Can I get a picture where it doesn't look like you're thinking of ways to drown me?"

I cracked a smile. "Sorry," I said, and he crinkled his nose at me before taking a photo.

Once he was finished, I handed him back his jacket. "You should get back in before they notice how long you've been missing," I said.

"Yeah. Make sure you wait a couple minutes before coming back, right?" He looked around us, then stepped toward me. He placed a hand on my chest and pushed me gently backward until I hit the wall, and then, even more gently, pressed his lips against mine.

It was probably a good thing I had to wait a few minutes before heading back inside, because it took about that long for me to collect myself.

When I got back to the table, Will, who'd been making his way through his milkshake soup, waved at me. "Mm, Ollie, I was just telling them about the other day in music class, when Ms. Ellison showed us that YouTube video."

I sat down warily. "Oh yeah?"

"Yeah. Anyway, it was the most patronizing shit ever, right? Like, it had all these clips of high schoolers comparing pop stars to classical composers. It's like someone told Ms. E she had to try to 'relate' to us more."

"Sure it wasn't you, Will?" Darnell asked.

"Not me. Honestly, I find the classical stuff pretty interesting on its own."

"Oh, God, they're brainwashing you," Matt said, grabbing onto Will's arm in mock despair.

Will shrugged. "Hey, it's better than *German*. What a useless language. Who even speaks German here?"

"Yeah, who needs a foreign language when you can just waltz up to people and sing at them?" Matt asked, but he was grinning. That was the thing with Will. Even when he was being teased, everyone was always laughing with him, never at him. He was the last person who should've been scared of being judged, when you thought about it.

"Music is a universal language," Juliette said.

"See?" Will said, holding a hand out. "She gets it. Y'all are outnumbered."

"Three versus, what, six?" Matt asked. "You call that outnumbered?"

Juliette looked to her left. "Lara? Niamh?"

Niamh, who'd been staring into the distance and propping her head up with one hand as though to keep it from falling into her milkshake, jumped and refocused. "Hmm?"

"Come on, Lara," Matt wheedled.

"Hey, I stand with my girls," Lara said. "If Juliette thinks music class is cool, then music class is cool. End of discussion."

Will shared a mischievous look with me, and I couldn't help but grin at him. Under the table I sent him a text.

Apology accepted.

# 16

From that point on, I guess Will and I were kind of seeing each other. I say "kind of," because we never labeled it. That, and the fact that it was still a bigger secret than the aliens the government have locked in a warehouse somewhere. And let's be honest, the government definitely has aliens locked in a warehouse somewhere. The government is just being coy about it.

And that's what Will and I were doing. We were being coy.

Because coy meant "texting someone all day every day, calling each other to hear their voice, and making out in secret whenever possible, all the while pretending to be acquaintances," right?

Right. Yeah. We were totally being coy, then.

This year was probably the first time it'd actually been a letdown to go on winter break. I'd gotten used to seeing Will in the halls, in the cafeteria, in Music Appreciation. Suddenly, all I had was social media, texting, and the once or twice a week we met up to go for a drive somewhere private.

That's why, when he messaged me out of the blue asking if I was free one Friday night, I found myself calling Aunt Linda for permission for him to join me babysitting.

He arrived at the door armed with Twinkies, Doritos, and Pop-Tarts.

"What's this?" I asked as he came in.

"Mom would kill me if I came around without bringing anything. And I thought the kids might like some junk food."

"They're in bed, thank God," I said. "If you gave them any of that now they'd be up until six in the morning rolling around on the floor screaming nursery rhymes."

"Oh. Well, how do you feel about eating all this ourselves, then?"

"Extremely positive, obviously."

"Great. Also, they're sort of celebratory, too."

I paused by the door. "What are we celebrating?"

He shifted on the spot to readjust his hold on the junk food bounty. "I applied for the nursing program at the University of North Carolina."

"You did?"

"Yeah. I was tossing it around, but after we talked about it on Thanksgiving I decided I was gonna do it."

He looked hopeful. Hopeful and soft.

"Well," I said. "They'd be out of their minds not to accept you."

We decided to put on a horror movie—with the volume on as low as we could get away with—and I laid the junk food out on the coffee table while Will kicked his shoes off and set up on the couch under the blanket Aunt Linda kept there.

When I was done, he lifted the blanket so I could climb in next to him. "When do your aunt and uncle get back?"

"They're out to dinner. It's the first time they've done something nice like that for months, so I'm hoping they won't be in a rush to come home."

Will nodded, and ran a finger along my thigh. I shivered. "How's she doing?"

"Umm. Same. She seems a little more tired than usual, but she's got so many appointments and stuff it might just be that. I don't know if I'm reading into things or not anymore."

"Yeah, I know what you mean. I'm glad she got to go out for something fun for once, though. It's really good of you to always volunteer to babysit."

I shrugged. "She needs help. It's what we're here for."

He nodded, but he seemed distant as he turned to watch the movie. The thick black hood of his jacket was bunched up around his neck, and he was biting his bottom lip. He had the world's most beautiful lips. When the Great, Ethereal Being was putting together the blueprint for Will Tavares, it must have just figured out the winning formula for the exact shape, thickness, and ratio of the perfect mouth. Then it'd gone and put that perfect mouth on a mortal, just to show off.

Woops. I'd gone all slack-jawed staring at it.

The perfect mouth opened a little. Not too far above it, the world's most perfect pair of eyes—the origin story of which was probably similar to the mouth—were scanning my own lips. My too-small, not very defined, unremarkable lips.

He touched my jaw. "I always wish I could see inside your head," he said. "You always seem to be thinking so hard about something or other."

"It's not that interesting," I said. I meant to look at his eyes, but I was right back fixated on his mouth.

He leaned in. "I think you're extremely interesting."

The way he kissed me was ginger, like I was made out of tissue paper that could be torn with the slightest sudden movement. For a moment, my rational mind piped up that we should be careful, that Crista or Dylan could come out for a drink or something at any moment, and making out on duty was a little unprofessional, even if it was family duty. But then his fingers were weaving their way through the hair at the back of my head, and his other hand was squeezing my thigh, and—responsibility? What responsibility? Who cared? Crista and Dylan had to learn about birds and bees sooner or later, so win-win, right?

Even though the first time I'd kissed him had been, like, seven months ago, none of the novelty had worn off. Every time his lips met mine, it was the first kiss all over again. And again, and again, and again . . .

Before I knew it, I heard the movie credits playing in the back of my mind. I broke away from Will, shaking my head at the TV. "It's over already?"

"Looks like it."

"I didn't even watch any of it, though."

Will tipped his head to one side and ran a hand up my thigh. "I'm sorry to distract you like that."

"You should be," I said, leaning back on the couch as he came back up and over me, crashing his lips against mine.

Then a key turned in the lock, and we sprung away from each other with a fluidity that'd make an Olympic gymnastics team green with jealousy.

Aunt Linda and Uncle Roy were laughing when they

came inside. They looked lighter than I'd seen them in weeks. Aunt Linda beamed when she saw Will. "*Will*, hey, how are you doing? I haven't seen you in forever."

Will had gone pale, and he stared at Aunt Linda for way too long before replying. At first I thought maybe he was freaking out that we'd almost been caught making out, but then I realized, it wasn't that. He was just shocked to see Aunt Linda. The skinny, gray-skinned, slowed-down version of her.

"Hi," he said in a weak voice. "I'm good. How are . . . how are you?"

"I," she said, "am fantastic. We just had the best steak *ever*, at this new place that's just opened over on Main Street."

I had my doubts as to how much steak Aunt Linda had eaten, given her appetite lately, but I wasn't about to point that out.

"Bernetti Café?" Will asked. "We've been meaning to go there."

"Oh, you *should*. It's very romantic."

There was no way Aunt Linda thought the "we" in that sentence referred to me and him—she knew if Will and I had gone public she'd practically know about it before I did—so I had to assume she was doing it to tease Will. Or maybe to even normalize the idea for him.

Will blinked at me. I wondered if he was picturing us on a date, and if the idea was kind of nice or just terrifying. "Good to know," he said finally, which didn't give me anything to go on. I would've asked him, but I was suddenly scared of what he might say.

Will and I packed up and left at the same time. It was only then that we noticed we hadn't even started to eat any of the junk food.

"She looks different these days, huh?" I asked once we were out of earshot.

"Yeah. I know you said she's been worse, but it was something else seeing it."

"And this was one of her good nights."

"God, Ollie, I'm sorry."

"Don't be. Don't. She's here, and we're here, and we're just going to keep getting through."

We stopped when we got to the door of my car. "It was nice to see you tonight," Will said. "How about we go for a drive tomorrow? We can go back to that place in the woods."

Well, it wasn't a candlelit dinner, but for now that was fine. I could take it. Especially given how much I'd enjoyed the last time we went to the woods, a few days before. "Yeah. All right. Lock it in."

He studied me, and all at once I got what he meant about wishing he could peek inside someone's mind.

"Can't wait."

"What was this, exactly?"

Mr. Theo stood over Will's desk, holding up the pile of essays he'd marked over the break. He didn't look angry as much as exasperated. I watched from across the class. The biweekly installment of Will vs. Mr. Theo was like tuning in to a soap opera you'd been following for months. It was trashy, but the dialogue was quick, and the drama was high, and you couldn't quite look away even if you had more important things to be doing.

Will cocked his head to one side. "Looks like my essay to me. You asked us to hand them in before Winter break, don't you remember?"

Matt snickered at the back of the classroom.

"I asked for an essay on symbolism and literary techniques. You gave me an essay on how *Lord of the Flies* is an allegory for Trump's America."

"An allegory is a technique! You said so yourself, sir, just last lesson."

"*One* technique, in an essay that was supposed to discuss four at a minimum. And it quite clearly isn't one of the techniques the author employed to tell his story, as *Lord of the Flies* was written approximately a century ago."

Will glanced over his shoulder at Matt and smirked. "Well, I don't know, Mr. Theo, maybe this Golding guy was telepathic."

"You mean clairvoyant. Will, if you want to use a homework task as an outlet for a political rant, there are many appropriate subjects. As it stands, English lit is not one of them. Rewrite it. Get it back to me Monday."

"*Someone's* a republican," Will muttered over the lunch bell, not quietly enough so that he couldn't be heard. Mr. Theo chose to ignore it.

Will shot me the briefest look as he went off with Matt. Maybe to see if I was laughing, or shaking my head. Honestly, I was kind of doing both.

I headed to the cafeteria more slowly, drifting along while I thought about the drive Will and I were going to take after school. Having something like that to look forward to made the days seem so much faster.

"Niamh's been keeping a secret," Juliette said in a singsong voice when I finally sat down at the lunch table.

Niamh looked up, alarmed. "Not now."

"Why not?"

"Darnell's gonna be here in, like, thirty seconds."

"So spit it out."

Niamh half-stood in her chair to eye the basketball guys, who were still filling their trays, then she sat abruptly and splayed her hands out on the table. "Okay. So we stop talking about this as soon as the guys get here, but I got signed by Enchantée Models. I found out in first period."

"What?" I asked.

"Ho-lee shit, Niamh," Lara said. "For real?"

"Yes, for real. An agency for real wanted me." There was an edge to her voice, but Lara didn't rise to the challenge. She just lifted her root beer in a one-sided toast.

"And they have strong ties in New York," Niamh went on, "so they said I might get a casting up there sometime."

"Niamh, that's amazing," I said.

Niamh was mostly looking at Lara, though. I'd thought that bad blood was behind them, but apparently not quite yet. If Niamh was looking for an apology, though, I wasn't sure if she'd get one. "Also," she said, "I've decided I'm not going to diet for it."

Lara met her eyes now. I mean, she wasn't dumb. She got the point. But she just waited for Niamh to go on.

"I didn't tell you guys because I didn't really know how to bring it up, but I found out a little while ago I have polycystic ovary syndrome," Niamh said. "I was getting really sick, and I wasn't losing weight even when I was exercising a ton, so I ate a lot less, and it made me really exhausted. And PCOS can make you feel exhausted to begin with, so I was making the problem worse by over-dieting."

"Oh, Niamh, I'm so sorry to hear that," Juliette said. "How did you know? Like, did you get tested because you couldn't lose weight?"

"No. I got tested because I kept skipping . . . periods." She lowered her voice, and her eyes flashed toward me as she said it. Her mouth twisted, and I realized she was embarrassed to talk about this with me there. I wasn't sure if I should be looking away like I hadn't heard, or something, but I decided that'd be significantly weirder and settled for nodding. "Like, I'd get it one month, then the next few it'd disappear. And obviously I couldn't be pregnant. But Mom has it, too, so she had a hunch. Turns out she was right."

"So, what does that mean?" I asked. "Is it . . . like, is it bad?"

What I meant to ask was, can it kill you? But I felt like that wasn't the most tactful question.

"Well, it's not amazing. Like it could affect my fertility, and it's going to be something I'll have for life. But I've seen my mom handle it, and it's manageable with medication and a healthy lifestyle. Which, I might add, is why I'm not going to crash diet anymore. I figure I used to focus on the wrong thing. I was so desperate to lose weight, and it was like fighting a losing battle. But now my goal is to exercise for strength, and eat the right things so I don't feel so tired and grumpy all the time. I'm already at a higher risk of diabetes and heart issues now that I have this, so I can't afford to cut out whole food groups just so I might lose a pound or two. I do know losing weight can potentially help with some of the symptoms, but it's much harder for people with PCOS. I'm working with my doctor on that, though, so I don't need anyone else monitoring me or commenting on what I do and don't eat."

It was officially the longest speech I'd ever heard Niamh give. By the end of it she looked triumphant, if a little nervous. Finally, she added uncertainly, "Health is more important, okay?"

Lara was utterly engrossed in her mac and cheese. When

she finally looked up, she had to face Juliette, Niamh, and me all giving her expectant stares. She rolled her eyes, but I didn't miss the shame that flashed across her face at first. "Yeah, I agree with you," she said to Niamh. "Good call."

Well, it was as much of a win as Niamh was ever likely to get from Lara. In any case, it was the closest I'd ever heard Lara come to admitting she was wrong. It came just in time, too, because the basketball guys arrived seconds later to pull extra chairs over and crowd our table. Let it never be said that the basketball guys weren't excellent wingmen. They were obviously hanging around like fruit flies so Darnell could see Niamh.

The group of them were laughing about something, though, and for once Darnell's attention wasn't on Niamh. He was zeroed right in on Will. So was Matt, actually. As they took their seats and lined up their lunch trays, the rest of the guys gravitated in to hear the conversation, with Will in the center of it all.

"So, is there something going on there again?" Matt asked Will, his voice all gooey and teasing.

"What do you mean?" Juliette asked before I had to.

Will's face made it immediately obvious he'd been keeping something from me. He looked like a rabbit who'd been unceremoniously teleported out of his burrow and dumped before a fox. Caught off guard and full of dread.

Guess I was the fox.

Matt, totally oblivious to Will's tension, cracked open a can of Coke. "He's going to the dance with Jessica," he said in a teasing, singsong way.

Well, if that wasn't the worst song I'd ever heard.

I didn't mean to look at Will with quite the level of despair that I think ended up on my face, but there was only so much self-control a guy could have when slapped with that kind of news. Will visibly winced when he met my eyes, and he covered up the movement by bending over his tray and shoving mac and cheese in his mouth. "Werr jush frensh," he said around a full mouth, before launching into a coughing fit.

"Mmm, but does she know that?" Darnell asked.

Funnily enough, that was just what I wanted to know. Well, that, and who the hell did Will think he was to keep this from me?

Did I not deserve to hear that from him?

Wasn't that my right?

Well, actually, that was kind of a good question. The problem with not labeling something was that what you could and couldn't expect was kind of gray. Was it unreasonable of me to expect Will to let me know if he was going to a dance with someone else? Or even, maybe, to ask if I was okay with that? Or did he owe me nothing, because he wasn't my boyfriend?

That didn't feel good.

"If she doesn't know it, she's gonna get a rude shock," Will said.

Darnell cackled. "Listen to this heartbreaker."

Will raised an eyebrow. "I'm just saying, you don't pass up your chance at all this and then get to change your mind later."

"Damn right," Matt said. "Make her regret it."

"He doesn't have to make her," Darnell said. "She's gonna regret it the second she sees him in a tie."

Huh. For some reason I'd always assumed Will dumped Jess, not the other way around. Did that mean he'd still loved her when they broke up? And how long ago *did* they break up, anyway? Was it possible I'd been some sort of summer rebound for Will to get over her? A thick vine of jealousy snaked around my stomach.

"What about you, Ollie?" Matt asked, and I snapped back to attention. "Going to the dance?"

He didn't ask if I was going with anyone. I guess he figured the answer to that was obvious. To go to this dance with a date, you had to be asked by a girl. It shouldn't have bothered me, but my cheeks started burning up anyway. It hit me that, back home, I never had to feel like I was lesser than everyone else. My school would never have held a dance that stuck to gendered rules. I would've been in the same position as everyone else—wondering if someone would ask me, or maybe figuring out if I even wanted to be asked.

But the point was, at my old school, no one would've assumed I didn't have a date to something because of my sexuality.

Well maybe they'd assume I didn't have a date because I was a super-awkward introvert who spent the whole of eleventh grade with a haircut that made me look like a toddler who'd played with scissors, but that was valid. At least that was, like, equal opportunity rejection.

I was too busy blushing at the table to notice Lara lean forward at first. Then she said, "I asked him," and I snapped straight back to the present.

Pardon? She asked me? Was I asleep at the time? Because I sure as hell didn't remember this. Maybe she'd whispered it from outside the door while I was practicing bass in the music room or something.

I was stunned, but not so stunned I missed Matt's face fall. "Really?"

Lara stabbed at her mac and cheese. "Really. He scrubs

up better than most of the guys here, and I'm planning on bringing it. We'll look great in the pre-dance photos, don't you think?"

The thing about Lara's particular brand of irony was that you could never quite tell if she was playing with you or not. The guys seemed to agree; Matt kind of smiled, then half-frowned, then smiled with his eyebrows drawn together. "Well, if you're planning on bringing it, then I'm gonna have to make sure I drop in to check it out for myself," he said finally.

Smooth. Safe reply.

Definitely sounded like he'd wanted Lara to ask him, though. Or maybe I was imagining that.

"You wouldn't want to miss it, Patterson," she said, and Matt actually bit his lower lip while he held eye contact with her. I got the strangest feeling Matt was going to picture her saying that while making out with his pillow or something later that evening.

"So, anyway," Will said without looking at me. "That new Marvel movie's out this weekend. Anyone down?"

"What, you wanna go to the movies?" Matt asked. "Sure you don't wanna just go with Jess?"

Somewhere inside of me, a dark cloud of wrath, rage, and indignation started twisting my intestines into sailor knots.

"No," Will said.

"Besides, since when do we pay for movies?" Darnell asked around a mouthful of salad.

"Exactly," Will said. "My parents just got a new TV, it's, like, seventy-five inches or something ridiculous. We could stream it."

"Are we invited?" Niamh asked.

Darnell brightened. "Ye—"

"Sorry," Will interrupted. "Guys' night only."

"So, Ollie's invited?" Lara asked with a pointed gaze.

Well, from the look on Will's face, you'd have thought she'd suggested burning the place down in a crazed satanic ritual once the movie was over.

"Seems kind of rude to bring it up in front of us if you're not going to ask us," Juliette said mildly.

"Like we'd want to haul ass all the way out to Napier to watch a blurry camcorder copy of another superhero movie," Lara said. "I'm sure we can find something actually entertaining to do with our Saturday night, girls."

I wasn't exactly sure if I counted as a girl in this scenario, but I nodded anyway.

After lunch, I caught up with Lara and walked next to her for a few steps, trying to get up the nerve to ask her.

She got there first. "You come here to dump me?"

"What? As my date, you mean?"

"Well I don't mean as your girlfriend."

I paused. "I wanted to know if you were serious."

"Duh. Do you have anyone better to go with?"

She was walking faster down the hall now and I had to scramble to keep up. "Not really."

"Yeah, well, neither do I. So let's coordinate outfits and look better than both of them, all right?"

She stopped her near-sprint and turned to face me, one eyebrow raised in a challenge.

Well, shit. Who would've thought Lara would be asking me to a dance? And who would've thought I'd ever say yes?

But I was about to, wasn't I?

I shrugged, and folded my arms. "All right."

In my pocket, my phone buzzed, and I pulled it out while Lara blatantly peeked.

Friday, 12:32 PM

Meet me in the parking lot after
school?

The parking lot was mostly empty by the time Will sheepishly appeared and shuffled to my car. He offered me a weak smile that I didn't return. I just leaned against my hood and waited.

"I wanted to tell you," he said in a low voice as soon as he got close enough.

"Yeah, well, you didn't."

"I was going to next time I saw you."

"You saw me yesterday. You didn't say a *thing*. You didn't have any trouble telling the guys."

"I didn't, I swear. Jess told Matt."

"Why did she tell Matt?"

"I don't *know*, Ollie!" he said, flinging his hands up in frustration. "I'm sorry, okay?"

"Sorry you didn't tell me or sorry you're going with her?" I asked, my voice hard.

He blinked at me. "It doesn't mean anything," he said. "I promise."

"Yeah."

"I would go with you if I could."

I tried to smile, but my muscles worked against me. The thing is, he could. He was just choosing not to. And whether they were good reasons or not, he was still choosing not to go with me. And if he absolutely had to do that, fine, but couldn't he go alone?

I probably should've said that to him, but I didn't for two reasons. One, because I was terrified he'd hear me practically beg him to do something important for me and still say no. Two, because I didn't want him to go alone because I asked him to. I wanted him to go alone because he truly believed that if he couldn't go with me, he didn't want to go with anyone.

"I can't wait to see you all suited up," Will said in a quiet voice. "I really do wish I could go with you."

He was looking at me in this intense way. No one had ever looked at me like that before. Like I was the most special person in the world, and he'd only just realized.

I opened my mouth, and a whole bunch of really appropriate things were supposed to come out. Something along the lines of "Thank you," or, "I'll text you later," or, "It's super cold out here, huh."

But then my mouth—completely of its own accord, may I add—did something really stupid.

It said, "I love you."

Will and I both froze. I don't know which of us was more shocked, to be honest. Where the hell had that even come from? Of all the times I could've picked, and I'd gone with "right after being told he's going to the dance with his ex-girlfriend." I didn't have a clue why I'd said that. *Why did I say that?* I was so angry, and hurt, and I came out with *that*? If your meal has a freaking toenail in it, you don't ask for a dessert menu. If your not-really-boyfriend does something selfish that makes you feel worthless, you don't tell them you love them.

I guess I'd wanted to hear him say it back. Because as long as he loved me, then the other stuff didn't matter, right?

Right?

He gave me a sort-of-smile, but it was more of an "I don't know how to make this less awkward" smile than an "oh my God the guy I love loves me back" kind of smile.

Mayday. Time to bail out. Immediately. "Well, anyway, I—"

"I really, really like you," Will said at the same time.

"Oh." Wow, that came out more high-pitched than I'd hoped. "Cool. That's really—"

"I care about you a lot."

*"Awesome."* I had to leave right now or it was going to be super obvious I was upset. "Thank you. Wow, it's, uh, super cold out here, huh? Hey, I actually have this huge essay due Monday and I really need to get home and start on it. So, I'll text you later?"

Nailed it.

Will studied me for so long I thought he was going to try to let me down easily. I sent him a firm message with my eyes. Don't. Do not. Please pretend I never said I love you. Please ignore it for me.

"Yeah, sounds good," he said finally. "I'll see you later."

Then we walked away from each other.

Wait, so he was just going to ignore it? The *audacity.* I tried not to look like I was stalking my way to my car, even though that's exactly what I was doing.

Okay, so maybe I didn't want to pretend I'd never said it. But I didn't want to hear how much he liked me, either. I wanted to hear he loved me.

Why didn't he say it?

Had I said it too soon? How soon were you supposed to bring that up? Why hadn't I done some research on this first? I'd never said I love you before, I didn't know how it worked. I mean, we'd been a thing for seven months now, on and off. It was reasonable to love someone by seven months, right? Wasn't it weirder that he didn't love me yet?

Oh my God, he didn't love me.

My hands were shaking as I got out my keys, and it took me three tries to slot one into the ignition. As soon as the car started, a Letlive song blasted out at full volume. I smacked the power button so hard I hurt my hand. It didn't matter, though. I just needed to leave. Now.

I got out of the parking lot and drove over several streets. I didn't know which way Will took home, but there was no way he'd come down this many side streets. Still, I weaved my way through a few more to be safe. I drove aimlessly for a while, then my breath started catching in my throat. I managed to pull to the side of the road, swore as loudly as I could, and then smacked my fist against the dashboard.

But yelling and hitting things didn't make it go away. Images started swirling around and around and around. Will screwing up his face at the thought of dressing like me. Turning his back on me at the beginning-of-school party. Looking at me across the cafeteria then looking away. And those endless weeks of silence after summer.

He could've logged into his accounts on someone else's phone, I realized suddenly. I'd accepted his excuse at the time, him being grounded and all. But so what? Why didn't he try harder? If he really cared about me, why didn't he find a way around the rules, even if it was only to let me know why he'd be AWOL? Surely he'd realized what I'd be thinking when he disappeared. How I would've felt. Why didn't he care enough to find a way to reach me?

That was the point. He didn't care enough. Because he didn't love me then.

And he didn't love me now.

# 17

"Now we need one in front of the fireplace," Mom said, dropping her phone down by her side. Lara and I were standing in the living room, ready to head to the dance, and we were quickly realizing the dance was still quite a while away at this rate. Mom had already taken photos of us on the front porch (to take advantage of the golden hour), by the back door (because the pane has a really lovely design), and sitting together on the couch (because I just like the way those kind of photos look, Oliver). "Oh, but just wait, I need to put the vase back up. I took it down to dust, now where is it?"

"No one's going to be looking at the vase, Cathy," Aunt Linda said from the couch, cuddling the faux mink blanket around her. "Not with these two sexy young things front and center."

Lara grabbed her powder-pink skirt and ruffled it for Aunt Linda, posing for a picture no one was taking. Aunt Linda held up a finger and pulled out her own phone.

"Hold on, we need some photoshoot music if we're taking this seriously." A few seconds later and the opening bars to "Can't Fight the Moonlight" played.

"Little vintage, don't you think?" I asked.

"Watch yourself, I danced to this at my prom," Aunt Linda said.

"Exactly. Vintage."

"I'm ignoring that."

Mom came back into the room with a vase full of fresh flowers she'd stolen from the neighbor's yard that had grown over into ours. "Here. Perfect. Now, I'll just get you two to stand over here."

Mom adjusted us like props while Aunt Linda merrily belted out LeAnn Rimes in the background. She was in particularly good spirits today. Aunt Linda, I mean. Mom was a ball of stress.

Mom took a few more photos of us—flash on and off—while instructing me to smile "more naturally, no, *naturally*, you look like you're in a political hostage video." Lara got no criticisms or critiques. Lara was made for the camera, apparently.

"Ollie couldn't have gotten a more beautiful date, Lara," Aunt Linda said when we were finally set free.

"She means because you're beautiful, I assume, not because I'm so hideous you're the best I could possibly do," I said.

"You sure she didn't mean because I'm hopefully the last time you'll have to take a girl to a dance?" Lara asked innocently.

"Partly," Aunt Linda replied, holding up a finger. She struggled to sit up straighter on the couch for a moment, then, panting, she clasped her hands together. "But also, Ollie, are you hoping to get married one day?"

"Ah, yes, ideally, but we'll see. Why?"

She paused and turned LeAnn off. Apparently she meant business. "Because one day you'll be all dressed up and taking photos with the person you love more than anything in the world. And I just want you to know that I'll be there. Maybe physically, maybe not, but I'll be there either way. So when the day comes, you'll be getting a huge hug from me at some point. Be on the lookout for it."

"I won't need to be on the lookout for it, because you'll be there physically, and I'll know exactly when you're hugging me."

"You'll know either way," she said. Her voice was strained, and her eyes were glassy.

Seeing Aunt Linda cry made me tear up a little.

"It's okay, I'm okay," she said, flapping her hands then wiping under her eyes. "Argh. Sorry. You're just so handsome. I'm glad I got to see it."

Okay, so I was tearing up more than a little now. "I'm glad you did, too."

Even Lara's bottom lip started wobbling a bit. Huh. So she did have a heart. Then she smacked my arm. "Come on, perk up. You don't want to be blotchy in the photos, do you?"

Ah. That was more like it.

Lara and I managed to arrive fashionably late.

The school gym was spilling over with students, and the room was a sea of color. Interestingly, that color was mainly yellow. Dresses and ties, not decorations. Apparently it was the shade of the season. Not that I'd gotten the memo with my cobalt-blue tie.

Most of the room was dimly lit, with disco balls set up to mimic the effect of snowflakes falling. Along the walls hung glittery white flower arrangements, and about twenty large round tables filled the far end of the room. Half the seats were taken already, the places held by strategically placed clutches and handbags.

Not far away from us, Renee stood with a group of her friends. She was wearing a form-fitting, honey-colored dress, and had her auburn hair curled and scooped into a half-ponytail.

"A lot of people, here," I commented to Lara, who was too busy objectifying Renee to reply.

I had to scan the room for a surprisingly long time before I spotted Will. He stood over by the tables with Matt, leaning against a chair and laughing about something, with Jess nowhere in sight. He'd paired a tailored blazer with dark gray pants and a light gray T-shirt. Even though I wouldn't have dreamed of wearing a T-shirt to a dance, he didn't come off as informal, somehow. Just sexy as hell. Why was it that guys like Will were able to play chicken with the rules and come out on top? If I wore a blazer and a T-shirt, I'd look like I'd gotten disoriented halfway through dressing.

When Will glanced up, he happened to look straight across the room at me. I got the feeling he'd already known where I was standing. As soon as he caught my eye, his smile changed to become a little shy, and he ducked his head, still smiling.

I was giving him what was probably the dopiest stare I'd given anyone in my life when Lara yanked me by my elbow to cross over to the refreshments stand. Darnell and Niamh were standing closely together, and their hands kept brushing. It was extremely intimate, and romantic, and oh, look, Lara was leading us over there to break it up, how nice.

"Hey guys," Lara said. "Don't you both scrub up well."

I'd lost sight of Will on the way over here. As I tried to super-casually search for him again, I drifted out of the conversation. It was mostly small-talk, anyway—I got the feeling Niamh and Darnell were hinting that they wanted to be left alone for a bit. I'm sure Lara *got* the hint, it was more that she didn't so much *care*, was all.

The dance floor was pumping already. From the way some of the kids were dancing, it was pretty obvious at least some of them had pre-gamed in someone's backyard before coming here. In fact, now that I thought about it, Lara had more than likely smuggled her flask along somewhere. I guess she'd just figured I wouldn't say yes to any. Which, fair. I *wouldn't* say yes.

I was so busy people-watching, though, that I totally missed the part of the conversation where Lara excused herself to go talk to Renee. Except she must have, because suddenly she was over with Renee, and they were walking off somewhere together.

Which meant I was an unwilling third wheel, didn't it?

I turned slowly to Darnell and Niamh. Oh shit. I didn't know anyone else. I had no one I could go talk to. But I definitely wasn't wanted here. I cleared my throat. "So, how long have you two been here?" I asked.

"I've been here for about twenty, but Niamh got here a minute before you two," Darnell said. Like Niamh, Darnell didn't seem to possess the nastiness gene, and he said it with such a genuine, friendly smile I couldn't possibly feel awkward about it.

Except, yes, I could, because it was me, and I would probably feel awkward at my own ninetieth birthday party, surrounded by a room full of people that I'd loved and raised.

"You didn't come together?" I asked.

Apparently, that was the exact wrong thing to ask. Darnell pursed his lips and cringed, while Niamh opened her mouth into an *O* shape of doom. "Well, I don't know, I just think maybe it's a little early—"

"Right," Darnell added, when he clearly meant wrong.

"For that," Niamh finished.

"Okay, gotcha, cool," I said. *"Cooooool."*

This time, when I looked up, Will was standing about four feet away from me. I blinked and took a step back in surprise. "Um, hi?"

"Hey," he said. "What's up? Remember what we were talking about earlier today? It's over here. Wanna come see?"

I did not remember what we were talking about earlier today. Mostly because I was quite sure we did not talk at all earlier today. And talking to Will wasn't the kind of thing I tended to forget about. At least, I couldn't remember ever forgetting him.

Well, this was a bother. Frying pans and fire and all that. Niamh and Darnell were only too happy to wave me off, though, so off I trailed after Will to check out the thing we never talked about, crossing my arms over my chest.

"I have never seen anything more uncomfortable in my life," Will said. "It was like watching a donkey trying to make friends with some unicorns."

"Are you calling me a *donkey*?"

"A really, really amazing, awesome donkey. And if you weren't a donkey, I don't think I'd like you as much, because unicorns seem like they'd make a lot fewer jokes than donkeys," Will said, still walking. "Can you imagine a quirky unicorn?"

"I cannot imagine a quirky unicorn." My answer was clipped, but Will didn't seem to notice.

"Exactly. Unicorns are so vanilla."

"What's it like trying to dig yourself out of a hole this big, Will?"

"I'm struggling, but I've got less practice at it than you do."

I pressed my lips tightly together. We pulled up against the wall and both of us put our backs to it, leaving us isolated enough that we could talk in low voices without being heard. Will sighed and shook his head. "Sorry, that was meant to be a joke. What I meant to say is, you look amazing."

Oh.

I tried to smile, but my face fought back. Who knew heartache worked better than Botox?

A part of me wanted to bring up the other day, and apologize for saying I loved him and making things weird. Even though we'd seen each other a few times since then, neither of us had brought it up. And you don't just forget to mention something like that. Also, I couldn't help but feel like Will was overcompensating. He'd been acting a little too cheerful and upbeat lately, but it was like trying to hide a skunk spray with a spritz of perfume.

A pile of bricks sat in the pit of my stomach. My limbs felt weighed down, and my chest was filled with a weird, tight pressure that I could only relieve by exhaling. Again, and again. Which came out sounding like a series of passive-aggressive sighs.

Apparently, my emotions had a sassy attitude of their own. Note to self: never play poker.

The song changed over, and I recognized the first few bars. So did everyone else in the room, apparently, because a cheer went up and the crowd swarmed onto the dance floor like fire ants attacking an innocent gardener with a family.

Will shrugged one shoulder and nodded toward everyone. "Do you feel like diving in?"

I hated dancing so much—my style could best be described as "toddler bopping along to the Wiggles." But if the other options were either standing here alone or skirting around pink elephants with Will, then . . . *woo*, party, yay.

The dance floor was hot and crowded, and people weren't so much dancing as they were jumping around to the music. Luckily, jumping around to the music was actually within my rhythmic skill set, so I threw myself into it with a surprising level of enthusiasm for me.

All at once, Will and I ended up surrounded by Renee, Renee's boyfriend, Lara, and Matt, along with a few other basketball guys. For probably the first time ever, I didn't even feel self-conscious. It was actually fun. I was part of a group, and we were all singing loudly enough that my throat got scratchy after a few songs.

And Will was right beside me the whole time, his face bright while he threw his head back and his arms out. He was singing to nobody, but from the way he kept sending sidelong glances at me, it felt like an oddly energetic serenade. Then he caught my eye, gave me a mischievous grin, and turned to me to sing right at me, still jumping around to the music. And all at once it didn't matter that he wasn't out, or that he didn't care enough, or that I'd been vulnerable and let myself get trampled. For just these few minutes, it didn't matter at all.

So I sang back to him.

Suddenly, he stopped jumping and grabbed onto my arm, pulling me into him. For the wildest half second of my life I thought he was going to kiss me, but instead he said into my ear, "Look, look, look—over there. Darniamh!"

Straight through the middle of the dance floor, Darnell and Niamh were making out. Not just kissing, but French-kissing, hands in each other's hair, going for it. They didn't even seem to be aware they were surrounded by hundreds of their closest friends.

"Eurgh, *yes!*" I shrieked, grabbing Will back with one hand and pumping the other in a fist. "We called it."

"Anyone with eyes could've called it," Will said with a laugh that faded rapidly. I followed his line of sight to Matt, who was giving us a funny look. Like, a really funny look.

I let go of Will's arm the same moment he shook me off.

"I'm gonna grab a drink," he muttered, and stalked off into the sea of people without inviting me as a new song started.

Well, at least I wasn't alone on the dance floor. But suddenly I didn't feel like dancing anymore.

I forced myself to stay as long as I could stand it, so Matt didn't get too suspicious, then I bounced my way over to one of the tables. Bounced, because if I didn't put on fake cheer, I would've moped my way over like the love child of Eeyore and Squidward.

Once I was sitting down with my phone, I felt calmer. No one was paying any attention to me, anyway—they were all perfectly content having fun with each other. Why couldn't Juliette be here? She was the most dependable person I'd met in this town, and she'd gone and bailed on me in my time of need. And all just so she could attend the biggest audition of her life. *So selfish, Juliette, what do you think this is?*

My unlikely hero came wearing a floaty pink dress and a scowl. Lara flopped into the chair next to me and crossed one leg over the other, shoving her nails in her mouth.

"Why, hello," I said.

"She basically just turned her back on me," Lara said, purportedly to me, but mostly I think she wanted the opportunity to vent out loud in general. "Just shut me out of her romantic little twosome."

"She's dancing with her boyfriend?"

*"She's dancing with her boyfriend."*

"The sheer nerve."

Lara shot me an icy glare, and I turned back to watch the room.

The basketball guys stood in a group against one of the flower arrangements, posing with Matt in the center for a photo taken by Niamh. As she took the photo, Will held up a hand to keep her there and gave her his phone to take a second photo. The guys rearranged themselves into *America's Next Top Model*–type poses, with Matt lifting a leg in front of Will's chest—held in place by Will, naturally—and Darnell crouching next to them with his head tipped back dramatically.

If it had been another group, it would've been a funny, cute pose. But I got the feeling that, for these guys, the humor lay in the femininity, not in the drama. And the difference mattered, if you asked me.

Niamh went to hand Will's phone back to him, but Matt grabbed it first. The guys made a show of gushing over the photos, as Matt flicked through the options. Then, all at once, they burst out laughing, and Will went to grab the phone. Matt held it out of his reach, with one of the other guys blocking Will's lunge. Will shoved the guy roughly out of the way and snatched the phone out of Matt's grip, stuffing it into his pocket with a storm-cloud face. Will said something, and the guys fell about cackling.

Jess, who'd been hovering nearby, went over to the boys at this point. Probably to ask what all the commotion was about. I would've liked to know myself, to be honest.

Jess seemed like a nice enough girl, but she was the ex of my kind-of-boyfriend, so I irrationally disliked her. She had shoulder-length, straight black hair, dimples, and a perfectly symmetrical face. Her bright red dress was longer in the back than in the front, and she paired it with enormous black pumps.

She looked great. Awesome. I hated it.

But I was about to hate it quite a bit more, because at that moment she grabbed Will's hand and led him onto the dance floor. Probably to take his mind off whatever had just gone down. She was probably being really thoughtful and sweet. She was probably a thoughtful, sweet person if Will had dated her.

I freaking hated it.

I was in the middle of striking a deal with the Great, Ethereal Being to send her uncontrollable, unattractive food poisoning—I was willing to volunteer at an animal shelter, take my parents out to a nice dinner, *and* sacrifice my eternal soul if she just went home in the next thirty seconds—when Beyoncé's "Crazy in Love" came on. Will glanced over his shoulder at the basketball guys, then grabbed Jess's hand and slowly spun her around. When she finished he pulled her into him, his hands slipping down her waist to her hips. Jess seemed startled, but she laughed and went along with it, swaying her hips in time to the song, with their pelvises *way* closer together than any two platonic friends would consider reasonable.

"What the hell?" I murmured.

"What?" Lara asked, lifting her head. "Oh shit. Am I psychic or what?"

I glowered.

"Get a sense of humor, Ollie, I'm joking. But . . . hmm. Wow."

An out-of-breath Matt came over to our table and sat next to Lara, folding his leg so it pointed in her direction. "Hey, beautiful people," he said. "How's your night been?"

Jess had turned around so her backside was pressed against Will, and he leaned right into her, grabbing a handful of her skirt while they rocked, like he wanted to pull it right off her body. She twirled around to face him and put one hand in her hair, the other on his shoulder, and she brought her face close enough for him to kiss her, biting her lip and flirting the whole time. He didn't kiss her, but he didn't back away, either. And as far as I was concerned, he was about thirty seconds from kissing her.

My night was fucking swell, thanks for asking.

"I'm going outside," I said to Lara, before staggering across the back of the room to the side door.

Holy shit. Had that really just happened? Will, my Will, had just practically hooked up with his ex-girlfriend in public, where he *knew* I could see him. And barely twenty minutes after he'd been dancing with me.

How could he?

And how could I let him do this kind of thing to me again? How many times was I going to put up with Will doing whatever the hell he wanted, whenever it suited him?

The air in the parking lot was icy. I gulped it down in huge gasps until my head cleared up. The lot was deserted. The dance wasn't over for another two hours. It was too early for anyone to be leaving yet.

I wandered a few feet away from the door and sat heavily on the edge of the sidewalk. Screw tonight. And screw Will. I was going to make sure Lara had a way home, then I was leaving.

But after ten minutes I hadn't made a move to do anything of the sort. I just sat, feeling empty and numb and tired.

I heard the door open, and my first thought was it was Will, coming to apologize.

But Will wasn't wearing high heels. They clicked on the concrete, getting closer, until their owner sat down next to me in a rustle of pink chiffon.

I sighed. I was glad to see Lara, but I was disappointed she wasn't Will. Because that meant Will was still inside with Jess, not caring that I'd disappeared.

Lara sighed right back at me. "I think I know why Will was acting like that."

Because he was self-absorbed, self-interested, and devoid of empathy? "Why?"

"Matt just told me the guys found a picture of you on Will's phone. Wearing his jacket."

"Oh."

"They gave him a hard time about it. Apparently Will was trying to say you guys took the photo to show how silly you'd look in a jacket that big, but they didn't let him off the hook."

"Right. So he wanted to prove himself?"

Lara smirked. "Apparently. Because he's *so super straight*, right? 'Cause if you dry hump a girl that makes you straight.

I, personally, turn straight every time I kiss a guy, too. That's exactly how it works."

Well, I didn't miss the sarcasm that time. "Sometimes I think I don't like him very much."

Lara shrugged. "Hate away. I've hated Renee for over a year now, I think. Doesn't mean I don't love her."

"Isn't that a contradiction?"

"Nope. Apathy is incompatible with hate. Love works okay."

We sat in silence for a few seconds, then Lara kicked at a few loose pebbles. "Be careful, though. Sure, you can forgive someone for hurting you by accident, right? But if they keep accidentally ripping your heart out over and over again, doesn't mean they're terrible people, but it probably means you're better off getting to a distance where they can't keep doing that. Accidentally or not."

It didn't seem like she was just talking about Will.

"We're better than that, right?" I said.

"We damn well are."

I was so angry that Will could so easily hurt me, without any hesitation.

But it made me even angrier to know that I'd let him.

I'd *let him*. He'd made it perfectly clear that he couldn't give me what I wanted. So why had I stuck around? Why was I so willing to accept whatever scraps he handed out?

All this time, I'd been wondering when my needs would start to really matter to him.

Maybe I hadn't spent enough time wondering when my needs would start to really matter to *me*.

A cheer rang out from inside the hall as a Post Malone song came on. We glanced back, but neither of us made any move to get up, even though it was freaking freezing out here, and even though we were sitting kind of near the

Dumpsters, and something sounded like it was rummaging through them, and maybe it was a raccoon. We stayed outside.

"How come you asked me to come here with you? Really?" I asked to change the topic.

Lara examined her nails. "Like I said. Neither of us had anyone better to go with."

I couldn't help myself—I actually laughed out loud at that one. Was it possible that Lara's jabs weren't able to hurt me anymore? Or was it that I was starting to get the sense that her jabs weren't meant to be taken personally? "Flattering. Thank you."

Lara reached for her purse then, and I thought it was time to go back in. But instead she rummaged around in it, then paused with her hand still hidden inside. "Um. I got you something. For being my date."

I was fairly sure Lara buying me a present was listed as an end of times sign in the Bible, between false prophets and stars falling from the sky. Which was terrible news for humanity, but it did brighten my night up a little. "You did? Oh . . . I didn't get you anything."

"We're playing swapsies with oppressive gender roles tonight. That's the theme of this stupid dance, right?" she asked. "Anyway. Here."

She handed me a rose-gold chain, longer than the ones the girls wore. It didn't have a rose on the end, though. It had a dagger.

I turned it around in my fingers and fought a lump that had turned up in my throat unannounced.

"Daggers represent the polar opposite of roses," she said. "But they're paired together a lot, like in tattoos and stuff. When they're paired together, it's supposed to represent the balance of two different parts making a whole.

Because you kind of round out the group. And also, because you can't get our exact necklaces anymore."

I rounded out the group.

"Can I wear it?" I forced out.

"No, you're supposed to keep it in your pocket. Of course you wear it."

When it was fastened, the dagger rested on my chest an inch below my collarbone. I doubted you could see it with this shirt, but I felt like I must look completely different somehow. I felt different. Like I properly belonged somewhere I never thought I could.

Against that, Will dancing with Jess didn't seem so catastrophic. Not anymore.

The dagger made me brave enough to ask a question that would never have left my lips before tonight. "Hey, Lara? On the first day of school, when I told you guys about Will . . . how come you didn't tell me you knew him? You could've warned me."

To my surprise, she burst out laughing. "Come on, Ollie. We knew nothing about you. For all we knew, if you realized Will went to our school you'd out him to the class. I wanted to give Will a heads-up before you figured out what was going on so he could do some damage control if he needed to."

I tried to work through this new information. "Wait, so *that's* what you and Juliette were doing at the party?"

"Trying to. But Matt wouldn't let me get Will alone. He was all talk, talk, talk, talk, talk."

"But why'd you wait until the party to tell him?"

"I couldn't find him at school, and he didn't reply to my texts. Then I asked Matt, and he told me about the whole grounding thing. Remember?"

Of course. Will hadn't had his phone.

So the party hadn't been about humiliating me. It was difficult to wrap my head around, and to be honest I didn't completely buy it at first. "That seems awfully thoughtful of you," I said, raising a pointed eyebrow.

"No one deserves to be outed against their will," Lara said.

And this time, I believed her. Lara, who was secretly in love with Renee. Who laughed along with the group when they teased her about her party behavior like it was all one big joke. Who snapped when Will made a comment about my clothing.

Lara'd had no intention of letting me come into her school and out one of her friends.

And why shouldn't she have thought that? I'd outed Will to the three girls, after all. On purpose or not. The consequence was still the same.

I cleared my throat and changed the subject, a little overwhelmed. "Well, hey. If things don't work out with Renee, at least you can be *pretty* sure Matt's an option."

Lara barked another laugh. "Oh God," she said. "Oh, I used to have the biggest damn crush on him."

"Really?"

"*Yes*, oh my God, yes." She grinned. "I'm bi as fuck, Ollie, in case you haven't noticed. I swear, he's only paying me attention now because I like Renee. That boy only wants what he can't have."

Ugh. Straight guys.

"Can I confess something?"

Hearing those words come out of Lara's mouth felt odd. Like a vegetarian asking you to pass the meatballs, or a mermaid asking to borrow your shoes. Guilt + Lara = system error. And yet, here she was, looking at me with what was almost *definitely* a guilty expression.

"Shoot."

She shifted in place and lowered her voice. "Well, the first time Renee and I kissed, it was on a dare. And I already liked her, so, you know, jackpot."

"Right."

"Right. Then it was suddenly a really easy way to kiss her. *Let's do it on a dare, let's do it for this group of guys.* I used to think it was funny. Actually, not even that. I thought I was twisting the whole 'girls performing for guys' thing. I was using *them* to get what I wanted."

But she didn't sound so certain. "And now?"

"Well . . . what if I was wrong? What if I betrayed queer women by doing that? Even if it was for me, and I didn't give a *shit* what those guys thought, wasn't I still basically reinforcing the idea that my sexuality is just there to get a guy off? I mean, think of the crap people say about bi girls only wanting attention."

Oof. On the one hand, I felt like, as a guy, it wasn't really my place to give my thoughts. But on the other hand, I could see why she wanted to ask a gay person for advice on this one. I went slowly, and picked my words carefully. "I think if that's how you felt safe exploring your sexuality, that's valid. It's not always black and white for us."

Lara was silent for a long time. "She's never kissed me alone," she said finally.

I thought about how much that must hurt. How crushed I would be if Will only kissed me for someone else's entertainment. Even if he was only pretending that was why he was doing it.

The space between Lara and me felt heavy.

"Anyway," Lara waved a hand right through the blanket of unease. "Screw that. I don't exist for any guy's pleasure, and I'm not playing that game anymore. If Renee wants to kiss me, she can do it one on one. And she can do it *single*."

"*Yes*."

"Come on," Lara said. "We need to get back inside and show those two we can have plenty of fun without them. If you're lucky, I'll let you use me as a pole dancing prop, and you can show Will up."

I burst out laughing at that, and stood up. "All right. Let's do it."

# 18

Sunday, 1:51 AM

Meet me in the lake. By the end of
the jetty, to the right of your house.

*He meant* by *the lake, right? In had to be a typo, didn't it?
It was 2 A.M. He was lucky I woke up when he texted me.*

*But there was no one standing on the jetty. There was, how-
ever, a pile of clothes barely visible at the end of it.*

*I stole a quick glance around to make sure I was definitely,
certainly, totally alone, and hurried along the jetty.* Way to
make me feel exposed, Will.

*He was treading water just beyond the edge of the jetty, a
small, stark face smiling up at me from the black lake.* "What
are you doing?" *I asked.*

*"Perfect night for a swim, isn't it?"*

*"Don't you have to drive home in four hours?" I asked.
We'd already forced our way through our good-byes. I'd spent*

*the night sulking, and hoping I'd see him again, and coming to terms with the fact that I most likely never would.*

*"I'm not the one in the driver's seat. I can nap then. I wanted to see you again."*

*"Will . . ."*

*"Come in."*

*"But it's dark," I whined.*

*"I won't let anything eat you. I promise."*

*I hesitated. For nobody but him. I swear, nobody in this world but Will would be able to convince me to strip down and plunge into an icy, dark lake of death during the freaking witching hour.*

*But I did it, didn't I?*

*As soon as I was in the water, his arms were around my shoulders, and his lips were on mine. He kissed me like he'd never get the chance to do it again. And that's damn well how I kissed him back.*

*"Screw tomorrow," I managed, when I pulled away.*

*"It's gonna come, whether you want it to or not."*

*"I know. And you'll be gone, and you'll forget all about me in a few weeks."*

*Will laughed and shook his head. "I'll definitely never forget you. I don't think I've ever been this happy. That won't vanish just because we'll be—"*

*"On opposite sides of the country."*

*"It could be worse. You could live in, like, Australia or something."*

*"I might as well."*

*He kissed me again. Good-bye kiss number seventy-six. "Promise me we'll find a way to see each other again."*

*"I can't promise that."*

*"Then lie. Please."*

Will and I didn't exchange a word until music class the next day.

He gave me a small smile when he sat down next to me. Like he was hoping I might act like everything was fine, and the dance hadn't happened. "Hey," he whispered.

Hey.

I was seething.

"I don't want to see you anymore," I whispered back.

He looked at me with the expression of someone who'd been told their new puppy had been brutally murdered. Just as he collected himself to try to respond, class started, and he slumped back in his seat with a clenched jaw. He stayed like that until Ms. Ellison paused to hand out some booklets she'd made. Then, still looking at the front of the class as casual as anything, he said under his breath, "Please don't do this."

I ignored him.

"*Ollie.*"

I ignored him.

"I'm so sorry. I feel really awful about last night."

Not awful enough to call me, or pull me aside and explain, or to not do it in the first place.

"Can we talk about this later?"

I ignored him.

When the bell rang, I continued to ignore him, and managed to storm off to my next class without Will being able to do much in the way of begging. Made partly more effective by the fact that Will couldn't say a word where anyone else could hear, and school halls weren't conducive to privacy. At lunchtime, I was strategic, and used this to my advantage by going to the cafeteria instead of the music room so he couldn't get me alone.

I'd expected the basketball guys to sit with us, especially after Niamh and Darnell's consummation of sorts last night, but the roses had our table to ourselves today.

"It's because Darnell and I had a . . . talk last night," Niamh said once all three of us had sat down. "I told him I'm moving to New York next year."

"And?" Lara asked.

"*And,* I think he had this picture of us staying here and raising a little family one day or something. He said he's never wanted to live in a big city. So, honestly, I don't know where we stand. I know he doesn't want to come with me next year, but we haven't really decided to call it quits, either. We're in limbo."

"Betwixt and between," I said. "That's the worst."

"Is that a poem?" Niamh asked.

"Darnell is an idiot," Lara said, pointing a french fry menacingly at Niamh. "Besides, the problem isn't the city. If he got a job offer there I bet you he'd move in a heart-beat. He's just intimidated by the thought of following around a strong woman while she chases her career instead of the other way around."

"Preach!" said Niamh, raising her Diet Coke in a toast.

"I think the dance might have been cursed," I said. Niamh nodded earnestly.

Lara gave us withering glances. "Um, the opposite, you mean? The dance cleansed us of the toxic baggage we were dragging around with us. Now we're all available, un-attached, and no longer bogged down by immature para-sites leeching love from us and not giving back anything more substantial than a lackluster quickie in a storage closet."

"You and Renee had a quickie in a storage closet?" I asked.

"It's a figure of speech."

"I don't think it is."

"Well, all the established figures of speech are so overdone."

"Yeah, that's what makes them figures of speech. If they're not overdone, they're just something someone said one time."

"Ollie," Lara said sweetly, "you can be really irritating sometimes. Has anyone ever told you that?"

"Other than myself? Nope."

The bad news was that the rose-gold dagger necklace I had around my neck wasn't enough to ward off a Lara attack. The good news was that this was probably the most I'd ever spoken at the lunch table. I felt more comfortable than usual, too.

Maybe the night before hadn't been a total write-off, then.

Will messaged me to meet him in the parking lot again, but I had no intention of doing that. I made a beeline for my car as soon as I left the building.

Footsteps smacked on the ground behind me as I put my hand on the car door. "Ollie, wait, please."

He just could not let this go, could he? Honestly, I'd thought I'd get out of here without having to deal with him, given how crowded the parking lot was right now. With students spilling out left, right, and center, I'd have put all sorts of bets down that Will wouldn't risk chasing me down.

But here he was, chasing me down.

"At least *talk* to me," Will said. "Let me explain."

"You don't need to," I said. "Lara told me. The guys found the photo of me on your phone."

"Right."

"Right," I said. "So unless there's something really, really convincing that I don't know, there's nothing else to explain."

Will looked befuddled. "But then you have to know it wasn't personal, right? I had to throw them off."

"You didn't *have* to do anything."

Will looked around to see if anyone was close enough to overhear. "Can we get in the car?" he asked.

I rolled my eyes and jumped into the driver's seat, slamming the door. Will followed after me on the passenger side, with less slamming. "Ollie, if I didn't, they would've been suspicious about us," he said once he'd closed his door. "Matt would never let me live it down, he'd be after me every time I ever hung with you, like at lunch, or outside school, or—"

"And so what? Let him think what he wants. It's not like he has proof."

"You don't get it."

"Oh, don't I?" I asked. "Do I not have any idea what it's like to be gay?"

"You," he said over me, "came out in *fucking* California. I'm not saying it wasn't hard for you, but you have no idea what it's like to grow up here. I knew, like, ten gay jokes before I even knew what being gay *was*. My friends would never be able to accept it, okay? Do you think Matt will suddenly go out and buy an Ally T-shirt?"

"Just say it's not like that, then! You don't need to get with a girl to prove there's nothing going on with me."

"They're always, always digging, Ollie. I told you how they used to joke about you, right? You don't know the half of it. You aren't friends with them. You don't know what they're really like."

"But that's the point," I said. "I'm *not* friends with them. But they've been friends with you for ages. They know you. They *like* you."

"Exactly. It's different for you, because they haven't known any other version of you. You're wearing a fucking *necklace* right now, and no one's said shit. It's, like, your thing. But it's not my thing. My thing is being a basketballer, and being one of the guys. You think I'd get away with coming to school tomorrow wearing a necklace with a pendant on it?"

"Look," I said. "I get why you're scared, honestly. Of course you are. Coming out is *scary*, and—"

"I'm not ready to come out!" he shouted.

"I am *not asking you to*," I said, slapping the steering wheel in frustration. "But if I'm with someone, yeah, I fucking expect that they aren't going to go dirty dance with someone else to prove a point, or insult the way I dress or act in front of their friends."

"I said I'm sorry!"

"I don't *care* if you're sorry! I didn't want an apology. I wanted you to think of me, and care about how I'd feel, before you did something horrible. But you didn't. So how can I keep doing this if I know the thought of breaking my heart isn't enough to stop you from doing something *no one* is forcing you to do?"

"I did it *so* we can keep hanging out without—"

"No, *no*, don't try to act like last night was for my benefit. Why don't you just admit last night was one hundred percent about you being terrified someone might figure things out, and zero about me?"

"So what if it was?" Will asked. "Am I not allowed to be scared?"

"Of course you are. But that's the problem. If you're so worried about what people might think that you need to do shit like *that* as a response? How am I supposed to be with someone who could do that to me?"

Will folded his arms and shook his head. Apparently he had no reply. Which only incensed me more.

"You treat me like dirt. You've noticed that, right? And every time you apologize, I think it'll be different this time, but it's *never different*. You genuinely do not seem to give a shit about whether I'm okay."

"That's not true—"

"*It's true, Will!* I would *never* do something I knew would hurt you. Not to save myself from embarrassment, or to throw people off my tracks, or *anything*. I just wanted that from you."

"I didn't—"

"*I just wanted you to care,*" I cried. My throat felt clogged up, and I knew I'd start crying any second now, so I chose anger. Better than sadness. And hurt. "But you didn't, and you don't. So, get the *fuck* out of my car and leave me alone."

He paused for a while, and I shoved my key in the ignition. "I said get out of my car. I need to go babysit the kids. I'm already late."

He nodded. Silently, blinking, he climbed out of my car and walked across the parking lot with his arms still folded tightly across his chest. A junior accidentally stopped in front of him, and Will shoved his way past with way more force than he needed to, lowering his head as he went.

And so, Will and I commenced operation: silent treatment.

It was hard to say who was ignoring who, because we both put our best effort into pretending we had no idea who the other was. No texts, no eye contact, no speaking in class. It was too late for him to move desks in Music Appreciation, but he pettily started sitting as far to one side of it as he could, with his back turned at a slight angle so he didn't even have to see me in his peripheral vision.

It wasn't so bad during lunch, at least, as Darnell suddenly didn't seem to want anything to do with Niamh, so the basketball guys kept to their own table. Which sucked for Niamh, but it was hard to feel *too* sorry for her, because I was too relieved I didn't have to field awkward silences from Will when all I wanted to do was eat a chicken panini in peace.

When Juliette had come back to school, high on life after nailing her audition at the Conservatory, she'd said it was like walking into the aftermath of a nuclear holocaust. "How did *all three of you* get into *this* much drama in the two days I was off school?" she'd asked when we finished filling her in during homeroom.

But we adjusted to the absence of the guys quickly enough, and after a couple of weeks we'd settled into a new vibe. A we-don't-need-any-men (except Ollie, he's all right) vibe. And everything was fine. You know, not epically great or anything, but fine. Right up until the day Juliette started sobbing into her cheeseburger at lunch, plumb out of nowhere.

Lara looked mildly alarmed at the sudden display of emotion, and Niamh and I sprang into action right away.

"Oh my God, what's wrong, honey?"

"Hey, what's up? You all good? Nah, you're not all good; why'd I even ask that? What *happened*?"

Juliette buried her face in her hands and gave a frustrated, sobby groan. "I didn't want to talk about this. I thought I was *fine*."

"Yeah, fine as a man who's been gently corrected on the internet," Lara said, crossing one leg over the other.

Juliette peeked through her fingers. "I got a rejection letter yesterday."

I blanched. "From the Conservatory?"

She nodded.

"Oh no. Shit."

"I thought you said the audition went well?" Niamh asked.

"I thought it *did*! It was the best I'd ever played. The best I'd ever played, and it still wasn't good enough." With that, she broke down in tears again, and I shuffled my chair around so I could awkwardly pat her back.

"Those schools are *so* selective," I said. "Honestly, Valentina probably could've gotten rejected from half of them."

"She would *not*. She could get in anywhere because she's amazing, and I *suck*, and I'm going to be *stuck here*."

"Did you apply to any other schools?" Niamh asked quietly.

Juliette shrugged at the table. "I applied to Juilliard, but I didn't even get an audition. And also NC State."

"I didn't know they had a good music program," I said.

"They don't. It was supposed to be my backup school. Like, worst-case scenario. But I didn't . . . think that would actually happen."

I was crushed on her behalf. It didn't make any sense to me. Juliette *loved* the clarinet, and she was *so* talented and passionate and dedicated. How could it be over? Just like that?

Lara suddenly looked taken aback, but not in regards to Juliette. She was looking at something behind me. I turned around just in time to see Renee swoop in like a witch without a broom, brandishing a phone instead of a wand inches from my head. "Lara, seriously, enough."

Juliette, Niamh, and I exchanged wary glances, while Lara stuck out her bottom lip to plead ignorance. "Enough what?"

"Texting me, and calling me, and asking me to hang out. You need to get a hobby or something."

Underneath Lara's defiant nonchalance, there was a hint of confusion. "I don't know what you—"

"*There is nothing going on between us,*" Renee said, far more loudly than she needed to. She glanced behind her, and I looked back to see her boyfriend watching from a few tables over. All at once, it made sense. This was a show, put on for his benefit. "How much clearer can I make myself?"

Lara's mouth dropped open, and I wondered if Renee had made even the slightest attempt to be clear about that before this moment. "Wait, so are you saying you *don't* wanna get married?" Lara asked, sarcasm mode officially activated. "This is so out of nowhere."

"I'm *sorry*, Lara, but I'm *straight*, okay? I don't think of you like that. At all. You've got the wrong idea."

Renee was practically shouting now. The buzz from the tables around us had died down, and a few students had looked back to more effectively eavesdrop on the argument. If "argument" was really the right word for this situation—in fairness, Lara seemed to almost be goading Renee more than fighting back.

"Well, clearly," Lara said. "I guess *something* must have confused me there. Can you think what? It's on the tip of my tongue, but I just can't—"

"You need to *stop it*!" Renee yelled.

"No, *you* need to stop it," I said quietly. The thing is, though, I didn't mean to say it. It was out of my mouth as quickly as I thought it. I froze as Renee turned around to face me, her face red and furious. This was not good. I was not a confrontation kind of person. More of an "eating popcorn in the very back row, out of the firing line" kinda guy.

As she opened her mouth, though, Niamh jumped in. "Renee, if you want to talk to Lara, fine, but screaming at her in public is *not* a good look."

"Yeah, so you might wanna get the hell away from our table before the rest of us scream back at you," Juliette added, her face still blotchy and red, but her voice steady. "And trust me, we can scream louder."

Renee looked between us and scrunched up her mouth. She seemed to be weighing the pros and cons. Juliette raised an eyebrow at her and she scowled, before turning back to Lara. *"Stop texting me,"* she said in a low voice.

"You got it, sweetie," Lara said, turning back to her lasagna like the conversation was a little too boring to hold her attention.

Even when Renee disappeared, Lara did an impressive job of holding her composure, despite the obvious whispering and looks from the tables surrounding us. Even the basketball guys were looking over, and they were practically on the other side of the cafeteria. Matt was staring right at Lara, like he was trying to catch her eye. He looked concerned.

"Sooo . . ." Juliette said.

Lara rolled her eyes and thrust her phone at Juliette. "There. You tell me if what I said warranted that."

Juliette and Niamh tipped their heads together to look at the screen. I didn't bother joining them. I just looked at Lara and waited.

"That was basically gaslighting," Lara said.

"What's that?"

"When someone tries to twist what really happened to make you think you're losing it." She shoved lasagna into her mouth. "Trying to make me look obsessed with her like she wasn't *actively* leading me on that whole time."

Juliette and Niamh reemerged. "She was flirting with you," Niamh confirmed.

"All the way up until the part when you got annoyed that she's flirting with you while dating a guy she has *zero* intentions of breaking up with," Juliette said, a little more loudly than she needed to. Probably so the nearby tables would overhear Lara's side of the story, I guessed.

But Lara shook her head. "Don't. I don't need anyone else to know what happened. I could care less what they think."

*Couldn't care less,* I corrected internally. But I kept it to myself. Now didn't seem like the time.

"But still," Juliette pressed. "That was completely out of line. I have half a mind to go over there and read this thread out to her whole table."

Lara shrugged. "It's fine. Really. I guess I just thought it might mean something to her," she finished, the same way someone might say, "I guess I thought it was going to rain today."

Yeah.

I knew how that felt.

# 19

Lara sat on the brick wall bordering the school's entrance with a straight back, her heeled boots crossed at the ankles, and her sky-blue dress spread out beneath the iced coffee she clutched in her lap. Juliette, Niamh, and I stood, drinking our own coffees, flanking her. Today, she was a queen, and we were her guards. We stood together, always. We had the necklaces to prove it.

Like any queen, she drew the crowd's attention as kids passed us on their way into school. But the too-long looks and hushed whispers weren't awed. Some were curious, some were almost fearful, and some were judgmental.

We stared each one of them down until they kept moving.

Everyone knew by now, of course. Anyone who hadn't been there in the cafeteria would've found out through the whisper network yesterday afternoon. There would be people throughout the school who'd never met Lara, but who now knew intimate details about her sexuality.

Would have it in their minds when and if they *did* meet her. Would have an opinion on her, and who she was as a person.

I knew how that felt. Shit. Absolutely shit.

I spotted a group of black-and-white moving across the parking lot. Will, Darnell, and Matt. I angled my body toward Lara so I wouldn't have to pretend to be incredibly interested in the roof when Will walked past in order to avoid awkward eye contact.

*"Ask her."*

The whisper came from a group of girls I vaguely recognized from Biology. One of them, a girl who wore her mousy blond hair in a ponytail, had on a T-shirt that said CHOCOLATE IS THE ANSWER, BUT WHAT WAS THE QUESTION? Her friends gave her a shove, and she giggled, then dared to look up at Lara on her throne. "So, we wanted to know if you were lesbian when we all got changed together backstage at the Sophomore Showcase?"

Lara made a point of gradually turning her head to take the girl in. "Oh, good fucking morning, Charlotte," she said, high-pitched and perky.

Charlotte's friends shifted in place, but they held their ground. "It's a fair question," Charlotte said. "I mean, if you *were*, it's pretty bad that you didn't say anything. We had a right to know who we were changing in front of. Some of us were *naked*."

Lara laughed into her drink, causing the coffee to bubble. "God, you're right. It's a wonder I was able to restrain myself around you all once you stripped down to your grandma underwear."

"So, you were?"

"What, you think I went to bed straight then had

the world's most convincing sex dream and woke up craving—"

"*Don't* say it."

"*Vagina, clit, beaver*—"

"You're *disgusting*."

"The *furry furnace*," Lara cried, kicking out in front of her. Charlotte shrieked and leaped backward. "What, are you ashamed to be a girl or something, Char?"

"Charlotte. And no, I don't think that. But I did think it was interesting that you all start hanging with the new kid, and suddenly you're gay, too."

Of course I'd get dragged into this. Of course.

"There's nothing sudden about it, *Charlotte*," Lara said.

"That's all I wanted to know. In that case—"

"In *fact*," Lara said over her, "I was *screwing your mother* the day you had your first Lifetime channel, straight-ass kiss with Todd Ferguson."

"I always knew you were a slut, but I didn't take you for a—"

"I don't think you want to finish that sentence." It was Matt, storming through the stream of students, closely followed by Darnell and a nervous-looking Will.

"This is none of your business," Charlotte said, but her voice had lost some of its thunder.

"Like hell it's none of my business. You're standing in front of *my* school spewing some crap to *my* friend, when you and I both know your mama would wash your damn mouth out if she heard you saying that kind of shit. So go on if you want to, but I *will* be recording it, and I *will* send it straight to my ma, who'll make sure yours sees it by first period. They work in the same building, *remember*?"

Several students had slowed down to watch the drama

unfold by now. Charlotte looked like she had half a mind to keep going, but her friends had the sense to grab her by the elbow and drag her inside the building. Gradually, the crowd dispersed, and Matt went to stand below Lara.

"I don't need defending," she said.

"Oh, I know you don't. But you *always* get to go in with the smackdowns, and I've hated that girl's face since seventh grade when she bribed her way into being class president."

"You just wanted a little masculinity boost."

"Trust me, my masculinity didn't need any boosting." Matt leaned one arm against the brick wall. "But, seriously, fuck her. If she or anyone else gives you shit, let me know, all right? That shit's not cool, and I'm not afraid to play dirty."

Darnell must have noticed the admiring look Niamh was giving Matt, because he jumped in with, "Yeah, me, too. Who cares if you're into girls? The world keeps spinning, you know?"

My attention went straight to Will at this, and I searched his face for any sign that he was surprised by his friend's words. But today he was unreadable.

And just for a moment, I hated him a little. Because, I guess, after all this, a teeny part of me still hoped he would magically realize he didn't have to be terrified of what would happen if his friends figured things out. Then, ideally, he'd understand how much he'd hurt me, with the whole thing culminating in some sort of grand gesture to prove he truly did care all along.

But that was just a fantasy. A nice fantasy, sure, but no more real than a million other fairy tales.

God, what I wouldn't give to live in a fairy tale, sometimes. Or even just a romantic comedy. In them, this wouldn't fly. Like, imagine if Prince Charming had picked up the glass slipper and decided the city was too big to scour it for someone who fit the damn thing? Or if Prince Phillip saw Maleficent blowing fire all over the forest and went nope, fuck that, too risky? Or if Prince Eric was all like, "Hmm, I *could* fight the giant octopus sea witch from my nightmares, but then I could *also* sail home and return to eating fish I now know are sentient, safe in my denial and *cognitive goddamn dissonance*!"?

But they wouldn't, they *wouldn't* have done any of that, because in stories guys fight. They fight for the person they care about, and they don't give up, ever.

In real life, though, sometimes you beg for them to care, and they just don't. And then they go quiet.

And they let you walk away without much of a fight at all.

Two weeks after the Renee disaster—debacle—devastation . . . whatever-you-wanted-to-call-it, Lara had apparently decided she was ready to move on.

Part of me would've called it quick, but then I was still moping around after Will like he was my prophesized, meant-to-be true love and not just a summer fling that wasn't evergreen, so maybe I had no grasp on how long it was supposed to take to move on after heartbreak.

How did I know she was ready to move on? Two things. One, that she was suddenly, inexplicably flirting with Matt at lunch on the odd occasion when the basketball guys visited the table, dragged over by Darnell who always seemed to have one question or another he *had* to ask Niamh. And when I say Lara was flirting, I don't mean the natural banter that had caused Will and me to give birth to *Larmatt*. I mean licking her spoon like she was a RedTube star, burning holes into his pecs with her stare and grabbing his arm every time she spoke to him as though to trap him into conversation.

Even more bizarrely, Matt seemed suddenly, inexplicably *uninterested* in Lara's flirting. He barely held eye contact with her, kept giving her tight, short smiles, and only spoke to her to answer her many, many questions.

So, basically, it looked to me like Lara's interest was fueled by Matt's disinterest, which was fueled by Lara's interest.

And I thought Will and I were messy.

The second thing was more straightforward. Later that same day, I was pulling in to my house after school— for once, I didn't have to go to Aunt Linda's. She'd been emergency free for a little while now, knock on wood, and so the night was going to be me, Netflix, and a whole bag of mini Reese's Pieces. Anyway, I'd just turned off the ignition, when Lara messaged me.

**Monday, 3:04 PM**

Can I tell you something?

Lara never messaged me. Not outside of Snapchat, which barely counted. This was totally out of the blue, without any initiation from me. So sure, I was intrigued. I put my car into park and messaged her back.

**Monday, 3:06 PM**

Shoot.

Before I could even pull my keys out of the ignition, she replied. Guessing she'd typed it out before I'd had the chance to text back.

**Monday,** 3:06 PM

I'm kind of over Renee. It doesn't
hurt like it did, at least. Also, can
you keep a secret?

**Monday,** 3:07 PM

What?

**Monday,** 3:07 PM

It's seriously a secret. But I don't
know, I was thinking about Matt
after our talk at the dance . . .

**Monday,** 3:08 PM

Oh my God, you're
rebounding.

**Monday,** 3:08 PM

I am not!

Well, maybe.

But does it matter if I am? So
what? We're seventeen, it's not like
we're going to marry the people we
date right now. I'm just having fun.

Plus, he's hot.

**Monday,** 3:09 PM

I mean, yeah. He's totally
hot. Especially when he was

throwing down with that
Charlotte girl.

Monday, 3:09 PM

Hands off!! Do you think I should
go for it?

Monday, 3:09 PM

Will it make you happy?

Monday, 3:10 PM

I don't know, Ollie, I'm not a damn
psychic! But it might.

I couldn't help but laugh at this. What a way to go
through life. Trying out crazy things on the off chance
that they might make you happy. It totally went against my
personal philosophy of overanalyzing everything and only
taking risks when there was a 5 percent or less chance of
failure. But maybe Lara's take had merit. I messaged her
back while hopping out of the car.

Monday, 3:10 PM

Good enough for me. Hell
yeah you should go for it.
Have as much fun as you can
until it's not fun anymore. And
if that never happens, even
better.

Monday, 3:11 PM

Hah. I always have as much fun as I
can. What's the point otherwise?

I cracked a grin at her reply as I pushed open the front door with my hip, my backpack sliding down my shoulder. I jumped to correct it, steadied myself, and paused to find my parents sitting in the living room.

They both should've been at work.

I let my backpack slip all the way down my arm, and I dropped it on the floor by the door. I wanted to walk right back outside, climb into my car, and drive back in time. Because I knew with horrible certainty that I wasn't ready for whatever my parents were going to say next.

But I had to go into the room. I shuffled to the couch and sat down heavily.

Silence.

I spoke first, because my parents kept looking at each other to check who should break it to me. Like I needed anything broken to me. Like I still didn't know what was coming.

"When did it happen?" I asked.

Amazingly, they looked relieved. At least neither of them had to say it out loud, I guess.

"Around lunchtime," Dad said.

Oh. Lunchtime. She'd been dead for several hours. And I hadn't even noticed the cataclysmic shift. I would've thought I'd notice. Somehow.

"She had a pulmonary embolism. Really, we're lucky it happened like this," Mom said in a tight voice. "It, ah, it was fast. And, we, um, we were told her condition was going downhill. And that she would be in a lot of pain, soon. A *lot* of pain, Ollie. And she didn't want to be in pain like that. No one does. That's no way to spend the last few weeks you ever get. And she got to spend her last few weeks with us, walking around, eating, laughing."

I stared at the ground.

"A lot of people in her situation end up with a blocked intestine. All they can do in their last weeks is lie in bed and wet their lips. That's such a horrible way to go. We're so lucky Linda didn't have to go through that, sweetie."

Was she trying to comfort me? Because the tone of her voice was so pleading, it seemed more like she wanted me to tell her that yes, all of that was true, and this definitely wasn't the worst day any of us had ever lived through.

I tried to speak, but nothing came out. I cleared my throat and tried again. "Okay."

We sat in silence. I felt like we should be hugging each other, or sobbing or something, but I didn't feel like crying. I didn't feel anything except stunned. What were we supposed to do now? Seriously, what? Did we go around to Uncle Roy's and comfort him? He probably didn't want us there right now. Not just yet. So, what, did we talk about our favorite memories of Aunt Linda? Oh, God, no, *memories*, all we had were *memories* now. That didn't feel real yet, though. It was like it was happening to someone else.

Okay, so, then, what? Did we just . . . turn on the TV? Do the dishes? Take showers? Did I do my homework? None of it felt right.

I waited for my parents to direct the next steps.

But maybe they didn't know what to do now, either.

It was too hard to look at my parents' stricken faces, so I picked at a hangnail instead. Was it bad that I didn't feel sad? Did that mean there was something wrong with me?

Maybe I was like the main character from *Dexter*. Like, maybe I was immune to death and pain, and I could theoretically spend the rest of my life killing people who I thought objectively deserved to die, and I'd never be even a little damaged by any of it.

Mom stood up first. "I'm going to call Grandma and Grandpa again," she said.

By that, she meant Dad's parents. Her parents had passed away when I was little. They'd had Mom when they were super old, like, almost forty.

Which meant that out of her whole family, Mom was the only one left now.

Mom pulled down her blouse and left the room. She was still wearing her work outfit. Usually when you think of grieving people, they're in their pajamas, and maybe a dressing gown, and their faces are red and blotchy. Mom's face was blotchy, but outside of that, she could run a board meeting now and she wouldn't seem out of place.

Dad, too. Even more so, because it didn't look like he'd been crying, either. No red spots in sight.

"Is there anything nice you'd like for dinner?" he asked.

"Pardon?"

"We won't be cooking tonight, but you can pick. We'll get anything you want. Takeout," he added as an afterthought.

"Um . . ."

"Have a think about it." He got up, too, then. "Are you all right?"

No. Yes. No. ". . . Yeah."

"Great. I'm just going to sort some things out upstairs. Let me know if you need anything, all right?"

With that, he escaped, too.

Now it was just me, and the living room, and an enormous, deafening silence.

I should probably call someone, I guessed. My first thought was Ryan or Hayley, but I hadn't talked to them that much lately. It's not that we had a problem with each other, we'd just kind of drifted.

Lara and I didn't have that kind of friendship. Same with Niamh.

I could call Juliette, but she'd been so down lately, it didn't feel fair to load her up with all my problems. Besides, she'd probably overcompensate by being super perky, or taking me out for ice cream or something, and I didn't want perkiness, or ice cream. Or sympathy.

What did I want, then? It's not like I could call someone and they'd wave a wand so Aunt Linda wasn't dead anymore. And that's the only thing that could really help right now.

Mom trotted downstairs with a USB, and plugged it into the TV.

"What are you doing?" I asked.

She sat herself down next to me and grabbed the remote. "We're going to remember some of the good times."

That did *not* mean what I think it did, right? "Mom . . ."

"Because Aunt Linda would not want us to be here moping. We need to laugh. We need to remember how good things could be. All the lovely, lovely memories she's given us."

The TV flickered onto a home video of us all back in San Jose. I remembered this. Aunt Linda had come to visit when Crista was just a year old, long before Dylan was even born. They'd come during summer break, and stayed for about a week or so, and I'd had to sleep on the couch so they could have my room.

The video started in on Aunt Linda feeding baby Crista in a high chair. She looked so different. Well, Crista did, too, obviously, but I'd forgotten how thick Aunt Linda's hair used to be. Her skin was deeply tanned, and she had hardly any wrinkles. I guessed she would've been in her late twenties.

"Oh my God, Roy, not *now*," She laughed into the camera, shooing it away.

"Here we have the mother covered in what appears to be baby vomit *and* baby food," Uncle Roy's voice said in a terrible David Attenborough impression. "It's her way of blending into the scenery, which is, incidentally, *also* covered in baby vomit and baby food, in order to sneak up on her young."

"I'm telling you, it's the *broccoli*," Mom's voice said. The camera swung around to face her typing something on her laptop. Probably work emails. That was the year she'd been hired as the manager of some accounting firm, back when she'd still liked that kind of role. I remembered her working at all hours of the day—and weekends—just to keep up with it all. "Ollie used to regurgitate anything with broccoli in it. Didn't matter how well I blended it, soon as it hit his mouth, *bleurgh*."

Next to me, Present Mom burst out laughing. I glanced at her without cracking a smile.

"I'm not letting Crista grow up to be a picky eater," Aunt Linda said, raising her eyebrows and turning back to put another spoonful in Crista's mouth. Crista promptly spat it back in her face in a raspberry, and Roy lost it, laughing so hard the camera ended up pointed at his feet.

"Yeah, well, how'd that work out for you, Lin?" Mom asked the screen. "She gave up on that as soon as she had Dylan."

"Mom."

"I told her, you have your resolve while they're little, but eventually you realize it's *so* worth it to cut the crusts off if it saves a three-hour tantrum every lunch!"

"*Mom*."

"Yeah, honey?"

"Don't you think, um . . . it's a little soon to be watching videos?"

She looked confused, like there was no reason in the world I should think such a thing. "Well, when is it not too soon? What's the rule on that, Oliver?"

I didn't know, but I was pretty sure "three hours after the death" was universally too early to laugh fondly about things. "Sorry. I guess I mean, maybe I'm just not ready yet."

Mom nodded. "That's fine, sweetie. I'm going to watch some more, though. Because that's what I need right now. I just need to watch some . . . some movies, okay?" Her smile was dangerously watery. "What is it you need right now? Is there something I can do for you?"

I needed to not be able to hear Aunt Linda's voice like she was still fucking alive. I needed to not discuss dinner plans with Dad. I needed to do something, *anything*, other than force a smile and act like everything was fine. I needed to not be here.

"Would it be all right if I went to see some friends?"

Mom nodded vacantly. "Yeah, of course, sweetie. Just be home by nine, okay?"

She didn't even ask me where I was going. She was 50,000 percent not okay. Maybe I shouldn't be leaving. But then she pressed Play again, and Aunt Linda was tasting the baby food to prove it wasn't that bad, and I had to go, I *had* to. So I wrenched my keys off the accent table and ran to my car.

I didn't have a clue where I was driving to. I had nowhere to go. At first I drove aimlessly, zipping in and out of side streets, and then I found myself pulling over to find his address on Google maps.

It didn't make much sense for me to go to him. In a lot

of ways, even Lara or Niamh would've been more appropriate, because at least we were on speaking terms. But he'd met Aunt Linda, and knew just how sick she was, and had listened to me night after night in the summer whispering into the darkness how scared I was she might die.

I just had to see him.

Will's house was no less intimidating in the daytime than it'd been on Thanksgiving. I pulled up, stared at it, and swallowed, heart pounding. There was no sense turning back now, though. It wasn't exactly a small trip.

I just wasn't quite brave enough to go up to the door. So I called him.

"Are you at home right now?" I asked.

"Yeah?"

"I'm outside."

"You're . . . hold on."

He hung up on me. Then the front door swung open, and Will emerged from the house and started down the driveway. I got out of the car in a daze and stood by it, hugging myself until Will reached me.

I think he knew as soon as he saw my face. *"Ollie,"* he breathed, holding out his arms. I launched myself into them like this wasn't weird, and we hadn't spent the last few weeks pretending each other didn't exist. As soon as I felt his hands on my back I burst into sobs. "Oh, Ollie, no. I'm so sorry."

He led me, crying and coughing and shaking, straight through to his room without even bringing me past his parents to say hi. Mom and Dad would've disowned me if they'd known I'd been so rude, but at that moment I honestly couldn't have cared less. He left me there for a minute or two while he went down and explained to his parents, then he came back upstairs and sat with me in silence.

When I finally calmed down enough to speak, Will and I had been sitting on his bed for about fifteen minutes. He hadn't tried to push me into talking, at any point. He'd just sat, his shoulder pressing against mine, with his hands in his lap.

"I just don't know what to do," I said. "What do you *do* when this happens? My parents are acting like everything's fine, and they wanted to go get dinner, and Mom put on home *movies*—"

"Movies?"

"*Movies* of Aunt Linda! Isn't that the most fucked-up thing you've ever heard?"

Will clasped his hands together soberly. "That's pretty ridiculous."

"It just doesn't feel real, Will. Everything is really distant, and blurry, and it's like I'm dreaming but I don't think I am. Am I? I'm definitely not dreaming, right?"

"You're definitely not dreaming," he said. "I'm sorry."

"It's okay. It's fine. But also, it's not okay, because she's *dead*, and that's real. That's real life. It's real life from now on, too. For every day, from now until forever, she's still going to be dead when I wake up every morning. How do I do this? I don't know what to do."

I was crying again now, and Will put his arm around me to pull me into him. Not in a romantic way, just comforting. The way I'd really wanted my parents to comfort me.

"What do I *do*?" I asked again. Like Will somehow had a magical solution to all of this.

"Whatever you need to," he said quietly.

I rested my head on his shoulder. I hadn't realized how

heavy it felt until then. My jaw was aching, too. From crying? Had I been gritting my teeth? I used to do that a lot when I was younger, until I'd chipped a tooth and the dentist made me sleep with a mouth guard. "It was just out of nowhere, you know? I mean, it wasn't *totally* unexpected, but I thought we'd have more warning. I thought she'd start looking really, really sick, and we'd know it was coming. I can't even remember the last conversation we had. I think it was about spoiled milk."

I sobbed all the way through the last sentence, so hard I could barely stammer the words out.

"It's not fair," Will said.

*"No,* it's *not* fair."

"No."

And in the weirdest way, even though I felt like I was being buried alive by grief, it was the tiniest bit more bearable now. Just having Will back me up, and agree with me, and not try to make me look at the bright side, or remember the nice times, made me feel less like I was alone in this. Even though Will barely knew Aunt Linda, I felt like he was right there with me in the darkness. Waiting with me for as long as I needed to be there.

Eventually, I wiped my eyes with the back of my hand and sat up. "I'm sorry. I just came over here out of nowhere, and you probably have a ton of homework, and you haven't even had dinner—"

"It's—"

"I should've at least texted, or—"

*"Ollie."* He grabbed my hand, and I looked down at it, startled. "It's fine. I'm glad you came. You can stay as long as you want."

I nodded, and gently took my hand away. "Thank you. I should get home, though."

He walked me through to the living room, where his parents were watching *Inception*. They'd reached the scene where everyone was banging around upside down in the corridor, but they paused it when they noticed us.

"Hi, Ollie," Mrs. Tavares said. "Will told me about your aunt. I'm so sorry to hear. Please let us know if there's anything we can do."

Mr. Tavares nodded and gave me a tight smile. "It's good to see you again, Ollie. I thought after Thanksgiving we might start seeing your face around here more often."

I had a sudden flashback to Mr. Tavares practically walking in on Will and me. I forced a fake laugh.

"Oh, and Will," he said mildly. "I know tonight was a bit of a special situation, but please remember our rule about not closing bedroom doors."

Will blinked at his dad like he'd spontaneously combusted or something. Swallowing, he gave a stiff nod, and walked me to my car.

The whole way, he stared into the distance without a word.

"You okay?" I asked.

"We don't have a rule about not closing bedroom doors for friends. Only for girls. Me and the guys hang out with the door closed all the time."

Oh. Uh-oh. "I'm sorry . . ."

He shook his head. "Don't be. It's not your fault. I'll just . . . see if he brings it up again."

His words were reassuring, but his face said otherwise. Will did not want to go back inside that house.

I hesitated at the car. Part of me wanted to hang around to make sure Will wasn't having an internal breakdown, but if we stayed out here for too long wouldn't that look even more suspicious? What if his dad felt the urge to come out here and tell us to wrap it up? "Okay. Well could you please text me in a bit, then? To let me know if he does bring it up again or not?"

Will nodded. "Sure. And you text me later to let me know you're okay, all right?"

Oh. Of course. For the briefest moment I'd forgotten about Aunt Linda. Then it came flooding back, fresh as if I'd only just found out. But I was not going to cry. Not now. It could wait approximately eight seconds. "Yeah. All right."

All right.

# 20

Home felt like a graveyard.

I was given the rest of the week off from school, which was a relief because I had developed a startling habit of crying without warning. Sure, I cried about Aunt Linda, but then I also cried at a dog adoption advertisement on TV, sobbed because I realized I'd be missing a math quiz on Thursday when I *hated* math, and bawled for about twenty minutes drinking orange juice one morning because it made me think of how Saint Nick used to give oranges to poor children and how some people never get oranges while I'd taken them for granted my whole life.

I wasn't the only one crying, either. It's what Mom did most of the day now. She'd gotten over that initial, way-too-optimistic reaction quite quickly. I didn't *like* seeing my mom cry, but it was less unsettling than her unnaturally loud laughter on that first day. Dad was less of a crier, but he didn't smile once. We were somber through the funeral preparations, and through the funeral itself on

Friday, and while we went through the motions of living, trying to figure out what that looked like now.

For my parents, at least, living looked like doing everything they could to help Uncle Roy and the kids. Which, that Sunday, meant cooking up an army's worth of soup, lasagna, and casseroles for them to freeze and reheat as needed.

"Ollie, can you fill the rest of these Tupperware containers?" Mom asked. She was covered in splatters of tomato sauce, had a splodge of gooey cheese in her eyebrow, and one of her sleeves was rolled up haphazardly. Her eyes were puffy from crying on and off half the morning, and her hair hadn't been washed in a few days now, so she wore it scraped in a messy bun.

"Yeah, of course." I took over for her and started scooping casserole into various-sized containers. "How about you go take a minute upstairs before we bring this all around?"

She hesitated, and Dad walked into the kitchen and made shooing motions with his hands. "You have your orders. We'll cover things in here."

Silently, she nodded and disappeared, leaving Dad and me alone in the kitchen.

He started to load the dishwasher. "Thanks for being such a champ with helping out your mother and me."

"No problem."

"Really, you've been a champ all year."

I paused and looked over my shoulder. He was bent over the dishwasher, hiding his face, but his voice had sounded unusually tight.

I clipped the lid onto another container and added it to the cooler we'd been stacking all the food into. "Well, when someone you love needs you, you step up, right?"

When Dad finally turned back around, his eyes were glossy. "Right. Yeah. That's right."

At Aunt Linda's—well, I guess I shouldn't call it that anymore . . . it was Uncle Roy's now, right?—the kids were set up in the living room in front of *Coco*. I didn't know if Uncle Roy realized it was a movie about deceased family members in the afterlife, but I didn't want to trigger anything by bringing it up. Who knows, maybe he thought it'd be helpful for the kids to watch it to process the last week.

Uncle Roy thanked my parents over and over again for the food. It turned out every family in the whole town had had the same idea, though, because his freezer was already so overflowing there was no way to cram any more food in. In the end, they decided to fill the cooler with ice, and set it up in the corner of the kitchen as a second refrigerator.

All three adults seemed to be actors in an improv play. Not very convincing ones, either. They smiled like they'd learned how to from written, step-by-step instructions. They talked about anything, *anything* but Aunt Linda, but she was in everything they said anyway. *I've been having trouble sleeping.* Because he'd been crying. *The kids go back to school and preschool on Monday.* Because they, too, had taken the week off to mourn, and were now expected to somehow return to life like there wasn't an enormous gaping hole in the middle of it. *Ah, no, I didn't get around to watching the series finale.* Because he used to watch the show with Aunt Linda—she'd told me—and I guess he didn't know how to watch it knowing she'd never find out how it ended.

Ever.

I slumped down on the couch with the kids. *Coco* had been such a big movie last year. What would be the next Pixar hit? Whatever it was, Aunt Linda would never get to know it. Even if it was bigger than *Frozen*, she'd never know it existed.

Any song that came out from this week onward, Aunt Linda would never hear. Not once.

Everything she was ever going to know about had already happened. Britney Spears could be voted the new president of the United States, and Aunt Linda would never know. The government might finally admit they have aliens in a warehouse, and Aunt Linda would never know. The world would keep moving, and tragedies would happen, and beautiful things would happen, and we'd invent things and grow and Aunt Linda would never see any of it.

And . . . God, I was so selfish and self-absorbed, but while I was completely devastated about Aunt Linda, I was also scared for myself. I mean, I knew about death, obviously, but it had always been in the abstract. Now it felt startlingly real. Real people I knew would die. All of us. Every real person I knew would die.

And I would die, too.

One day, I would see the last thing I was ever going to see. And the next day, someone would release a song I'd never hear. Statistically, the most amazing events that would ever happen in the world would probably happen sometime in the far future, and I'd never get to know about it. So many beautiful, wonderful things would happen one day, in a world that didn't have me in it. And I didn't want the world to keep going if I wasn't in it. I mean, obviously I *did*, it's not like I wanted to take everyone else down with me. But the idea of just being here, and then not being here, and the world not really caring that I was gone was so . . . it just . . . it made me feel hollow.

Will would laugh at me and call me goth if he saw me, because I was probably filling all those existential stereotypes right now, but seriously, what was the point? What was the *point*? Of any of this? If we were all going to just vanish at a moment's notice, why bother even trying while we were alive? It's not like we'd be able to remember any of it once we were dead.

I kicked off my shoes, brought my knees up to my chest, and tuned back in to the movie.

A part of me expected the kids to ask me questions about the afterlife, like if that's where their mom was, and if she was a skeleton now, or something. But they didn't. They were weirdly quiet. Like, weirdly quiet. Crista, who never took a break, just stared at the TV. Or, really, she stared *through* the TV with glazed-over eyes, snuggled into her bright pink beanbag.

Dylan, sitting in a beanbag covered in pictures of *Thomas the Tank Engine*, was clutching a bottle without drinking out of it. I sat up, confused. Since when did he ditch glasses and mugs? "Hey, Dyl. I haven't seen that bottle in a while."

"It's *my* bottle."

"Yeah, I remember it."

"*My bottle.*"

"Yeah, I know."

"You can't have it."

"That's fine. I don't want it."

"*You can't have it. It's my bottle.* IT'S MY BOTTLE, I WANT IT, IT'S NOT YOURS!" he screeched, curling up into a ball on his beanbag. Crista barely glanced at him. "IT'S MY BOTTLE! MY BOTTLE, MY BOTTLE!"

Oh shit. "Dylan, yeah, it's your bottle. I'm no—"

"DON'T TAKE IT!"

"I'm *not*!"

"IT'S NOT YOUR BOTTLE, OLLIE! NOT, IT'S NOT, IT'S NO—" He broke off and started full-blown wailing, screaming the room down and summoning a demon from the pits of Hades's lair.

I hopped to the floor and went over to try to calm him down. "Hey, hey, Dyl, it's okay."

He swiped at me with the bottle. "NO! NO!"

"I'm not—"

He threw the bottle at me, and it hit me square in the forehead. Nearly knocked me the hell out, too. *"Dylan!"*

In response, he roared at me, his little face purple with rage. I held the bottle out to him and he knocked it out of my hand and started kicking in the air, screaming as loudly as he could.

Crista kept watching the movie like this wasn't even happening.

I stood up, helpless, and Uncle Roy came into the room. I was about to explain, but he didn't look surprised at all. "Hey, kiddo," he said, picking up a still-kicking-and-screaming Dylan. "It's time for your nap."

"NONONONON—"

"Yes. Say good night to Ollie and Crista."

"—ONONONONONO—"

"Good night, Ollie. Good night Crista."

Dylan's screams faded as he was carried unceremoniously out of the room.

"Good," Crista said without looking up. "He was hurting my ears."

I sat back down on the couch, my own ears ringing. "Sounds like he's missing your mom."

"Yeah."

"How are you doing? Are you feeling okay?"

She looked up now. It was clear from her face that she was irritated with me. She cocked her head. "Ollie, I can't hear the movie."

"Oh. Sorry."

So we watched it in silence. We were both handling it pretty well, until the part where the kid sings the gut-wrenching song to his abuela about remembering people who have passed. Then I lost it.

At least I had the good sense to excuse myself from the room, though, so, specifically, I lost it in the hallway. I pressed my back against the wall and sank to the floor, crying as quietly as I could. I didn't want to be here in this house knowing Aunt Linda would never be in it again. It was *her* house. We came here when we visited *her*. It'd been *her* house my whole life. This wasn't right. None of it was right.

Someone sat down beside me. Mom. I hadn't even heard her come in.

"Hi, my gorgeous man," she said. "Not doing so well?"

I sniffed and shrugged without meeting her eye.

"It's hard being here, huh?" she asked. I nodded, and my chin started shaking as I tried to hold the sobs in. "It'll get easier. That's the beautiful thing about the universe. It puts you through trials, but it never gives you anything you can't handle. We grow from these things."

I let my head hit the wall and rolled it around so I could meet her eyes. "Mom. This didn't happen to teach us all a lesson and help us to grow."

She darkened. "Ollie, that's not what I meant and you know it."

"This isn't beautiful. It's ugly, and pointless. That's the

thing, Mom. There *was* no point. She's dead, and there's nothing fair about it. She had one life, and it's done, and that's it for her, and that's it for us. It didn't make anything *better* that she died. How can you still believe there's meaning to all of this? What, what you think something out there in the universe looked down from the clouds and found our family and said, 'Hmm, you know what? Fuck this family in particular.' Crista and Dylan don't get a mom anymore, and Uncle Roy lost the person he loves, and she doesn't get to ever be old, and there is *no. Reason. For. It.* It was just a waste. The end. Sorry if I'm not happy about it."

She stared at me, and something in my stomach tumbled. "You think I'm *happy* about this?" she asked in disbelief. "She was my sister. She was my baby sister."

All my steam ran out at once, and I wilted against the wall. "Mom . . ."

She went to speak, then she shook her head, got to her feet with a frustrated grunt, and walked away from me.

I made it through the first day back at school okay. Or, at least, I made it through the morning. No breakdowns, no freak-outs, no terrified contemplations of my own mortality.

The girls were appropriately gentle with me when I came back. Even Lara didn't have any sassy digs. Just lots of questions about how I'd been, and a fair bit of concern. I'd been ignoring the majority of their texts all week. Ditto for the one condolence text each sent by Hayley and Ryan. Conversation just seemed to take up so much energy. Energy I didn't have.

At lunch I went to the music room instead of the cafeteria. Juliette had seemed disappointed when I rushed past her to grab a slice of pizza to go, but what could you do? Even though I'd made it through, the effort of being *okay* and *engaged* all morning had been more exhausting than I'd realized. I'd thought I was okay to come back to school, but that didn't mean I could dive straight back in with no adjustments. A little alone time wouldn't be amiss.

When I grabbed the bass guitar, though, I realized I didn't feel like playing. I just wanted silence. So instead, I flopped onto the floor with my back against the wall, pulled the bass guitar into my lap, and drummed my fingers on the body.

It was nice to be somewhere quiet. I loved the girls, but I just wasn't close enough with them to be sad. Sure, I could be a downer for a day or two, but what if it took longer than a day or two? What if I was down for weeks, or months? What if I was never chirpy again? What if I needed to glare, and snap, and be lost in my thoughts? What if I just needed to cry?

Alone in here, I could be any of that. I could feel every negative, terrible, aching feeling at once, and I didn't have to be self-conscious about it or try to put on a mask so someone else didn't feel dragged down.

But now that I had the freedom to cry, I couldn't make myself.

Someone had put a new poster on the wall to join the other inspirational quotes. MUSIC COURSES THROUGH OUR VEINS, FROM THE SMALLEST ANT TO THE LARGEST WHALE, it proclaimed in enormous, scarlet comic sans font. In the background was what I assumed to be a Photoshopped image of an ant about to be stepped on by an elephant's foot. Either the dimensions were all off, though, or it was some kind of mutant superhero ant, because it was almost the size of one of the elephant's toenails.

Literally, what the hell did that quote even mean, though? And why was it paired with an image of an ant about to die?

Guess the music that flowed through its veins was a funeral march.

I almost laughed at my astonishing wit, but then I started thinking about the music at Aunt Linda's funeral, and the laugh slipped away.

There was movement at the side of the room, and I looked over to find Will entering. I hadn't seen him much since the night I'd driven to his house. He gave me an unsure smile. "Hey. Can I come sit with you?"

I patted the floor next to me. "Come in."

He lowered himself to the ground and crossed his legs like a kindergartener. "How are you doing?"

He meant well, but holy *hell* did I not want to talk about it. I'd spent so much time speaking about the death, and how terrible I felt, and how pointless all this bullshit was. At home I felt like I couldn't talk about much else. But I had nothing new to say. Repeating myself wasn't helping anymore. For once, just for once, I wanted to talk about something meaningless.

"Hey Will?" I said instead. "Do you think ants have hearts?"

He studied me for a long time. "I . . . haven't ever thought about it."

"Well, it's just the poster there talks about ant veins, and veins usually bring blood to hearts, right?"

He looked where I pointed. "That is a really depressing picture."

"*Right?* Oh my God, it's not just me. I think it's the most unmotivating motivational poster I've ever seen."

"You could say it's an uninspirational poster. Also, why

ants? If we're going from smallest to largest, you can go way smaller than ants. What about ticks? Or bacteria?"

"Bacteria don't have veins, I guess."

"Honestly, Ollie, I don't think ants do, either. I really don't."

I couldn't help but start to smile at that. "Oh no, I think you're right."

"*Do they?* Now I don't even know. Hold on, I'm googling this shit."

I giggled and put my guitar on the ground next to me, then leaned over to look at Will's phone. He opened an article and scrolled down the page. "And it's a no," he said. "No veins. No blood."

"Hey, no, they have blood."

"Yeah, colorless weird fluid. Not the same thing."

"You can't go around erasing insect blood because it isn't the same as yours."

"Watch me."

I tipped my head to one side and fiddled with my necklace, a grin still lingering on my lips. Even though I felt a little guilty for laughing, it felt good. So, so good. "Did you come here to check on me?"

"Eh, yes and no. I figured you probably wanted some space, so I wouldn't have usually come by, but I actually wanted your advice on something."

Interesting. "Yeah?"

"So, Lara's always seemed at least a little into Matt. But then apparently she was into Renee. So I'm wondering what's going on there?"

I mean, it wasn't exactly what I'd expected. I stuck out my bottom lip and thought about the best response. Lara had told me she liked Matt in confidence, so I didn't want to give that up. But maybe I could still play Cupid.

Before I could speak, though, Will groaned. "God, I'm such an idiot. Sorry, you must think I'm being ridiculous right now. You have bigger shit going on than who Lara likes."

Well, kind of. But it was such a nice distraction from all the bigger shit. "No, seriously, it's fine. She was into Renee, but I'm pretty sure that's all over. Why do you ask?"

"Because Matt thinks she's a lesbian."

*Oh.* "Nope. She's bi."

"Right, I thought she might be," Will said. "Matt's had a thing for Lara for ages now, but I think he thinks there's no point anymore."

"Oh, I'd say there's plenty point."

Will bumped my shoulder. "How would you feel about explaining that to Matt?"

"Me? What, now?"

"Yeah? He'd believe it coming from you. I don't think they see me as the resident expert on identities, you know?"

On the one hand, I'd been enjoying myself in here. And even more so with Will for company. I'd take sitting in here talking absolute nonsense with him over heading back out to the crowded, noisy cafeteria. Or, at least, I usually would. But a not-so-small part of me really wanted to help Lara out. Because maybe I kind of really liked her now, and maybe I kind of really wanted her to know I'd done something for her.

"All right," I said, hopping up and holding out a hand. "Let's do it quick, though. The bell's about to go off."

Will took my hand and let me pull him to his feet.

The basketball guys were sitting at their own table today. Without the girls to break them up, it was basically a sea of black-and-white jackets. Suddenly joined by me in my new salmon sweater and tan skinny jeans, here to break up the monochrome. I'd chosen the sweater that morning because it felt like it'd cheer me up to wear something other than black and khaki this week. Did it work? Not . . . really. No.

"Hey, what's up, Ollie?" Matt asked. He was giving me an expectant look, though. I guessed Will had told him why he went off to find me. Well, no point beating around the bush. Besides, if I told him what was really up with me, it'd probably make the whole vibe uncomfortable and depressing. So.

"Do you like Lara?" I asked.

A few of the guys snickered and tittered, but Darnell shot them a warning look and they shut right up. Matt shrugged and leaned back in his seat. "Yeah, but it's whatever. She's into girls, so, that's cool, you know?"

"She's into guys, too."

He gave me a quizzical look. "I thought she was a lesbian now, though?"

"She's bisexual. If she's with a girl that doesn't make her a lesbian. She's still bi no matter who she's dating."

Matt nodded slowly, and the tiniest, most secret smile crossed his lips. "So, are you saying she might be into me?"

"I'm saying I think checking in with her is probably a good idea. She might be a little pissed that you've been giving her the cold shoulder, though, just a heads up."

Darnell and Matt shared a quick smile. "You're in, man," Darnell said, holding up a fist for Matt to bump while the other guys laughed and made catcall noises.

Will watched them with an intense look, his brow furrowed and his lips pressed together in a thin line. I couldn't read his expression.

"Oh, also?" I said, this time looking right at Darnell. "You need to stop with the back-and-forth stuff. It's not cool. Either you want to be with Niamh, or you don't, but don't pretend you're just coming over to the table because you had a question about homework."

Darnell opened his mouth but didn't manage to spit anything out. Will used his hand like a megaphone around his mouth. "Called *out*."

As for me, I was impressed with myself. When did I get so brave?

I guessed the last couple of weeks had changed me. Suddenly, it didn't seem so terrifying to look stupid in front of a group of guys who, for the most part, didn't mean much to me. Other than Will, anyway, and I knew he wouldn't judge me for it. There were worse things that could happen than being a little embarrassed.

And life was too short to play chicken with something as important as the person you loved.

# 21

"You leave in an hour," I said.

Will, who had his head resting against my bare chest, tilted his head up to look at me. "Hmm."

"One hour, Will."

He made a face and traced a finger along my stomach. Our skin was dry now. If you didn't know it, you wouldn't have been able to tell we'd been in the lake thirty minutes earlier.

"Will you walk me back to mine?" he asked.

"You want me to sneak out of my own house at four in the morning, walk you around the other end of the lake, then sneak back into my house?"

". . . Yes?"

"Of course I will. Don't know why you felt you had to ask."

It took us longer than it probably should've to get dressed—mostly because Will kept rudely interrupting the process to kiss my legs, and stomach, and arms one last time before I covered them back up—but eventually we managed to get ourselves looking kind of presentable. We slipped outside fairly easily, *thanks to my silent front door, and then started walking. My legs felt like they belonged to a turtle. Everything weighed so much more than it should've.*

*It had gone too fast. All of this had gone too fast.*

*"Do you have to go?" I asked.*

*"Do you?" he shot back.*

*"Please visit."*

*He grabbed onto my wrist and stopped me from going any farther. "Seriously, we need to make a promise now, okay? One of us will make sure we visit the other as soon as we can."*

*"Okay."*

*"We can't just say it, though, we have to do it. I don't want this to be over. Maybe it doesn't have to be, right?"*

*I shrugged. I just didn't know the answer to that.*

*"We need to stay in touch. We need to keep talking, and we'll figure something out. Maybe I can get down there for spring break or something. Or maybe you'll come back to visit your aunt, and we can organize to meet up somewhere."*

*I had a horrible feeling I was about to cry. All I could do was give a short nod.*

*Will cupped my face with one of his hands and stared at me with serious brown eyes. "Please don't lose contact, okay? I need to see you again."*

"Did you know your heartbeat changes rhythm when you listen to faster or slower music?" Will asked.

"Nope. That's pretty cool, though."

"Yeah. And the cornea is the only body part that doesn't get oxygen from blood. It just sucks it in, right from the air."

He was sitting crossed-legged on a spare chair in the music room, flicking through the biology textbook he balanced in his lap. That day, his excuse to hang with me in the music room was an upcoming test. I'd thought the book was a prop, but, to my surprise, he actually sat down and started reading it when I picked up my bass. I wasn't sure if it was because he really wanted to ace the test, or if he just found it really boring to listen to the same bass line repeated over and over again. I wouldn't blame him if it was the latter, but then I had to wonder—why did he always come to visit me here at lunch when I spent three-quarters of it ignoring him to practice music?

"And blood flows through your veins *so fast*, it only takes twenty seconds for a blood cell to do a whole lap," he went on. "That's funny. I always pictured blood as cruising along at, like, a walking pace."

"It spurts out pretty fast if you cut yourself badly," I said.

"Yeah, but not, like, a-hundred-miles-an-hour fast," he said. "Think about how small a blood cell is compared to your whole body. And it only takes *twenty seconds*. That would be like us doing ten laps of a football field in twenty seconds."

"I guess. But it's all relative, right?"

He blinked into the distance. "I don't even know anymore. My brain hurts."

I riffled through the folder of sheet music I'd been compiling for Absolution's upcoming gig and selected a song I wasn't having much trouble with, but that was a little more impressive sounding than the last couple I'd practiced. So maybe I wanted to show off a little with Will in the room. Was that such a crime? It had to be a misdemeanor at most. "So, are you actually studying?" I asked.

"*Yes*. Sort of. This textbook has little bubbles in the corner of the pages with fun facts about the human body. I've been making my way through those."

"Let's hope they're examinable," I said. I banged the sheet music against the stand to knock the papers into place, before lining them up to start rehearsing.

"Hey, Ollie?" Will said just as I picked up my bass. "I've been thinking."

Well, the bass went right back down at that. "Hmm?"

He took so long to answer, I was gearing up to prod him into speaking when he finally spat it out. "I was angry at you for a while because I thought you should understand that I had to act in certain ways because I'm not out. So, when you didn't take my side, I thought it meant you didn't have my back."

To say I was surprised to hear that was an understatement. It hadn't even occurred to me that Will could have seen it that way.

"But," he went on, "I thought about how I'd feel if you acted like you didn't know me, or danced with someone else or whatever. And then I got it."

"Got what?"

I mean, I knew what, from the tone of his voice, but I wanted to hear him say it.

"That I was being a fucking asshole to you."

We sat in silence. I didn't want to say it was okay, because I didn't know if it *was* totally okay. Not yet. But it was nice to hear him acknowledge that. And also, I had a bit of thinking to do. I'd been upset because I wanted him to care about me more. But if he'd interpreted my behavior as *me* not caring enough, even if I didn't agree with what he did, still, maybe that was a little more forgivable. At least, it was better than him just totally disregarding my feelings.

Will broke the silence in a small voice. "Do you wanna come over after school sometime? As friends," he added quickly.

I couldn't stop the surprise from flashing across my face. After that reaction from his dad the last time, I'd assumed visits were blacklisted now. Anything that seemed to make people suspicious had to be off-limits with Will. I'd been working hard on accepting that, and not getting too close or assuming it'd change, and here he was pulling the rug out from under me. Why did he always manage to catch me off guard, no matter what I expected from him? "What about your parents?"

"We can keep the door open."

I hesitated. "It seems like your dad might suspect something, though."

"I know. But I miss hanging out with you, and I'd like to see you more."

I thought about it. "How about you come over to mine sometime? I'm only five minutes away from school."

Will gave me a huge smile that warmed my stomach. "Okay."

I made as if to start playing, but he spoke again. He was lucky he was cute, or I'd have to kick him out for distracting me when I had a deadline. "Hey, also, uh, are you busy Friday? We're playing the regionals round."

Right, because *that's* how I wanted to spend a Friday night—watching guys throw balls at each other's heads and congratulating each other on their excellence and athletic prowess when they managed to throw the ball in *just* the right way. Thrilling. "I can't, sorry. I have this gig with Absolution on Friday."

His face fell so suddenly I kind of felt guilty. I hadn't realized he actually cared about having me there. But I wasn't lying—I *did* have a gig. And it wasn't exactly optional attendance. Anyone who didn't think bass was important hadn't tried listening to a punk song without it. Picture a chocolate sundae without any sauce, or a movie without any extras in the background. It'd work, technically, but the overall experience would lack a certain oomph.

"Oh. That's fine. I hope it goes well."

"I'd like it if you could come to the show, though. Maybe after the game?"

He could've thrown a tantrum about me missing the basketball game. Told me he was too busy with his own life to come to something that was important to me, just like I was too busy to go to his. But, like he always did, Will nodded immediately and said, "Of course."

Then he went back to studying.

"How come you're not in the library?" I asked suddenly.

"What?"

"It'd be easier to study in there, wouldn't it? Quieter?"

He hesitated. "Is this you hinting you want me to go?"

"No, I swear. I'm honestly just curious."

"Oh. I don't know, I just like spending time with you."

"But why do we always do what I want to do? You could ask me to go to the library with you, you know."

Will gave me a funny, questioning smile. "I don't mind?"

But that was the thing. He didn't mind. He never minded.

Over the summer, Will had eagerly sat with me while I introduced him to all the bands I liked, without giving the bands he listened to the time of day. He'd taken up Music Appreciation, a subject he was never going to naturally excel in, because he wanted to see me without the judging eyes of his friends. When I'd escaped from the cafeteria to practice, Will followed me there, happy to sit by while I did my thing, even though there were probably a dozen ways he'd rather be spending his lunch.

And for the first time, it occurred to me that I'd asked

for plenty of things from Will this year. Some things he'd given, some things he wasn't ready to.

Then I heard Aunt Linda's voice somewhere in the back of my mind. *You only have control over your own actions. But what have you done to meet him halfway?*

Nothing.

I'd never even gone to one of his basketball games.

And he'd never guilted me about it. Not even once.

Now that I thought about it, I hadn't gone out of my way to do something just for him that didn't benefit me in any way. I'd been so focused on what I wanted from Will that I'd never really stopped to think about what he might want from me.

What did that say about me?

Juliette had set up a vision board.

I reminded myself to introduce her to my mom some-time, while she stood in front of the board in jeans and socks. Niamh, Lara, and I sat in a row on her bed, a well-behaved, captive audience. The girls were about to get ready to head to the basketball game. And I was, to be honest, not sure what I was doing. I'd already dressed and prepared for the gig, but sound check didn't kick off until later that night. I'd been planning to hang out with the girls until they left for the game, at which point I might grab some dinner and go hang at home alone for an hour or so.

But, before that, it was vision board time.

"So, here's a little kid with a clarinet," Juliette explained, indicating one of the printouts she'd pinned to a poster board. "That represents my plan to get an after-school job teaching clarinet. I could use the money next year, and it should strengthen my application, and make sure I'm forced to keep practicing."

The three of us nodded agreeably.

"The picture of the A-plus paper represents the fact that I am going to *nail* my subjects next year. I want the strongest GPA I can swing if I'm going to get into the Conservatory."

More nodding.

"And, of course, we have the Conservatory itself over here. I'm gonna spend all year studying, and practicing, and *perfecting* myself before the next round of auditions. I'm not gonna be going to any *frat parties*. I will be committed."

"No frat parties?" Lara asked skeptically.

"Okay, *some* frat parties. But mostly, next year's version of Juliette is a girl on a mission. I am good enough to get in—"

"Yes," I said firmly.

"And I am not going to let myself be locked out of where I wanna be, and where I deserve to be. I don't have connections, and I don't have parents who can make donations to the school right before application day, but I do have talent. I am going to be so perfect, they won't have *any* excuse to turn me down next year."

"*Yes*, Juliette!" Niamh said.

"Just because I didn't get in on my first shot does *not* mean I have to give up my dream. It only means I have to work that much harder than some people to get there."

"If anyone can do it, it's you," I said, and Juliette skipped forward to bowl me onto her bed in a bear hug.

"Can I borrow your eyeshadow?" Niamh asked Juliette, getting to her feet and wandering over to the desk. "We'll need to go soon."

"Why do you want eyeshadow for a basketball game?" Lara asked.

"It's a big game for Darnell. He's been walking on air all week."

"Wait, so you two have been talking again?" Juliette asked. She bent in front of the desk to pull out a few palettes, crusty with dried makeup powder, and handed them to Niamh along with an eyeshadow brush.

"Yeah, we have. I think he needed some time to process the New York thing, but he called me a little while back and apologized."

Huh. So he had listened. That, or the guys had shamed him into it after I left the table that day. Either way, I was basically Jerry Springer now.

"Anyway," Niamh went on. "It's a big deal for him, all right? This is the first time they've ever gotten into the regionals round."

Something pricked at me. Something that felt an awful lot like guilt. "I didn't realize it was such a big thing," I said.

"Huge," said Niamh as she held a compact mirror up to work a purply-taupe color onto her lids.

I looked down at my hands. So that's why Will had seemed so gutted when I'd turned him down. Now that I thought about it, the way he'd asked me to go along was way too casual. The kind of casual that only comes out when the speaker wants to sound like something that's really important to them doesn't matter at all.

It turned out I could be pretty oblivious when it came to the person I apparently loved.

How many times had I said to Will that I just wanted him to do something because he cared about me, not because I asked him to?

So why hadn't I done this for him because I cared about him?

I should be there tonight.

"You know, sound check doesn't start until a bit later," I said. "I wouldn't be able to stay for the whole game or anything, but maybe I could come for the first quarter or two."

Juliette squealed and abandoned zipping up her knee-high boots. "Yes, Ollie-oop! Come with us, it'll be so much fun."

Even if it wasn't fun, which I seriously doubted it would be, Will wanted me there.

And it wasn't always about me.

Admittedly, the vibe at the game was pretty exciting, even for someone who didn't care about sports. Most people in the crowd either wore or held something with their school colors, and banners and streamers waved around wherever you looked. On our side of the stadium, the Collinswood High cheerleading team was putting on a much more impressive—if less adorable—show than I'd been treated to on Thanksgiving, complete with flips, lifts, and twirling.

On the court, both teams were already out doing warm-ups, the squeaking of their sneakers on the waxed floor echoing throughout the stadium. I spotted Will right away among the sea of black and white, the number four splashed in bold white lettering on the black of his jersey. His wavy dark hair was already plastered to his red forehead with sweat, and the rest of his light brown skin seemed to glow under the bright lights. He was completely focused on his teammates as they did some sort of group drill that involved dribbling and passing six balls around the team at once. There was some sort of pattern, I'm sure, but to me it just looked like balls flying everywhere, and I kept expecting someone to take a ball to the head. But no one did. They were coordinated and calm.

Especially Will. But that was probably my bias showing. The game itself started not long after we got there. It was hard for me to follow the rules of who was supposed to go where, and what kind of moves were allowed, but at least I had the gist of things. And the gist was, this was probably going to be a close game. Fifteen minutes in, and so far the pattern had been home score, away score, home score, away score. The boys from Frankston High—the team in green and white—played well, but so did we. Some of the sheer bodily feats, the dodging, sprinting, blocking, and leaping, were kind of blowing my mind. It was one thing to watch it on TV, but it was another to see it happen in person. Here, you could really tell just how high someone soared off the ground, and hear the thud of colliding shoulders if two guys got in each other's way.

And *Will*. He was amazing. Totally focused on the game at all times, he threw himself into things, not a single cheeky smile in sight. If any of the Frankston guys were unlucky enough to come up against Will defending him, it was almost guaranteed they'd lose the shot. He didn't jump to intercept balls so much as fly.

In fact, by halftime I was almost sorry I'd have to leave soon. Watching him out there gave me a rush of pride that I hadn't quite expected. But if I was going to make it to sound check, I couldn't hang around for more than another fifteen minutes or so.

It was during halftime, though, that Will spotted me in the stands for the first time. He'd tipped back his head to take a swig from his water bottle, right after leaving some sort of strategy talk led by the coach and Matt, when his eyes locked onto mine. His blue plastic bottle went right back down to his side, and his lips spread into a slow smile. I tucked my hands between my knees and rocked to the side a bit, to say, *"Yes,* you got me here, happy?"

From the looks of things, he sure was.

I hung around for the beginning of the second half, and then turned to Juliette. "I'm gonna have to head off—" I started, when her back snapped straight and she let out a gasp, pressing her hand over her mouth.

I whipped around to see Matt rolling along the floor near the farthest hoop. When he stopped rolling, his body was totally motionless.

"Oh my God," Lara said, half-standing in her seat.

The coach, the referee, and a teacher ran onto the court to crouch by Matt's side. Will sprinted over at the same time, trying to look through their shoulders to check on his friend, with Darnell coming up behind him. Someone in the crowd screamed over a wave of urgent murmuring.

Then, thankfully, Matt kicked out a little, and the adults rolled him over. The crowd clapped and whistled with relief, including the sea of green and white on the Frankston side of the stands. Matt was conscious again, but dazed, and they slowly lifted him under his arms to a sitting position. They seemed to do a quick examination to see if anything was hurt, then painstakingly helped him to his feet and walked him off to the sidelines. The coach sent one of the guys on the bench on the court in his place. Lara jumped to her feet and hurried down the steps to meet Matt.

"What happens now?" I asked the remaining girls. "Do we finish the game?"

On the court, Will hooked his hands behind his neck and watched after his friend, looking distressed. The coach went over to him and said something, and Will nodded, wiping his forehead with the back of his arm. "All right, guys, huddle up!" Will shouted, and the rest of the team fell into a semicircle.

"Yup," Juliette said. "Will's vice-captain. We can play on. Matt seems okay, at least."

"They should've put him on a stretcher or something," Niamh said, shaking her head at the referee and the teacher, who were still chatting with Matt on the bench while Lara hovered nearby him, frowning. "He could have a concussion."

I agreed with Niamh, but he *did* seem all right, at least—he laughed at something, even with his hand pressed on the back of his head, and scooted over to make room for Lara to sit with him.

The referee blew the whistle, and the team moved into their places on the court, Will shouting out short instructions to everyone.

Will had to act as captain for the rest of the game. I couldn't leave him now. No way. And, really, did it matter if I missed setup and warm-up? It wasn't ideal, but hopefully Izzy and the guys would understand if I explained there'd been an emergency here. I'd still be able to make it for the gig itself, easily. I shot Izzy a quick text, then settled back into my seat.

The rest of the game was just as close as the first half. The crowd got more and more invested as the end drew closer, screaming and whooping and booing, and even standing up to cheer at one point when Darnell managed to land a shot from almost halfway down the freaking court. And every time the whistle blew for a break or time-out,

Will glanced up at me, to check if I was still there. I was so glad I was.

There was only about fifteen seconds left on the clock when I realized we were going to win. Even I was into the game now, cheering and clapping along with everyone around me as Will passed to Darnell, who passed to number twenty-two. It looked like this guy was going to land a shot, but as it left his hands it was intercepted out of nowhere by a Frankston player, who dribbled the ball a little down the court. Then, way too far away for it to possibly go in, he took a shot. And then, impossibly, it *did* go in, increasing their score by three points and putting them one point above us on the scoreboard.

"*No!*" I shouted, and Juliette swore emphatically beside me.

We only had a few seconds left. There was no way we could win now, right? The ball was passed quicker than I could keep up with down the court. Back and forth, back and forth. Then, one of the Frankston guys went to pass to another, but Darnell quickly dodged around the front to block the second guy from receiving. The ball bounced out of bounds, and Darnell crossed the line to take the pass. He bounced the ball a couple of times, scanning the Collinswood team. He brought the ball in, and it looked like he was going to pass to a blond guy who broke free of his own defender. But then, Will tore through out of nowhere, and Darnell shot the ball at his chest. Will grabbed it, flipped around, and in one fluid motion took the shot.

It went in with a swish of the net.

I knew from the roar of the crowd surrounding me that it had been a winning shot. The scoreboard flipped over to put us one point ahead of Frankston. A few seconds later the buzzer sounded to signal the end of the game, and the Collinswood team swarmed inward to Will and Darnell, hugging them and clapping them on the back, shouting with joy.

Then a couple of the guys lifted Will onto their shoulders. Unlike the way he usually acted around that group, though, he didn't look self-impressed or cocky. Actually, he looked kind of astounded.

"Come on," Niamh said to me, grabbing my hand.

"What?"

"We're going down there, come on!"

We weren't the only ones going onto the court, but it clearly wasn't the norm for people in the crowd to spill in around the players, though. It seemed like more of a close friends and family thing. But Niamh tugged me, pulling me after her down the stairs. Then she broke away from me and ran to Darnell, who picked her up and spun her around.

Will spotted me as the guys lowered him to the ground. I hung back on the edge of the court, suddenly self-conscious. I didn't want to ruin this for him.

But he came over anyway, approaching me with long, confident strides. "Hey," I said when he got closer. "That was *amazing*, I—"

He cut my sentence in half by grabbing me by the shoulders and kissing me.

I let out a squeak of astonishment. This was the exact last thing I could've expected to happen at that moment. Well, maybe that wasn't true. Maybe the *last* thing I expected would've been the grand entrance of the Great, Ethereal Being, floating in on a cloud and playing the accordion while a group of warehouse aliens performed an interpretive dance to the tune. But in the realm of things that were actually possible, Will throwing his arms around me and kissing me hard on the mouth in front of everyone who mattered ranked approximately number one million, five hundred and fifty-two thousand, three hundred and seven. Point five.

He broke away, and didn't even check to see who was looking. He just locked his eyes on me. "I love you," he said.

There were no words. I couldn't think of a possible way to reply to this. I just stood in dumb shock. Then I looked around on Will's behalf. About half of the basketball team had paused in their tracks, staring at us with open mouths. For them, this was probably *less* expected than synchronized dancing warehouse aliens, I guessed. In the stands, Juliette was beaming down at us. And Will's parents, who'd gotten about halfway down the stairs to congratulate him, were simply standing and watching with blank expressions.

I turned back to Will who, it seemed, was purposely not looking behind him to check on people's reactions. "Why aren't you at your gig?" he asked.

Why had the world suddenly tipped upside down? What, exactly, was going on? "Uh, I skipped sound check. It starts in fifteen minutes."

"Did you drive here?"

"Yeah."

"Come on." He grabbed my wrist, and now it was him who was dragging me. This time, toward the side door. Dizzy with shock, and suddenly surged by an adrenaline rush, I broke into a run with him, as we pushed through the door and broke into the cold evening air to sprint across the parking lot to my car.

# 22

I could barely focus during the gig. Throughout the whole performance, I fixed my attention on the table at the back of the room where Will sat. For the first couple of songs, he sat with his shoulders hunched over, making himself small. All I wanted to do was throw my bass on the ground and run across the room to hug him and tell him everything was going to be fine, but I couldn't.

Then, during song number three, Darnell, Matt, and the girls burst through the front doors of the Lost and Found in a group. Will watched them through dull eyes as they filed into his booth. I was desperate to know what they were saying, but heartened by the fact that the girls were there. I couldn't imagine Matt giving him a hard time without Lara tearing him a new one, and there was no way Darnell would say anything that might upset Niamh.

But still.

The worst part was later in the set, when Will's parents entered, pulling their coats tightly around them. As soon as the rest of the group saw them enter they scattered to stand against the far wall, giving the family some privacy. I wondered if Will had told them where he was, or if they'd figured it out.

I wondered if they were mad.

Sayid and Emerson definitely noticed how distracted I was, because they kept looking at me with pointed expressions. I just gave them a smile and shook my head. *Don't worry. I'll explain later.*

They were probably the last few kids left in school who hadn't yet heard about what'd happened at the game.

Finally, we played our last song. The place cheered for us—including Will's parents—and the band started packing up. I began rolling up an aux cord as Sayid checked his phone. His eyes went wide, then he looked straight at me. It wasn't hard to figure out what he'd seen.

"Hey, Ollie," he said, shoving his phone back in his pocket. "If you need to go and speak to Will about something, don't worry about the rest of the equipment. We've got this."

"Are you sure?"

"Yeah, buddy, go."

So, my head spinning with tension, I went.

I dragged my feet, waiting for Will to make eye contact with me and indicate if it was a good idea for me to come sit. He gave me a nod, so I swallowed, sent a quick prayer to whatever the hell might be listening in, and sat at the booth next to him.

Mr. and Mrs. Tavares both smiled at me, which was the biggest relief ever. Even if the smiles were a little tighter than usual.

"You did a great job up there, Ollie," Mrs. Tavares said. "You have a real talent."

"Thank you," I said. My voice came out as a thin sort of squeak.

An awkward silence fell over the table. I don't think Will's parents knew what to say. And I *definitely* didn't know what to say. Did I ask if everything was okay? Apologize for kissing their son? Bring up Will's amazing shot at the end of the basketball game that now felt like it'd happened sometime the year before?

"Are you kids going to be out for a while?" Mr. Tavares asked.

Out as in, out of the closet, or out as in, out celebrating?

"Yeah—the rest of the team is partying at Reese's house. I think Matt and Darnell want to swing by," said Will.

Okay, yup, out celebrating. Glad I didn't reply with "I'm planning on being out permanently," then.

His parents nodded, and Mrs. Tavares looked to me. "Would you make sure Will gets home safely after?" she asked.

Unless I was very much mistaken, that sounded like something a parent might say to her child's boyfriend. "Yeah, yeah, of course I will."

"Thank you. We're going to head home," Mrs. Tavares said, scooting out of the chair. "We still haven't had dinner. But, Will?"

He jumped.

"Remember what we told you."

As they walked out of the building, their heads bowed together so they could speak in low voices, I turned to Will. "What did they tell you?"

His eyes were glassy, and he drew in a ragged, shaky breath. "That they both love me."

Oh.

Oh, thank God.

Juliette was waving to catch my attention across the room, to see if their group could come back over. I held up my pointer finger. "And what did Matt and Darnell say?"

Another deep breath. "More or less the same thing?"

"That's great. So why don't you seem okay? Aren't you happy?"

"I just, uh, I'm just waiting for something bad to happen."

All the adrenaline and excitement from earlier seemed to have trickled out of him. His eyes were puffy, and his shoulders tense, his hands curled up into fists in his lap.

Under the table, where no one in the room could see, I grabbed his hand. "Nothing bad's going to happen. That's it. You're through the bad part."

"But what if my parents were just pretending to be okay because they're in public? You saw them; they weren't exactly jumping up and down with joy."

"They said they love you. They asked me to bring you home. Do you think they would've done that if they didn't want us to be around each other?"

He grabbed a napkin off the table and squirreled it away into his lap so he could pick at the edges. "No. I guess not."

"Are you okay?"

"I'm okay. I am."

His smile was less shaky now. I returned it, and bumped our knees together. "So . . . you kissed me."

"Yeah."

"In public."

"Yeah."

"We weren't even together, though."

"I'm sorry," Will said. "I'm an asshole. I wasn't even

thinking straight. It's just, I was high off winning the game, and you *came*, and it just made me realize that you had my back, and also I don't think I knew how badly I wanted you there until you were. I've been meaning to ask if we could try again, but I didn't know how to when I couldn't promise anything. I wasn't ready yet, and I didn't want to drag you down with me while I figured myself out."

"I shouldn't have said that. You weren't dragging me down because you needed to take your time."

"No, but I wasn't in a place where I could give you what you needed."

I nodded. "So what changed?"

"I don't know. A few things. Like, my dad being suspicious enough to ask me to keep the door open, but not demanding I tell him what was going on or steer clear of you. And also, Lara coming out, and Matt still wanting to be with her even if she likes girls, too. It made me feel a little braver, I guess. I was still scared, but I was tired of being scared. The not-knowing was getting worse than the thought of just jumping in and dealing with whatever happened."

"And now the hard part's over," I said. "Your parents know, and your best friends know. And they still love you."

"Yeah. I really think they do."

I took a deep breath. "And so do I."

This, I was pretty sure, was finally an appropriate time to say that. And Will didn't reel away from me, or panic, or scramble to respond. Instead, he grabbed my hand and tilted his head back so he was looking at the ceiling. It seemed like he was trying to force his tears to slip back down their ducts. "I don't deserve it."

"But I do anyway."

He let out his breath like every bit of tension in his body

seeped out with it. "I love you, too. I think I always did. I was just scared of what saying that might mean."

"And now you're not?"

"Not even a bit, Ollie."

After everything. Meeting by chance, and falling too fast, and breaking up, and falling again, and pushing him away. All of it. This was the first time anything to do with us felt calm and rational. There was no impulsivity in this moment, or thrill of being discovered, or the passion and lust of discovering someone. It was just us. Two people who weren't strangers anymore, and who were now well versed on all the things that could stop them from working out, and who'd maybe figured out a way to fit together anyway.

Apparently tired of waiting for us, the rest of the group made their way back over to the table as one.

"All right, well, they didn't look too angry," Matt said, waving at the door with one hand.

"Nah, not angry," Will said offhandedly, the affectionate tone of his voice gone right out the door. Some things never changed. "They're chill."

He kept hold of my hand under the table, though. So. *That'd* changed.

"Oh, sweet. And, uh," Matt said, turning to me with a flourish. *"Hi, Ollie."*

"Hi, Matt."

"I cannot believe this has been going on since summer, *summer*, and no one thought to loop me in," Matt said, obviously joking. "That is a bad start. We have bad blood now, Ollie, I'm sorry. You'd better do a fine job getting on my good side from now on. Everyone knows the best friend gets to call the shots in a relationship."

"Who died and made you his best friend?" Darnell

asked, bouncing his head to one side in disbelief. "But for real, why *didn't* we know?"

Will shrugged, self-conscious.

No. Nope. Not good enough. "When was he supposed to tell you guys?" I asked. "When you were making jokes about who wants to marry me? Or when you were throwing shade at him for *grabbing my arm* at the dance? Or, maybe when you were laughing about us being boyfriends if he mentioned something about me at lunch?"

Darnell's mouth went into an *O* shape, but Matt looked affronted. "Ah, hell, man, we were just joking," he said to me. He looked to Will for backup, but Will wouldn't meet his eye. "Wait, Will, we weren't being serious. We didn't think you were actually . . . like . . ."

"But I was," Will said. "I'm bi, I think. Just like Lara."

"I'm sorry. We seriously didn't know."

"Yes, well, maybe from now on we can cut the gay joke crap as a blanket rule," Lara said in a cutting tone. "How about it?"

"You've got it," Darnell said, and Niamh squeezed his arm.

"So," Juliette said. "Are we going to that party now, or what?"

We all looked at Will. He flushed red, and shrugged. He didn't seem capable of much else right now. "I dunno. People might be weirded out about before."

"Hell no, you have to go, you won us the game," Matt said. "If I'm going with a goddamn concussion, you're going."

"Is it the same thing, though?" I asked, and Lara choked back a laugh.

"But what if . . ." Will trailed off.

"You've got us with you," Darnell said.

"Yeah. Like they'd even try that shit," Matt added.

"Besides," Lara jumped in, grinning over at Juliette as she did. "Even if they did. We can scream louder."

"So, when are you telling Will?" Mom asked. She sat in the living room, clutching a steaming cup of black coffee, along with Uncle Roy and Dad, both of whom had beers in front of them instead of coffee. I was running in and out of the living room, packing my car with blankets, folding chairs, and a cooler filled with soda. I didn't know if everyone wanted Coke, or Diet Coke, or root beer, or Dr Pepper, or Mountain Dew, so screw it, I was taking all of it.

"Tonight. I told you it was tonight." I grunted under the weight of the cooler as I shuffled it through the propped-open front door to load into my trunk. I kicked something unidentified, and I peeked around. A marble. "Crista, I told you to pick up your marbles, people can slip on those things!"

"Oops! Sorry, sorry, sorry."

"You should be," I said under my breath, fighting a grin as she abandoned her iPad and scooped up the stray marble. What kind of new-age kid played with marbles these days, anyway? Wasn't that a little vintage?

Not that I was going to hold it too hard against her. It was only pretty recently that she'd started poking her head out of her turtle shell again. A laughing, noisy Crista, tormenting Dylan and running around the house experimenting with new toy setups was far preferable to the quiet, nonchalant kid she'd turned into after Aunt Linda passed away. It wasn't that she didn't miss her mom anymore, of course. She still brought her up. All the time, in fact. It was just that she'd adjusted to the idea that life would keep on going without her mom, and she'd finally decided to catch back up with it.

"I know it's tonight, but *when* tonight?"

I blew my bangs out of my face and shrugged. Honestly, did it matter when? "I don't know. I'll wing it."

"Don't do it in front of everyone," Mom said.

"Uh . . . why?"

"Because. He should get the chance to react in private before everyone else jumps in, okay?"

Dad tapped the neck of his beer against his chin. "Clearly, your mother has never forgiven me for proposing in front of a crowd of strangers," he said.

"Well, all I'm saying is you're *very* lucky I was going to say yes, anyway," Mom shot back.

"Good thing I'm not proposing," I said. "All right. I've got to go, so—"

"Ollie, can I play your guitar while you're gone?" Crista asked.

I hesitated in the entryway.

"I'll supervise," Uncle Roy promised. "Only very *gentle* guitar playing tonight, all right, Crista? We aren't in a rock band. If Ollie comes back to find another scratch on that thing he might lock you up and throw away the key."

He pulled Crista into his lap and tickled her while she shrieked with laughter.

"Fine." I smiled. "Supervised rocking out only. Deal. But if it's scratched, you'll have to take her place in the dungeons."

"Duly noted."

With that, I sprinted to my car, and practically broke the time and space barrier on the way to Will's. Why was it that I managed to be late for *everything*?

"What took you so long?" Will asked as he climbed into the passenger seat.

"Hey, count yourself lucky I'm here at all. Napier is a hell of a long way to go for a drive-in movie."

"It's worth it, I promise. Where are the others?"

"They all went in Matt's car in the end. I totally missed out on the road trip."

"Those motherfuckers." Will grinned.

"But it kind of works out, because I have to talk to you about something," I said. I put the car into Park and flipped around in my seat. Mom *did* say to do this in private. And this was the only moment of privacy we'd be getting, so.

Will looked wary. "Oh no, what?"

There was no point dragging it out. "I got into the University of Southern California."

"Oh," Will said. He cleared his throat and gave me a forced-looking smile. "Wow, Ollie, amazing. That's really great. When did you find out?"

"A couple of weeks ago."

He drew his brows together. "What, and you just kept it a secret this whole time?"

"Well, I wanted to wait and see, first."

"For what?"

"If I got into NC State."

He waited, shrugging to tell me to go on.

"And I did," I finished.

". . . And which one are you going to pick?"

"What would happen if I picked USC?"

He swallowed, looking hurt. He'd gotten into the nursing program at the University of North Carolina not long ago. An amazing school, but it couldn't have been any farther away from California. "Well, we'll figure it out. It's far away, but it's not impossible. We can keep an eye out for cheap flights and do weekend visits whenever we can. I'll come up and stay for breaks, if you're happy to let me crash with you—obviously, you can stay at mine whenever you want, but LA is more exciting than Chapel Hill, so—"

"So you wouldn't want to break up?" I asked.

"What? *No*." Will's eyes went wide, and he reeled back a little. "Do you?"

"No, not at all. Plus, it wouldn't be necessary, because I'm going to NC State."

"*What?* Wait, seriously? You're not joking?"

"Not joking. I just wanted to make sure that was still what you wanted."

"Are you trying to kill me? You're so ridiculous, why wouldn't I want that?"

I shrugged like I didn't know, but I did. Because after a year of everything being uprooted again, and again, and again, I was constantly bracing myself for something else to fall apart so I could somehow preempt it.

But Will didn't fall apart, or reject me. Instead, he grabbed both of my hands and grinned so wide he could've auditioned to be a suitcase model on *Deal or No Deal*. "So, we're going to be, like, a thirty-minute drive from each other next year?"

I nodded, and he threw his arms around me and hugged me so tightly he nearly squeezed my lungs out of my mouth.

"Thank God," he whispered.

Picking NC State hadn't exactly been a no-brainer—I still missed California, and the people, and the culture. Not to mention the weather. But I couldn't deny that the day I'd gotten my offer letter for NC, I'd felt like a set of fifty-ton weights I'd been lugging around since I got the USC offer had been lifted. Partly because of Will, for sure.

But not just for Will. My parents had decided to stay here for at least another year to keep an eye on Roy and the kids, for a start. And even though I missed Ryan and Hayley, they weren't really my *group* anymore. They didn't know what I did with my days, and I knew barely anything about theirs. We'd kind of grown apart. And maybe that was okay.

Sayid, Emerson, and Izzy had been offered places at Duke, NC State, and UNC. Juliette and Lara were both going to NC State. And for all I'd sulked and cried when I found out I was moving here, North Carolina had grown on me.

My friends had grown on me.

Living near my cousins, uncle, and parents suddenly seemed more important than living near the beach. Aunt Linda might be gone, but I still had everyone else. And I'd come to realize I wasn't guaranteed a lifetime with any of them.

Funny how much seven months could change.

As soon as we pulled into the parking spot next to Matt's car, Will launched himself out and ran over to the others. *"Ollie's going to NC State!"* he shouted, so loudly that a few families looked over at us from the hoods of their cars.

"Hey, that was supposed to be my news." I grinned as the girls let out a chorus of squeals and screams. Even Matt and Darnell cheered, as Niamh threw her arms around Darnell in celebration, rocking him from side to side.

Will dug through the trunk of my car and started pulling out the collapsible chairs we'd shoved in there. "Nah. It's my news, too."

Niamh let go of Darnell as Will joined the guys, then she came over to dig around in the trunk of Matt's car. She was dressed in her usual workout gear, and had her hair pulled away from her face by a fabric headband, presumably left over from an afternoon gym session. "So," she said, passing me some blankets. "I have something to say as well."

"You do?"

"Yup. I got cast in a mascara ad in New York. I'm going up to do a photoshoot for it over a weekend, soon."

I gaped. "Oh, my God, Niamh, that's amazing. Congratulations."

"Thank you." She wrapped her blanket around her shoulders and pulled it tight. "I put it down to the photos I took a few weeks back. It's amazing how much having some *energy* again improved my pictures."

"Freaking awesome. What does Darnell think?"

She glanced over at him. He was sprawled in his own chair, chatting easily with Matt and Lara, who were set up on the ground on a beanbag chair Matt had insisted on bringing along. I'd argued it'd get covered in mud and grass, but apparently it'd been a lifelong dream of Matt's to watch a drive-in movie from a beanbag chair, so who was I to crush it? "Darnell's supportive. He still doesn't want to move there, but he said he's happy to try long distance while we figure it out. So, I guess we'll see." Niamh gave a happy giggle, then wandered back over to join Darnell.

Who knew if they'd manage to make it work? But that wasn't the point, was it? We had no way of knowing what the future held. People changed their minds, people passed away, people moved unexpectedly. The only thing we could ever really do was play it by ear. And if this was what Darnell and Niamh wanted right now, then I was totally on their team.

Back by my car, Will focused on trying to push our chairs closer together while I stood by with our blankets.

"Wait, are you two together?" asked an unfamiliar voice.

I thought the question was being directed at me, and I instinctively took a step closer to Will while I looked up. But the speaker was a blond guy I didn't recognize, standing in front of Lara and Matt, who were technically sitting in the beanbag chair together, but really enough of Lara's legs were over Matt's that you could say she was using *him* for a chair.

"Yeah, we are," Matt said. "Couple weeks."

"I thought you were into girls now?" the guy asked Lara. He wasn't giving her a hard time, exactly; he looked genuinely confused.

"I'm bi," Lara said, before elegantly giving him both a sweet smile and the finger. "Not that it's any of your business, is it, Xavier?"

Matt shrugged, beaming. "You heard the lady. Move along."

The guy looked between Lara and Matt, and then his gaze trailed over the rest of the group, who were all watching him pointedly. He rolled his eyes. "I was just asking, chill. No need to be so sensitive."

"*Good-bye,* Xavier," Lara said firmly, and this time he walked off.

"Go Lara," I said under my breath, and Will and I shared a secret smile while he took a blanket from me.

We tried a few different setups, but settled on loading both blankets on top of us, holding hands under them. Then, as the movie started playing, Will shifted and put his arm around my shoulders.

It was, I realized, the first time we'd sat like this in public since the lake.

So maybe I owed Disney an apology.

Maybe our Happily Ever After hadn't worked on the

first shot. And maybe Happily Ever Afters weren't a singular event. Maybe they were something you had to work at, and build, and never give up on, as long as they were something you still wanted.

And, maybe they weren't perfect. It wasn't like having Will right here and right now somehow erased all of the terrible things that had happened this year. And it didn't prevent terrible things from happening in the future. Sometimes in life, terrible things happened. And sometimes really, really amazing things happened. And sometimes, those things all kind of happened at once.

But screw tomorrow.

Even if no one could promise that everything would work out perfectly, right here and now, in this exact moment, it was perfect.

And right here and now was the only thing that ever mattered anyway.

# Acknowledgments

This, my second book, is different from my debut novel in a lot of ways. In other ways, it's similar. The most notable of which being that this book, like my first, didn't happen by itself. It may take a village to raise a child, but to birth a book baby? *That* takes multiple friends, family members, publishing professionals, and readers, spanning three continents!

To Moe Ferrara, my agent. For being the first person to get my words, for always being there for emotional support, and for helping me make good books great. I wouldn't be here if I hadn't met you. Thank you as well to James McGowan and the rest of the Bookends team for their advice and support!

Thank you to Sylvan Creekmore, my super-awesome-amazing editor, who totally got what I was trying to do, remained completely unflappable even when I went into high-anxiety mode ten or twenty times in a row, and who wasn't afraid to tell me if a joke that was hilarious to me made absolutely no sense. This has been the most amazing experience, and I'm forever grateful to have you as my editor.

To the entire team at Wednesday Books: Good God, you're all superstars. I wish I had a recording of every time I've gushed to a friend about the professionalism, passion, and expertise within the Wednesday Books office. I can't express how grateful I am to be able to call myself a part of the Wednesday Books family. Every one of you has made this experience everything I could have ever hoped for. Special thanks to DJ DeSmyter, Dana Aprigliano, Alexis Neuville, Jessica Preeg, Sarah Schoof, Sara Goodman, Anne Marie Tallberg, NaNá V. Stoelzle, and Caitlyn Averett!

Thank you to Kerri Resnick, my cover designer, and Jim Tierney, who illustrated. Thank you for giving me a cover that made me cry.

To the earliest readers of *Only Mostly Devastated*, who responded to my emergency call for a lightning-fast turnaround time to beat the Thanksgiving publishing break; Lee Kelsall, Ash Ledger, Sophie Cameron, Julie Tuovi, and Tere Kirkland. Thank you all for reading this book at its roughest, and for giving me the frank feedback it needed at the time.

To Ash and Julia Lynn Rubin: Our near-daily chats kept me from unspooling. Thank you both for being a safe space to rehash the same conversations over and over and over again when I needed it the most.

Thank you to The Lobster Garden girls Hannah Capin and Bibi Cooper, and to Cass Frances, Sadie Blach, and everyone else who allows me to scream into their Twitter DMs when it's midday for me and bedtime for them. Love you.

Thank you to my Melbourne writer crew, Katya De Becerra, Ella Dyson, Astrid Scholte, and Claire Donnelly, for always being there for a coffee or stronger beverage, depending on how intense edits were that week.

Special thanks to Sandhya Menon, Angelo Surmelis, Jenn Bennett, Kayla Ancrum, Cale Dietrich, Hannah Capin, and Mason Deaver: Your early support of this book meant the world to me, and I'm still pinching myself that authors as unbelievably talented as yourselves took the time to read the words I wrote.

To Mum, Dad, and Sarah: Thank you for being the best family in the world. For reading to me as a baby, for the library trips, for the encouragement. Shout-out to Mum for letting me hog the dial-up internet so I could publish my fanfiction when you needed to make phone calls, to Dad for reading The Faraway Tree series to me until your throat must have felt raw, and to Sarah for listening to every wild story plot I ever ran by you.

Cameron, thank you for giving me your patience, your silence when I needed it, your support when I needed that, and your ears when I demanded them. Thank you for letting me neglect the dishes when I have deadlines due, and for buying me surprise Nutella when it gets too much for me. Most of all, thank you for making home a safe haven.

To everyone who was on the bus the morning Moe called me to say we had an offer on this book: I'm sorry for startling you. I know that 7:30 A.M. is too loud to start screaming on public transport. I was very excited, and I hope you all forgive me.

And finally, to everyone who ever showed me what a broken heart felt like: What doesn't kill a writer gives her plenty to write about.

Read on for a sneak peek at
Sophie Gonzales's new novel

# Perfect on Paper

Everyone in school knows about locker eighty-nine: the locker on the bottom right, at the end of the hall near the science labs. It's been unassigned for years now; really, it should've been allocated to one of the hundreds of students in the school to load with books and papers and forgotten, mold-infested Tupperware.

Instead, there seems to be an unspoken agreement that locker eighty-nine serves a higher purpose. How else do you explain the fact that every year, when we all get our schedules and combinations, and lockers eighty-eight and ninety meet their new leasers, locker eighty-nine stands empty?

Well, "empty" might not be the right word here. Because even though it's unassigned, locker eighty-nine ends most days housing several envelopes with almost identical contents: ten dollars, often in the form of a bill, sometimes made up of whatever loose change the sender can gather; a letter, sometimes typed, sometimes handwritten, sometimes adorned with the telltale smudge of a tearstain; and at the bottom of the letter, an email address.

It's a mystery how the envelopes get in there, when it's

rare to spot someone slipping one through the vents. It's a bigger mystery, still, how the envelopes are collected, when *no one* has ever been spotted opening the locker.

No one can agree on who operates it. Is it a teacher with no hobbies? An ex-student who can't let go of the past? A big-hearted janitor who could use some cash on the side?

The only thing that's universally agreed on is this: if you're having relationship issues and you slide a letter through the vents of locker eighty-nine, you will receive an email from an anonymous sender within the week, giving you advice. And if you're wise enough to follow that advice, your relationship problems will be solved, guaranteed, or your money back.

And I rarely have to give people their money back.

In my defense, in the few cases that didn't work out, the letter left out important information. Like last month, when Penny Moore wrote in about Rick Smith dumping her in an Instagram comment, and conveniently left out that he did it after finding out she'd coordinated her absent days with his older brother so they could sneak off together. If I'd known that, I never would've advised Penny to confront Rick about the comment during lunch the next day. That one was on her. Admittedly, it *was* kind of satisfying to watch Rick perform a dramatic reading of her texts to his brother in front of the whole cafeteria, but I would've preferred a happy ending. Because I did this to help people, and to know I made a positive difference in the world; but also (and maybe even mostly, in this case), because it pained me to drop ten dollars into Penny's locker all because *she* was too proud to admit she was the one in the wrong. Problem is, I couldn't defend myself and my relationship expertise if Penny were to tell everyone she didn't get a refund.

Because no one knows who I am.

Okay, I don't mean *literally*. Lots of people know who I am. Darcy Phillips. Junior. That girl with the shoulder-length blond hair and the gap between her front teeth. The one who's best friends with Brooke Nguyen, and is part of the school's queer club. Ms. Morgan-from-science-class's daughter.

But what they don't know is that I'm also the girl who hangs back after school while her mom finishes up in the science labs, long after everyone else has left. The girl who steals down the hall to locker eighty-nine, enters the combination she's known by heart for years—ever since the combination list was left briefly unattended on the admin officer's desk one evening—and collects letters and bills like tax. The girl who spends her nights filtering strangers' stories through unbiased eyes, before sending carefully composed instructions via the burner email account she made in ninth grade.

They don't know, because nobody in school knows. I'm the only one who knows my secret.

Or, I was, anyway. Up until this very moment.

I had the sinking inkling that was about to change, though. Because even though I'd checked the halls for stragglers or staff members like I always did barely twenty seconds ago, I was thirteen-thousand percent sure I'd heard someone clear their throat somewhere in the vicinity of *directly the fuck behind me*.

While I was elbow deep inside a very much unlocked locker eighty-nine.

Crap.

Even as I turned around, I was optimistic enough to hope for the best. Part of the reason why I'd gotten by without detection for so long was the locker's convenient location, right at the foot of a dead-end, L-shaped hallway.

There'd been close calls in the past, but the sound of the heavy entry doors swinging closed had always given me plenty of notice to hide the evidence. The only way someone would be able to sneak up on me was if they'd come out of the fire escape door leading from the pool—and no one used the pool this late in the day.

From the looks of the very wet guy standing behind me, though, I'd made a fatal miscalculation. Apparently, someone did use the pool this late in the day.

Well, fuck.

I knew him. Or, at least, I knew *of* him. His name was Alexander Brougham, although I was pretty sure he usually went by Brougham. He was a senior, and good friends with Finn Park, and, by all accounts, one of the hottest seniors at St. Deodetus's.

Up close, it was clear to me said accounts were categorically false.

Brougham's nose looked like it'd been badly broken once, and his navy blue eyes were opened almost as wide as his mouth, which was an interesting look, because his eyes were kind of bulgy to begin with. Not goldfish level, but more like a "my eyelids are doing their best to swallow my eyeballs whole" type of bulgy. And, as aforementioned, he was wet enough that his already dark hair looked black, and his T-shirt stuck to his chest in damp, see-through patches.

"Why are you soaking?" I asked, folding my arms behind my back to hide the letters and leaning against locker eighty-nine so it closed behind me. "You look like you fell in the pool."

This was probably one of the few situations where a sopping wet, fully clothed teenager standing in the school hallway an hour after dismissal *wasn't* the elephant in the room.

He looked at me like I'd said the stupidest thing in the world. Which seemed unfair, given I wasn't the one who was wandering around the school halls literally dripping.

"I didn't 'fall in the pool.' I was swimming laps."

"With your clothes on?" I tried to shove the letters down the back of my skirt without moving my hands, but that was a more complex task than I'd anticipated.

Brougham surveyed his jeans. I used the brief distraction to ram the letters inside the band of my tights. In hindsight, this was probably never going to go far in convincing him he hadn't just seen me digging through locker eighty-nine, but until I had a better excuse, denial was all I had.

"I'm not that wet," he said.

Today was apparently the first time I'd heard Alexander Brougham speak, because until just now I'd had no idea he had a British accent. I understood his wide appeal now: Oriella, my favorite relationship YouTuber, once dedicated a whole video to the topic. People with perfectly good taste in partners historically had their senses addled in the presence of an accent. Setting aside the messiness of *which* accents were considered sexy in which cultures and why, accents in general were nature's way of saying, "Procreate with *that* one, their gene code must be varied as fuck." Few things, it seemed, could turn a person on as quickly as the subconscious realization they almost certainly weren't flirting with a blood relative.

Thankfully, Brougham broke the silence when I didn't reply. "I didn't get time to dry off properly. I'd just finished up when I heard you out here. I thought I might catch the person who runs locker eighty-nine if I snuck through the fire escape. And I did."

He looked triumphant. Like he'd won a contest I was only now realizing I'd been participating in.

That was, incidentally, my least favorite facial expression. As of right this moment.

I forced a nervous laugh. "I didn't *open* it. I was putting a letter in."

"I just saw you close it."

"I didn't close it. I just banged it a little when I was sliding the, uh . . . the letter inside."

Cool, Darcy, way to gaslight the poor British student.

"Yeah, you did. Also, you took a pile of letters out of it."

Well, I'd committed to this enough to shove them down my tights so I might as well follow this through to the end, right? I held my empty hands out, palms up. "I don't have any letters."

He actually looked a little thrown. "Where did you . . . I saw them, though."

I shrugged and pulled an innocent face.

"You . . . did you put them down your stockings?" His tone wasn't accusing, per se. More mild, patronizing bafflement, like someone gently questioning their child on *why*, exactly, they thought dog food would make a great snack. It only made me want to dig my heels in further.

I shook my head and laughed a little too loudly. "*No*." The heat in my cheeks told me my face was betraying me.

"Turn around."

I leaned against the lockers with a rustle of paper and folded my arms across my chest. The corner of one of the envelopes dug uncomfortably into the back of my hip. "I don't want to."

He looked at me.

I looked at him.

Yeah. He wasn't buying this for a second.

If my brain were functioning properly I would've said something to throw him off track, but unfortunately it chose that precise moment to go on strike.

"You *are* the person who runs this thing," Brougham said, confidently enough I knew there was no point protesting further. "And I really need your help."

I hadn't settled on what I believed would happen if I ever got caught. Mostly because I'd preferred not to worry about it too much. But if you'd forced me to guess what the person catching me would do, I would've probably gone for "turn me in to the principal," or "tell everyone in school," or "accuse me of ruining their life with bad advice."

But this? This wasn't so threatening. Maybe it was going to be okay. I swallowed hard in an attempt to shove the lump in my throat down closer to my thudding heart. "Help with what?"

"With getting my ex-girlfriend back." He paused, thoughtful. "Oh, my name's Brougham, by the way."

Brougham. Pronounced BRO-um, not Broom. It was an easy name to remember, because it was pronounced all wrong, and that had irked me since the first time I'd heard it.

"I know," I said faintly.

"What's your hourly rate?" he asked, peeling his shirt away from his chest to air it out. It thwacked heavily back against his skin as soon as he let go of it. See? *Overly* wet.

I tore my eyes away from his clothes and processed his question. "I'm sorry?"

"I want to hire you."

There he went again with the weird money-for-favors language. "As . . . ?"

"A relationship coach." He glanced around us, then

lowered his voice to a whisper. "My girlfriend broke up with me last month and I need her back, but I don't know where to start. This isn't something an email's gonna fix."

Well, wasn't this guy dramatic? "Um, look, I'm sorry, but I don't really have time to be anyone's coach. I just do this before bed as a hobby."

"What are you so busy with?" he asked calmly.

"Um, homework? Friends? Netflix?"

He folded his arms. "I'll pay you twenty dollars an hour."

"Dude, I said—"

"Twenty-five an hour, plus a fifty-dollar bonus if I get Winona back."

Wait.

So, this guy was seriously telling me he'd give me fifty dollars, tax-free, if I spent two hours giving him some advice on getting back a girl who'd already fallen for him once? That was well within my skill set. Which meant the fifty-dollar bonus was all but guaranteed.

This could be the easiest money I'd ever made.

While I mulled it over, he spoke up. "I know you want to keep your identity anonymous."

I snapped back to reality and narrowed my eyes. "What's that supposed to mean?"

He shrugged, the picture of innocence. "You're sneaking around after hours when the halls are empty, and no one knows it's you answering them. There's a reason you don't want people knowing. It doesn't take Sherlock Holmes."

And there it was. I knew it. I *knew* my gut was screaming "danger" for a good reason. He wasn't asking me for a favor, he was telling me what he wanted from me, and throwing in why it would be a bad idea to refuse. As casually as anything. Blink-and-you'll-miss-it blackmail.

I kept my voice as steady as I could, but I couldn't help the touch of venom that seeped through. "And let me guess. You'd like to help me keep it that way. That's where this is going, right?"

"Well, yeah. Exactly."

He'd stuck his lower lip out and widened his eyes. My own lip curled of its own accord as I took him in, any goodwill I'd been feeling toward him evaporating in one puff. "Gee. That's so thoughtful of you."

Brougham, expressionless, waited for me to go on. When I didn't, he circled a hand in the air. "So . . . what do you think?"

I *thought* a lot of things, but none of them were wise to say out loud to someone who was in the middle of threatening me. What were my options here? I couldn't tell Mom someone was threatening me. She had no idea I was behind locker eighty-nine. And I really, *really* didn't want everyone to find out this was me. I mean, the awkwardness of how much personal information I knew about everyone alone . . . even my closest friends didn't know my involvement. Without anonymity, my dating advice business was a bust. And it was the only real thing I'd ever achieved. The only thing that actually did the world any good.

And . . . god, there was the whole Brooke thing from last year. If Brooke ever found out about that she'd hate me.

She couldn't find out.

I set my jaw. "Fifty up front. Fifty if it works out."

"Shake on it?"

"I'm not done. I'll agree to a cap of five hours for now. If you want me for longer, it's my call to continue."

"Is that everything?" he asked.

"No. If you say one word to anyone about any of this,

I'll tell everyone your game is so bad you needed personal relationship tutoring."

It was a weak addition, and nowhere near as creative as some of the insults I'd thought of a few moments ago, but I didn't want to goad him too much. Something flashed so slightly across his blank face I almost missed it. As it was, it was hard to define. Did his eyebrows rise a little? "Well that was unnecessary, but noted."

I simply folded my arms. "*Was it* now?"

We stood in silence for a beat as my words played back in my head—they'd sounded bitchier than I'd intended, not that bitchiness was unwarranted here—then he shook his head and started to turn his back. "You know what? Stuff it. I just thought you might be open to a deal."

"Wait, wait, wait." I darted forward to head him off, hands up. "I'm sorry. I am open to a deal."

"Are you sure?"

Oh, for god's sake, was he going to make me beg him? It seemed unfair to expect me to accept his blackmail terms without any pushback or sass at all, and I was liking him less and less by the second, but I'd do it. Whatever he told me to do, I'd do it. I just needed to keep the situation contained. I nodded, firmly, and he took his phone out.

"Okay then. I'm at practice over at my swim club before school every day, and Monday, Wednesday, and Friday afternoons we do dryland training. Tuesdays and Thursdays I swim here at the pool. I'll grab your number so we can organize this without me hunting you down at school, okay?"

"You forgot 'please.'" Damn it, I shouldn't have said that. But I couldn't help myself. I snatched the phone from him and entered my number into it. "Here."

"Excellent. What's your name, by the way?"

I couldn't even *begin* to stifle my laugh. "You know, usually people find out each other's names prior to making 'deals.' Do you do it differently in England?"

"I'm from Australia, not England."

"That's not an Australian accent."

"As an Australian, I can assure you it is. It's just not one you're used to hearing."

"There's more than one?"

"There's more than one American accent, isn't there? Your name?"

Oh for the love of . . . "Darcy Phillips."

"I'll message you tomorrow, Darcy. Have a wonderful night." From the way he surveyed me, lips pressed together and chin raised as his eyes drifted down, he'd enjoyed our first conversation about as much as I had. I stiffened with annoyance at this realization. What right did he have to dislike me when *he* was the reason that exchange had gotten so tense?

He slid his phone into his damp pocket, electrical failure be damned, and turned on his heel to leave. I stared after him for a moment, then took my chance to rip the letters out of their extremely uncomfortable position by my underwear and shove them in my backpack. Just in time, too, because Mom emerged around the corner not ten seconds later. "There you are. Ready to go?" she asked me, already turning back down the hall, the clack of her low heels echoing in the empty space.

Like I was ever not ready to go. By the time she packed up her stuff, answered her emails, and got some sneaky paper marking in, I was the last student to leave this area of the school—everyone else was way down at the other end hanging around the art room or the track field.

Well, except for Alexander Brougham, apparently.

"Did you know students stay back this late to use the pool?" I asked Mom, hurrying to meet her stride.

"Well, we're in the off-season for the school team so I daresay it wouldn't be busy, but I know it's open to students Vijay gives passes to until reception closes. Darc, could you text Ainsley and ask her to take the spaghetti sauce out of the freezer?"

By Vijay, Mom meant Coach Senguttuvan. One of the weirdest parts about having a parent work at school was that I knew the teachers by their first *and* last names, and had to make sure not to slip up in class or talking to my friends. Some of them I'd known practically as long as I'd been alive. It might sound easy, but having John around for dinner every month, and at my parents' birthday parties, and hosting New Year's Eve for fifteen years, then suddenly transitioning to calling him Mr. Hanson in math class was like playing Minesweeper with my reputation.

I texted my sister Mom's instructions as I hopped in the passenger seat. To my delight, I found an unread message waiting from Brooke:

I don't want to do this essay.
Please don't make me do this
essay.

As usual, getting a message from Brooke made me feel like the law of gravity had declined to apply to me for a beat.

She was obviously thinking about me instead of doing her homework. How often did her mind wander to me when she started daydreaming? Did it wander to anyone else, or was I special?

It was so hard to know how much to hope.

I sent a quick reply:

> You've got this! I believe in
> you. I'll send you my notes
> later tonight, if it'll help?

Mom hummed to herself as we pulled out of the parking lot, unbelievably slowly, so as to not bowl down any unexpected turtles. "How was your day?"

"Pretty uneventful," I lied. Best to leave out the whole "I got hired and also blackmailed" thing. "I got into an argument about women's rights in sociology with Mr. Reisling, but that's normal. Mr. Reisling's a dickhead."

"Yeah, he *is* a dickhead," Mom mused to herself, then she gave me a sharp look. "*Don't* you tell anyone I said that!"

"I'll leave it off the agenda at tomorrow's meeting."

Mom glanced sideways at me, and her round face broke into a warm grin. I started to return it, then I remembered Brougham, and the blackmailing, and I wilted. Mom didn't notice, though. She was too busy focusing on the road, already lost in her own thoughts. One of the good things about having a perpetually distracted parent was not having to dodge prying questions.

I just hoped Brougham would keep my secret to himself. The problem was, of course, that I had no idea what kind of person he was. Wonderful. A guy I'd never met properly, who I knew nothing about, held the power to throw my business—not to mention my relationships—into havoc. That wasn't anxiety inducing at *all*.

I needed to talk to Ainsley.

Melbourne Actors' Headshots

SOPHIE GONZALES is a YA contemporary author. She graduated from the University of Adelaide and lives in Melbourne, Australia, where she currently works as a psychologist. When she isn't writing, she can be found ice skating, performing in musical theater, and practicing the piano. She is also the author of *The Law of Inertia* and *Perfect on Paper*.